W9-BYH-377

"Everyone has a temper sometimes. And Kenny Murdock is no exception." Exhaling an errant strand of light brown hair from her forehead, Tori continued, her voice still quiet yet firm. "Branding him a killer because of it is simply ludicrous."

Problem was, she wasn't buying what she was selling. She'd seen Kenny's face the previous afternoon. She'd heard the blatant threat he'd hurled in Martha Jane's direction. She'd felt the rage simmering inside him.

And now the woman was dead. Strangled by a piece of rope that sounded a lot like the kind he'd been using that very day to bundle sticks in Rose's backyard.

"Victoria is right," Beatrice said, her accent and her innate shyness making them all lean closer to hear. "What's that expression? Just because it looks like a duck and acts like a duck, it doesn't mean it's a duck."

Margaret Louise laughed, her hand slipping around the nanny's shoulders in a conspiratorial fashion. "They may say it like that across the pond . . . but here, in the States, if it looks like a duck and quacks like a duck, it *is*, in fact, a duck."

"Oh." Beatrice flashed a look of apology in Victoria's direction. "I'm sorry. I was only trying to help."

Tori reached out, patted the girl's hand. "I know. But don't worry. It will be okay. Martha Jane's killer will be found."

What that would do to Rose when it happened, though, was anyone's guess . . .

Pinned *for* Murder

Elizabeth Lynn Casey

BERKLEY PRIME CRIME, NEW YORK

THE BERKLEY PUBLISHING GROUP
Published by the Penguin Group
Penguin Group (USA) Inc.
375 Hudson Street, New York, New York 10014, USA
Penguin Group (Canada), 90 Eglinton Avenue East, Suite 700, Toronto, Ontario M4P 2Y3, Canada
(a division of Pearson Penguin Canada Inc.)
Penguin Books Ltd., 80 Strand, London WC2R 0RL, England
Penguin Group Ireland, 25 St. Stephen's Green, Dublin 2, Ireland (a division of Penguin Books Ltd.)
Penguin Group (Australia), 250 Camberwell Road, Camberwell, Victoria 3124, Australia
(a division of Pearson Australia Group Pty. Ltd.)
Penguin Books India Pvt. Ltd., 11 Community Centre, Panchsheel Park, New Delhi—110 017, India
Penguin Group (NZ), 67 Apollo Drive, Rosedale, North Shore 0632, New Zealand
(a division of Pearson New Zealand Ltd.)
Penguin Books (South Africa) (Pty.) Ltd., 24 Sturdee Avenue, Rosebank, Johannesburg 2196,
South Africa

Penguin Books Ltd., Registered Offices: 80 Strand, London WC2R 0RL, England

This is a work of fiction. Names, characters, places, and incidents either are the product of the author's imagination or are used fictitiously, and any resemblance to actual persons, living or dead, business establishments, events, or locales is entirely coincidental. The publisher does not have any control over and does not assume any responsibility for author or third-party websites or their content.

PINNED FOR MURDER

A Berkley Prime Crime Book / published by arrangement with the author

PRINTING HISTORY
Berkley Prime Crime mass-market edition / October 2010

Copyright © 2010 by Penguin Group (USA) Inc.
Cover illustration by Mary Ann Lasher.
Cover design by Judith Lagerman.
Interior text design by Laura K. Corless.

ISBN: 978-0-425-23789-2

BERKLEY® PRIME CRIME
Berkley Prime Crime Books are published by The Berkley Publishing Group,
a division of Penguin Group (USA) Inc.,
375 Hudson Street, New York, New York 10014.
BERKLEY® PRIME CRIME and the PRIME CRIME logo are trademarks of Penguin Group (USA) Inc.

PRINTED IN THE UNITED STATES OF AMERICA

10 9 8 7 6 5 4 3 2 1

In memory of Paula Stech,
a woman who taught me the true meaning
of strength and courage in the face of adversity.

Chapter 1

As all reading enthusiasts know, books improve your life in unimaginable ways. They provide a momentary escape from the mundane, serve as food for the mind, and at times when humming isn't a socially acceptable way of passing time with a less than interesting companion, books offer much-needed conversation starters.

That these bound feats of literature also make excellent stand-ins for doorstops, posture correctors, and hand weights is simply icing on the cake. But, like nearly everything else in life, books, when put to the test, have an area where they fail to achieve.

The ability to repel water is that area.

A test they failed in red-inked spades if the bottom row of shelves in Sweet Briar Public Library was any indication. Hard covers, paperbacks . . . it mattered naught. If they were less than a foot off the ground, they fell prey to the effects of the season's most impressive weather event to date, ushering in yet another undeniable fact. . . .

Roger—of the tropical storm variety—was obviously *not* a reading enthusiast.

Groaning, Tori Sinclair hoisted yet another saturated book onto the wheeled cart in the center of the narrow aisle and shook her head, the repetitive motion dislodging the last few strands of light brown hair from a ponytail that had seen better days.

"Has this ever happened before?" she asked as she peered through the nearly empty shelf at the plump woman on the other side.

"Sure as shootin'. Amelia paid us a visit 'bout three years ago but she was pretty easygoing as far as leavin' a mess behind. Before that there was Tom an' Richard an'"—Margaret Louise Davis wiped her hands down the sides of her black polyester pants and gestured to the dark-skinned girl two shelves to her left—"Gus. At least I reckon it was Gus. Though now that I say it out loud it doesn't sound right. Nina, do you remember the one I'm talkin' 'bout? The one that knocked the gazebo in the town square to kingdom come?"

"How could I forget?" Tori's assistant replied with a sigh, her petite frame slumping against the shelf of paperback mysteries that played host to authors with *H* names. "Gus was the worst . . . until this one blew into town, anyway."

"Land sakes these storm names are hard to remember. If I was naming 'em I'd give 'em good southern names that folks can recollect."

Tori smiled in spite of the destruction around them, her friend's words a bright spot in an otherwise miserable morning. "You mean like *yours*, Margaret Louise? Because you're right, it flows off the tongue like a champ. Much, *much* more easily than Tom or Gus."

Oblivious to the teasing tone in Tori's voice, the woman

nodded. "It does, doesn't it? And that's just the kind of name folks need to remember one storm from another." With a huff and a puff, Margaret Louise rose to her feet, her assigned shelf now clear of all water-damaged books. "Though I'm bettin' everyone on Rose's street will remember Roger with not a dab of trouble. He left them the kind of mementos that make forgettin' hard—name or not."

"Rose?" Tori grabbed the last three books on her shelf and stood, her feet guiding her around the local history section and into the fiction aisle Margaret Louise and Nina had been culling through all morning. "Is she okay?"

"Physically, yes. Though that cough she's had for the past six months or so doesn't seem to be getting better. Makes her sound like a sea lion most days." The woman motioned to Tori and Nina to follow, her sandal-clad feet making soft squishing sounds as she wound her way through cart after cart of damaged books en route to the information desk in the center of the library. "I've been after her to see a doctor for months now but that woman is as stubborn as a mule."

Margaret Louise was right. Rose Winters, the oldest in their sewing circle, was stubborn on a good day and downright ornery the rest of the time. But still, everyone loved the retired kindergarten teacher, not the least of which was Tori. In fact, aside from Margaret Louise— and her opposite-in-every-way twin sister, Leona—Rose was one of Tori's favorites. Especially when the eighty-something's bristles retracted in favor of a softer, more mist-inducing edge that reminded Tori of her own great-grandmother. Her *late* great-grandmother.

Blinking back an unexpected tear, she cut her hand through the air, the gesture successfully thwarting the inevitable ten-minute discussion about Rose and her failing health. It wasn't that she didn't care. She did. Very much. But the elderly woman's cough had nothing to do

with the storm or the accompanying damage Margaret
Louise had alluded to at the start. "We'll get her in to a
doctor one way or the other, even if it means calling in
reinforcements from the rest of the Sweet Briar Ladies
Society Sewing Circle. But we can talk about that later.
Tell me about Rose and her neighbors. . . ."

Margaret Louise cocked an eyebrow of confusion.
"Rose and her neighbors?"

"You just said they wouldn't forget Roger anytime
soon." Tori shot an exasperated look at Nina, her assistant's trademark shy smile giving way to all-out amusement at the spectacle that was Margaret Louise Davis.
Rolling her eyes skyward, she shrugged, her words willing her friend to get back on track. "You know . . . that he
left them souvenirs . . ."

"Mementos. I said, mementos."

She moved her index finger in a rolling motion. "And
those would be . . ."

"Busted windows, leaky roofs, damaged porches,
snapped trees, no power."

Tori's gasp echoed against the walls of the library.
"Busted windows? Leaky roo—but how?" She gestured
around the library, her gaze skirting the bottom layer of
shelves within range of the information desk before coming to rest on her friend's face. "I mean, I get that there
was damage—we have a hundred-plus books to serve as
proof of that. But structural damage like you just said?
How? Why?"

"The older parts of town weren't made to sustain
Roger's anger," Nina explained, her quiet tone making
Tori draw closer. "Duwayne said those homes—like them
ones Ms. Winters and her neighbors live in—never would
have been built today. They wouldn't pass code. But . . .
back when they were built . . . it wasn't an issue. Add that
in with decades of age and, in many cases, lack of upkeep
and, well, they're the perfect playground for a storm like

Roger." As if realizing she'd taken over the conversation, Tori's assistant looked at the floor, her dark hair slipping forward to cover her face as her words grew even more hushed. "'Least that's what Duwayne says, anyway."

"And your Duwayne is exactly right," Margaret Louise said as she picked up the conversation and ran with it. "Jake went over there first thing this mornin' to see if everyone was okay and he was shocked. Said he hasn't seen that much damage from a storm in a long time. He offered to help Rose but she refused . . . said she'd wait for Kenny to get to her."

"Kenny?" Tori asked.

"Murdock. Kenny Murdock. He's one of Rose's former kindergarten students. Only now he's 'bout Jake's age and minus the wife and kids."

Jake Davis was Margaret Louise's son and the husband of fellow sewing circle member Melissa. He owned a successful garage in Sweet Briar, which enabled him to put food on the table for the couple's seven children, Margaret Louise's pride and joy.

"Kenny's a bit of a strange bird. Might even call him a bit slow," Margaret Louise continued. "But Rose has championed that boy since he was no bigger 'n a corn sprout. Gets madder 'n a hornet when people dismiss him as being dumb. After she settles down she's quick to point out he has a different kind of smarts."

Tori drank in the information, adding it to her ever-growing mental book of Sweet Briar facts. She may not have lived there long, but—thanks to her sewing sisters and their penchant for gossip—she was figuring out how and where everyone fit in record fashion. Kenny Murdock was simply another name to process.

"Is he close to her as well?" Tori asked.

Margaret Louise nodded. "Slow, dumb, missin' a few marbles . . . whatever you want to call it . . . there's no denying the fact that Kenny cares 'bout Rose. And if

Kenny don't like you, you know it. That one can hold a grudge like there's no tomorrow. Trust me . . . I've seen it with my own two eyes."

Huffing and puffing, the woman hoisted herself onto one of the two stools that perched behind the information desk. "Anyway, over the past few months, I've been noticin' that it's harder for Rose to maintain that little flower garden she has along her walkway. All that bendin' and pullin' is gettin' too much for her. But the one time I said that, she nearly bit my head clear off my neck."

"She's still doing a good job, though," Tori pointed out, her thoughts traveling back to the last time they'd had a meeting at Rose's house. "Her mums looked spectacular, and there wasn't a weed anywhere. She puts the rest of us—or, at least, *me*—to shame."

"That's 'cause Kenny took over. He shows up when she's out there workin' and just quietly goes about the task of helpin' her . . . though his helpin' has become the lion's share of doin'."

"Then I like him."

A smile spread across Margaret Louise's face as a mischievous twinkle lit her eyes. "You haven't even met him, Victoria."

"I don't need to. Any man in his early thirties who shows up and helps an elderly woman with a garden is A-okay in my book." She took a few steps into the local history section and grabbed hold of a cart, the normally squeaky wheels muted somewhat by the saturated carpet. "I sure hope he's gotten there by now, though. I hate to think of Rose walking around in less than ideal conditions."

Margaret Louise waved off her concern. "Oh, he'd already been there. Even 'fore I sent Jake over. But you know how Rose is . . . she insisted he help Martha Jane Barker first. Seems her place was even worse off than Rose's."

Nina stiffened behind the counter.

"Nina? Are you okay?"

"I'm fine, Miss Sinclair."

She bit back the urge to correct her assistant's tendency to use her surname rather than her first name. It was simply no use. She'd been trying for months. "Do you know Martha Jane?"

Nina busied herself with the books on the cart, her head shaking slowly with each damaged novel she stacked on the counter. "Yes. I know Ms. Barker."

Tori looked a question at Margaret Louise only to receive a shrug in return.

"Am I missing something?"

"I'm black."

"I knew *that*, Nina," she said, the ensuing smile disappearing as quickly as it came as the reality of her assistant's words took root. "She has a problem with that?"

"Martha Jane grew up quite wealthy. And by wealthy I mean w-e-a-l-t-h-y. With servants. *Colored* servants," Margaret Louise rushed to explain as something resembling understanding spread across her face. "She's been known to snap her fingers around people of color when out and about."

Nina snorted.

Tori looked from Margaret Louise to Nina and back again. "Then what's she doing living next to Rose? That's hardly the kind of house that screams money."

"She don't trust nobody," Nina said. "She thinks everyone is out to get her money . . . to rob her blind. And when something goes wrong—either real or in her head—people of color are top on her list of suspects."

"Is that true, Margaret Louise?"

Her friend nodded. "She lives in that house as a way to throw people off . . . to think she's broke. But she ain't. And everyone knows it. Most folks suspect she's so paranoid she keeps her money hidden in her house for fear a bank would lose it."

"And she thinks that's *safer*?"

"Paranoia tends to multiply with age, Victoria."

"And she's turned that paranoia toward people like Nina?" She knew her voice was sounding shrill but she couldn't help it. The notion that someone would judge a person like Nina simply because of the color of her skin bothered her. Deeply.

Margaret Louise shrugged. "There might be something to that. But I think it goes deeper. I really do. Martha Jane doesn't like nobody—dark skin or not. Take me for instance. When I won that contest with my sweet potato pie, I brought some over to her. Rose asked me to . . . said Martha Jane wasn't feeling well and couldn't make the Re-Founders Day Festival." Shifting her weight more evenly across the stool, the woman continued. "So I did. But was she grateful? Was she happy that someone remembered her? No. She hollered at me for bringing a plastic fork instead of a real one."

Tori's mouth gaped open. "Couldn't she have just gotten one from her kitchen?"

"There weren't any colored folks around to fetch it for her," Nina interjected with an uncharacteristic edge to her voice.

"I think she's just plain rude. Regardless of color." Margaret Louise reached a reassuring arm across the counter and patted Nina's hand. "Then there was another time when Jake was out walkin' with Jake Junior. They were passing Martha Jane's house when Jake Junior— who wasn't more 'n four or five at the time—dropped his ball in her yard. When he went to fetch it, Martha Jane poked her head out the door and started yellin' at him for trespassin'. *Yellin'* . . . at *my grandbaby*. Can you imagine?"

"Then why would Rose send Kenny over to help her first?" Tori asked.

"Because even as cantankerous as Rose is, she still has a heart filled with gold. You know that, Nina knows that, we all know that. Besides, it won't be long before the drifters sweep into town. They're not more 'n twelve hours behind these nasty storms. And when that happens, that street will be good as new in no time. At least from a standpoint of looking all neat and tidy."

"Drifters?"

"The folks that move around, chasing work. They have no ties anywhere. They just show up, get work fixin' things, and then shove off to the next town, the next tragedy."

Tori considered her friend's words, her mind trying them on in various ways. "I guess that makes sense. I just wish there wasn't so much to do *here*." She waved her hand around the room, her shoulders slumping at the sight of the empty shelves and the water-stained walls.

As if sensing her sadness, Margaret Louise stepped down off her stool and offered Tori a body-squashing bear hug. "Don't you worry, Victoria. It'll all work out."

She supposed Margaret Louise was right. But still . . .

Stepping back, she nodded in spite of the quandary raging in her head. She loved the library, she really did. It was not only her source of income but her passion in life as well. But Rose? Rose was her friend. Shouldn't that take precedence?

"I—I just wish she hadn't refused Jake's help . . . or sent this Kenny fellow off so fast. She needs him, too. Even if her place isn't as bad off."

"As I just said, don't you worry 'bout Rose. If Nina is right, Kenny won't be at Martha Jane's place for long, anyway. In fact"—Margaret Louise glanced at the clock on the far wall—"he's probably workin' on Rose's place right now."

"But I thought you said her place was even worse off than Rose's." Tori flipped through the pages of several books and sighed. In the grand scheme of things, the library had gotten off lucky. Only the bottom row of books had been affected by the rain that had found its way through the building's less than perfect windows. It could have been worse. Much, much worse.

"I did . . ."

Grabbing a notebook from the shelf under the computer, Tori began jotting a list of things that needed to be done in Roger's wake—phone calls to make, damage to document, and a rug to dry. All things that could be done at varying times throughout the day *while* helping Rose . . .

"Because it *is* worse."

The calls she could make from her cell phone. The damage could be documented fairly quickly with the help of her camera. And, if she could get her hands on a power fan, the carpet could be drying all on its own. . . .

"*Much* worse."

Her friend's words filtered through her thoughts, suspending her list-making task momentarily. "Then how could this Kenny person be at Rose's already?"

"Because Ms. Barker wouldn't have let him in the door," Nina offered.

"Why on earth not?"

"Because he's black. Like me."

Chapter 2

As always, Debbie Calhoun's home was an oasis of southern hospitality, with its warm yellow walls, welcoming nooks and crannies, potpourri of delectable smells, and happy chatter of children playing in the background. It was, in a word, the epitome of home.

The fact that it belonged to one of the sweetest members of the Sweet Briar Ladies Society Sewing Circle was simply the icing on the cake. Icing Tori got to taste once every eight or nine weeks.

"I hear the library took a hit," Debbie said as she pulled Tori in for a hug. "Did we lose a lot of books?"

Inhaling the mixture of lilacs, flour, and vanilla that clung to the bakery owner's skin, Tori nodded. "We lost about ten percent of our collection. But it could have been a lot worse."

Debbie stepped back, studied her from head to toe. "And the rugs? The tables? The chairs?"

"They're all salvageable for the most part. The rugs will dry and the furniture is fine. In fact, if the windows had been in better shape, we wouldn't have suffered damage at all."

With a quick glance around the corner, the woman lowered her voice, her pale blue eyes rounding as she continued. "And the children's room? Is it—is it okay?"

She couldn't help but smile. The children's room, which was a project that had been near and dear to her heart from the moment she arrived in Sweet Briar, had become a source of pride for the town's most loyal patrons as well. Its story-filled walls, jam-packed shelves, and costume trunk had made it a destination of choice for parents and youngsters alike. "Miraculously, it was untouched. No water damage whatsoever."

Debbie released a sigh of relief. "Boy, will Suzanna and Jackson be happy to hear that. They were in an absolute panic when Colby told them the library had been affected by the storm." Tucking her arm inside Tori's, Debbie led the way down the wood-planked hallway that linked the entryway with the rest of the house. "You should have seen the way Jackson's lip quivered at the notion he might not be able to wear the Peter Pan costume while acting out his fight with Captain Hook. It nearly tugged my heart right out of my body, Victoria."

A swell of voices greeted them as they approached the hearth room on the backside of the house, the familiar sound a welcoming respite from a long and trying day. Turning to Debbie, Tori stopped just short of their final destination. "I have to admit, I was surprised when Margaret Louise told me we were still on for tonight. With the storm and the cleanup, it seems as if sewing would be the last thing on anyone's mind."

"Sewing is therapeutic, you know that."

"But Rose . . . shouldn't we be coming together to help her instead? We can sew and gossip another time."

"We don't gossip, Victoria. We *visit*."

"And *talk*."

"And talk," Debbie confirmed as she pushed a hand through her dirty blonde hair.

"About other people."

Biting back the smile they both knew was there, Debbie brought her eyebrows together in quizzical fashion. "Do we do that?"

Tori laughed, the sound echoing her arrival to the members of the circle assembled just out of view.

"Now go on in. I'll join you in just a second—after I make sure Colby has things under control with the kids."

"You *know* he does, Debbie. That husband of yours is nothing if not the absolute epitome of a Renaissance man."

A reddish hue crept across her friend's face as her ever-present smile grew still wider. "You're right."

"I know." Squeezing Debbie's hand, Tori turned toward the room that housed her fellow sewing comrades, a group of ladies who had opened their hearts and homes to her over the past six months. "Well, I'll head inside now and—"

"But that's not *all* I know," Debbie teased as she, too, began walking, her path taking her toward the front door and the knock that signaled the arrival of yet another circle member.

Tori stopped midstep. "What are you talking about?"

"Rose needs the therapy as much as anyone else."

"Rose needs—" She stopped, Debbie's words finally registering. "You mean she's here?"

"She's here."

"Why didn't you say so?"

"You didn't ask."

She considered her friend's words. "I didn't ask just now, either . . ."

"True. But I couldn't handle the worry on your face any longer."

Transparency had always been her downfall. "That obvious, huh?"

"That *endearing*." Debbie shooed her hands at Tori. "Now get in there before Dixie starts stamping her feet at my door, will you?"

Hoisting the strap of her tote bag higher on her shoulder, Tori grinned. "Feet stamping is better than finger wagging."

"Keep talking, Victoria, and I'll get both."

As Debbie headed toward the front door, Tori turned back to the hearth room, the promise of seeing Rose with her own two eyes propelling her forward. It was hard enough to imagine anyone picking through storm damage without a mate by his or her side. The thought of an elderly woman going it alone in less than perfect health was even worse.

"Oh, Victoria, we're so glad to see you." Georgina Hayes said by way of a greeting from her spot on the armchair to the left of the fireplace. "I had hoped to get over to the library today to check on things but I got sidetracked by fires that seemed to be igniting—one after the other—all over town."

Stopping just inside the doorway, Tori nodded at the town's top elected official, a tall, dark-haired woman with a no-nonsense set to her jaw. Despite the fact that the position was virtually a birthright thanks to her kinship with her mayoral predecessors, Georgina took her role seriously, looking after all things Sweet Briar.

"Compared to what I've been hearing, the library fared relatively well compared to other—"

"Fires? Did you say, fires?" Beatrice Tharrington looked up from the khaki-colored skirt she was sewing, her eyes wide. "Luke didn't hear a single fire engine all day. He busied himself with blocks all afternoon, crafting skyscrapers and some such things like that. Had he heard the hint of a fire engine, he would have abandoned building in favor of begging to go outside and watch. He's such an adventurous little bloke."

The youngest in the room, Beatrice often faded into the background among the more talkative members of the circle, her rare bursts of conversation—laden with a British accent in a roomful of southerners—tending to bring an awkward hush to the room and a subsequent flush to the nanny's face.

"I—I'm sorry. I shouldn't blather on like that."

"And why not? Blatherin' is good for the soul." Margaret Louise shot her hand into the air and motioned Tori toward the empty sofa cushion to her right as she continued to encourage Beatrice out of her cocoon. "Just ask Georgina."

"Ask *me*? Ask *me*? Isn't that the pot calling the kettle black?" Georgina huffed as she swiveled her body to the side and reached into the sewing box she'd propped beside her chair. "I don't blather. I *explain*. I *encourage*. And I do my best to *rally*."

"Rally what?" Leona Elkin lowered her latest travel magazine to her lap and peered at Georgina over the top of her glasses.

"My constituents." Turning back to Beatrice, Georgina took charge of the conversation once again. "When I mentioned fires, I meant in a figurative way, my dear. Every time my office would address a problem—such as a power outage or a downed tree—another would pop up in its place. Happened time after time. But 'round about noon, folks who weren't affected by Roger started showing up . . . asking how they could help those who weren't so lucky."

"Noon, you say?"

Tori turned her head to the right, smiled at the sight of Rose bent over the hem of a blouse in a lamplit corner. "Rose! I've been so worried about—"

"Noon," Georgina confirmed, cutting Tori off midsentence. "It sure does a mayor good to see her residents chipping in and helping each other through difficult times."

"Kenny showed up long before noon. Crack of dawn brought him to my door," Rose said proudly, her slipper-clad foot setting her chair to a gentle rock.

"Kenny?" Beatrice sputtered.

Rose's eyes narrowed. "Yes . . ."

The nanny sat up tall, her half-sewn skirt slipping to the floor in favor of a white-knuckle hold on both armrests of her chair. "K-Kenny? Kenny is *here*? In Sweet Briar?"

"Of course," Rose snapped. "It's where he's been since the day he was born."

Beatrice's face drained of all color. "He was born in Texas!"

Rose's eyes rolled skyward as a chorus of groans broke loose around the room. "Not *that* Kenny, Beatrice. Kenny *Murdock*."

Beatrice's shoulders slumped. "Oh."

Confused, Tori bypassed Margaret Louise's offer and sank into the closest chair she could find—one that put her directly next to her personal Sweet Briar encyclopedia. Lowering her voice to a barely discernable level, she put words to the question begging to be asked. "Um, Leona? What did I just miss?"

"*Miss*, dear?"

"With Beatrice . . ."

Flipping to the next page in her magazine, Margaret Louise's twin sister *tsked* softly under her breath before providing the answer Tori sought. "Beatrice is obsessed with Kenny Rogers."

She snorted back a laugh. "Kenny Rogers? You can't be serious."

Leona's gaze traveled across the room and stopped on Beatrice. "I can't?"

Tori followed suit, studying the disappointed woman with a new set of eyes. "Well, how obsessed is obsessed?"

"Have you heard her phone ring?"

She shook her head.

"'Islands in the Stream.'"

"Okay, but lots of people use songs as ringtones. It's really not that unusual, Leona."

"Do lots of people carry a picture of the person who *sings* their ringtone?"

Tori swallowed. "I don't know for sure but I imagine some do . . . if they really like that particular artist."

"Do they also insert their own face into the picture to make it look as if they've spent time together?"

"Insert . . ." Lowering her voice still further, she lifted her palms from her lap and held them outward. "Look, if I've learned anything over the past six months or so it's the importance of not judging people. So, she likes Kenny Rogers . . . big deal."

"If you say so, dear." Leona shifted her magazine to the end table beside her seat, then set to work plucking imaginary lint from her tweed skirt with perfectly manicured hands. "But as you well know, obsessions of that nature can get out of hand."

Leona was right. They could. And they did. But she also knew that obsessions of the dangerous variety weren't commonplace in a town the size of Sweet Briar, South Carolina. Surely the recent obsession-based abduction of Colby Calhoun—Debbie's author husband—had met the geographical quota for the next century or ten . . .

"What are you working on this evening, Victoria?" Rose's voice, frail and husky, broke through her wool-gathering, snapping her back to the here and now.

Setting her tote on the cushion between herself and Leona, Tori pulled a stack of multicolored fleece pieces from the bag. "I'm working on scarves for a women's shelter I used to volunteer at back in Chicago. Now that I'm living here, I figured this was a way I could contribute from a distance."

"How are you making them?" Margaret Louise bellowed across the room, her eyes narrowed to near slits as she bobbed her head in such a way as to provide the best view of Tori's project.

"Well, I'll stack these four long rectangles together in alternating colors—this one will be blue, white, blue, white. I'll sew a straight seam right down the middle," Tori explained as she held the pile up for all to see. "Then, it's just a matter of cutting from the outer sides toward the center seam to create a boa type effect."

"That'll be real pretty," Debbie said as she returned to the room and motioned the last of the circle members to the empty space beside Margaret Louise.

"I hope so," Tori said. "Some of these women have next to nothing. I figured this was something I could do . . . something that can make them feel pretty when they step outside on a cold winter's day."

Needles stilled and machines quieted as the circle members stopped to listen to Tori's description, the allure of a new sewing project reaching each of them in a way the others could understand.

"I got the idea from Melissa, actually." Tori laid the fabric across her thighs and looked around the room before focusing on Margaret Louise. "Is Melissa coming?"

The woman shook her head. "Not tonight. Lulu wasn't feelin' well after school today. I offered to whip up some of Mee-Maw's famous feel-better-brownies and look after the young-un so Melissa could get out, but she declined."

"I don't know how that one keeps from going stir-crazy with seven kids. I'd be in a padded room." Leona shook her head as she swept her hand across her lint-free skirt.

"If you had *one* you'd be in a padded room." Margaret Louise's laugh, hearty and loud, brought a smile to everyone's lips. "That's why you have no offspring, Twin."

Leona tapped her chin with a bejeweled finger. "I have Paris."

"Garden-variety bunnies don't count," snapped Rose.

"Paris is anything but garden-variety," Leona argued. "He's intelligent . . . smart . . . attractive . . ."

Rose rolled her eyes amid the pockets of laughter that sprang up around the room. "He's a *bunny*, Leona."

"He's more than that, Rose."

"Oh good heavens," the elderly woman grumbled in disgust.

"How many scarves do you plan on making, Victoria?" Beatrice asked, her quiet voice serving as a cease-fire in a war that was as much about personality differences as the topic at hand.

"As many as I can make. The shelter has beds for nearly twenty women on a nightly basis but they also do an outreach program that reaches another thirty to forty."

"You could make hats, too. Something that matches the scarf and keeps their head warm at the same time," Georgina suggested as she shifted in her seat. "Maybe add some sort of decoration or fringe."

Tori smiled, her own initial excitement for the project multiplying in the wake of Debbie and Georgina's enthusiasm. "I hadn't thought of that, but you're right."

"I got a lovely scarf and hat from a library patron when I was pushed out of my job," Dixie muttered as she shuffled her way across the hearth room to claim the empty spot beside Debbie.

Lifting her magazine from its resting place, Leona buried her face in its contents once again, a faint snort rising up from behind the glossy pages.

"*Must we*, Dixie?" Margaret Louise asked as she, too,

pulled a project from her sewing box—a tiny lace-edged bib for her youngest grandbaby. "You had talked about retirin' for months. It just happened a dab sooner than you'd planned. Besides, that was over six months ago."

"Six months I'd still have been working if the board hadn't hired Victoria behind my back."

"Do you like the children's room she created in the library, Dixie?" Georgina asked with an air of boredom to her voice.

"Yes, of course. But—"

"Do you like the book delivery she set up with the retirement home in town?" Debbie caught Tori's eye and winked.

"Of course, but—"

"Did Victoria make you lead storyteller for the pre-school crowd?" Beatrice chimed in quietly.

"Yes, but—"

"Then quit your blathering."

Dixie shot Georgina a dirty look. "Blathering?"

"Don't worry, it's good for your soul . . . isn't it, Beatrice?" Margaret Louise smiled triumphantly. "Besides, by being retired you no longer have to answer to a board."

"Amen," Dixie mumbled before shrugging her sweater-clad shoulders in Tori's direction. "How'd we fare with the storm, anyway?"

Six months ago, the use of the word *we* when referring to the library would have been a sign of her predecessor's continued bitterness and never-ending territorial claim on Tori's place of employment. But now, after rubbing elbows in their weekly circle meetings, she saw it more as a shared passion for books that inevitably placed them on the same team. A team Dixie was protesting less and less as the days wore on.

Pulling the fleece fabric to her chest she closed her eyes, breathed in the memory of the empty shelves she'd left behind in favor of a few hours of sewing-induced sanity.

"We lost everything on the bottom row of shelves . . . but it could have been worse."

Margaret Louise nodded her agreement. "When I showed up at the library this mornin' to help, I was expectin' things to be worse. But other than the books Victoria just mentioned, everything else will be good as new in no time. You mark my words."

Dixie released an audible sigh Tori not only understood but shared as well. "There's no doubt we were lucky. Especially considering the age of the building.

"In fact, from what I've been hearing all day long, the library got off lucky in the grand scheme of things. Some of the other older buildings in town didn't fare quite so well, isn't that right, Georgina?"

"I believe Rose can answer that better than anyone else." The mayor gestured toward Rose, the elderly woman's tired form reminding Tori of her evening's mission.

"Rose? Would you like to stay with me for a while? I have plenty of room . . . not to mention electricity," Tori said, her voice stopping just shy of pleading.

"Candles worked for my great-grandparents, candles will work for me." The retired schoolteacher's chin jutted forward with an air of resolution. "Besides, Kenny is right next door at Martha Jane's if I need anything."

"Kenny might not be able to handle the kinds of problems that come from storm damage like we've seen," Georgina cautioned gently, the hesitancy in her voice as much a reflection of her respect for Rose as it was anything else. "You know he can get a little unsettled when he feels trapped or unsure of himself."

"I know no such thing," Rose hissed as she pulled the flaps of her sweater more tightly against her body. "Need I remind you that book smarts don't always translate to life smarts?"

Tori watched her friend closely, the stress of the storm emphasizing the tremor in the woman's pale and bony hand. While she understood Georgina's overriding concern for Rose, she also couldn't discount the one thing she'd come to know about the group's matriarch.

Rose Winters valued her independence and believed in the power of loyalty—characteristics that were not only honorable but worthy of celebration as well.

"Could I stay with you, then?" Tori asked. "That way we could fix minor things while we're waiting for Kenny to finish up at your neighbor's house."

Large charcoal-colored eyes—magnified behind bifocals—turned to study her, a fleeting look of moisture the only evidence her offer had been heard. She continued on, enthusiasm for her off-the-cuff idea mounting with each word. "We could get things back in order around your home and I could pick your brain on ways to reach our school-aged patrons—the ones who are a little too big for the children's room but not necessarily ready for the adult section—"

"Excuse me, ladies, but there's a call for you, Georgina." Debbie's husband poked his head around the corner, a phone in his outstretched left hand. "It's Chief Dallas. Said it's important."

"Thank you, Colby." Excusing herself to the hallway, Georgina hurried out of the room, the phone held close to her ear as pockets of conversation resumed around the circle.

Tori considered prodding Rose for an answer but, in the end, opted to let the sewing work its magic on the elderly lady before approaching the subject once again. Sometimes patience and decorum were the best course of action. Instead, she asked for specifics about some of the damage her house had sustained, the woman's description bringing a renewed catch to her throat and a worry to her heart.

As if sensing her feelings, Rose met her eye with a

shaky smile. "Don't you worry about me, Victoria. Kenny is a marvel. He looks after me almost as he would his mamma."

"You've been good to him, too, Rose," Debbie said as she crossed her feet at the ankles before digging her hand into her sewing box and extracting three spools of varying shades of pink thread. "You've been his biggest champion, encouraging people to give him a shot in life."

Rose waved off their hostess's praise. "Too often people in this world equate everything with education. Even decency. As if being a compassionate human being is something taught in a book rather than the world at large. But regardless of his challenges in school as a young boy, Kenny has always been kind, hardworking, and honest to a—"

"I'm sorry for the interruption, but that couldn't be helped." Georgina strode back into the room, her now empty hand held tightly in a fist. Reclaiming her spot beside the fireplace, the mayor closed her eyes and rested her head against the seat back.

"Is everything okay, Georgina?" Debbie asked, voicing the inquiry mirrored on the faces of those around them.

Slowly, the woman opened her eyes, her gaze skirting the room's occupants before coming to rest on Rose. "There's been a robbery."

"A robbery?" Margaret Louise echoed.

Georgina nodded, her gaze still firmly rooted on Rose's face. "Martha Jane claims she was robbed in her own home."

"Good heavens, is she okay?"

"She's fine, Dixie. But she's fit to be tied and ready to press charges. *Now.*"

"She knows who did it?" Tori asked.

"Yes." Georgina broke eye contact with Rose long

enough to send a meaningful glance in Tori's direction. "She does."

"Who?" Rose stammered, her voice cracking under the stress of the day. "Who was it?"

"Kenny. Kenny Murdock."

Chapter 3

If she didn't know any better, she'd actually think Roger had a split personality. Persona A had been relatively tame, showing a hint of manners despite a propensity to make a mess. Persona B, on the other hand, had been nothing short of tyrannical, subjecting his victims to a host of ill-tempered behavior with absolutely no regard to the plight of the elderly or anyone else.

Standing in the center of Rose's prized sewing room, it was no secret which personality had come knocking on the elderly woman's front door. And like most unwelcome guests, he'd stayed entirely too long.

"Oh, Milo, I had no idea," Tori gasped from behind her hand as she surveyed the damage to her friend's home. "I mean, I knew she'd suffered more damage than we did at the library, but *this*? It's . . . it's insane."

The third-grade teacher, who was single-handedly restoring her faith in the opposite sex, slid his arm around her waist as he, too, took stock of their surroundings. "It's bad, there's no doubt about that. But it's fixable, Tori. And what's *not* fixable is replaceable from what I can see."

She willed herself to take a deep breath, to get her emotions under control, but it was hard. For years she'd seen televised images of damage sustained from storms, their impact dulled by the absence of a shared reality. But standing there, witnessing the fallout in person, was overwhelming if not downright disheartening.

"I mean look at this . . ." Tori squatted down in the middle of the room, her hand sweeping across the overturned sewing machine and wooden sewing box that had always reminded her so much of her great-grandmother's things. "Rose loved this room. She told me she could sit in here for hours sewing away the time."

"And she will again. I promise." Milo Wentworth swooped down beside her, turning her face toward his with a gentle hand. "We'll get that tree all the way down, replace the broken windows, and put everything back where it belongs."

She encased his hand with her own, the man's calming presence something she'd come to realize she not only needed but craved as well. Peering up, she studied the amber flecks that softened the darkness of his eyes. "But how, Milo? You work all day long at the school. Then, when the students are gone, you've got papers to correct and parent calls to field. And I'm tied up all day at the library. How on earth are we going to get this place in shape anytime soon?"

A slow smile stretched his mouth upward, the motion etching dimples in his cheeks. "I don't work *all* day, Tori."

Reaching up, she tousled the longish thatch of burnished brown hair that graced the center of his head. "You're a sweetheart to even think about coming over here after working with kids all day long . . . but I can't ask you to do that."

"You're not. I'm offering." Motioning around the room, Milo's eyes narrowed. "Trust me, I couldn't sleep any better than you could knowing that Rose is picking around one trip hazard after the other. It's not safe. For anyone, much less Rose."

Rose.

It was hard to look around, to see the shattered windowpanes and the overturned knickknacks that seemed to dominate the retired kindergarten teacher's home. But it had been even harder to see the utter disbelief on the woman's face when she heard the news about her former pupil.

Lowering her voice to a near whisper, Tori jerked her head in the direction of the closed door halfway down the hall. "You should have seen her face when Georgina said Kenny was being questioned for stealing. She was devastated and angry all at the same time."

"Rose adores Kenny. Has for as long as I can remember." Milo straightened up, his six foot one frame making its way across the tiny room to right a lamp that had tipped onto its side. "Celia used to say I'd be the same way one day when my own students are grown and out on their own."

She cast a sidelong glance in his direction, the mention of his late wife's name bringing a catch to her heart. Milo had been a widower for ten years, and Tori had never met his wife, a woman he'd been married to for all of about six months before cancer claimed her life. Time had marched on since then, of course, healing hurts and spotlighting new perspectives. But still, she couldn't help but hesitate when Celia's name was mentioned.

"Are—are you okay?" she asked, her shoulders bracing for some sort of revelation even she couldn't identify.

"Of course." Pulling her in for a hug, he rested his chin on the top of her head, the rumble of his words spreading outward from their point of impact. "We've talked about this, Tori. Things happen for a reason whether we understand that at the time or not."

He was right. When she'd found Jeff in the closet of their engagement hall with his pants down around his ankles, she'd been devastated, his inappropriate shenanigans with a coworker rocking her to the core and propelling her to run as far from Chicago as possible. At the time, she'd thought her life was over. Yet now, in hindsight, she realized Jeff's betrayal was the catalyst for something better.

Much, much better.

Shaking her thoughts from a path that had absolutely nothing to do with Rose, Tori forced herself to focus on the true topic of their conversation. "All the way here in the car, Rose kept saying the same things over and over again . . . 'Kenny wouldn't steal,' 'Kenny is a good boy,' 'Money holds no meaning for Kenny.'"

"And she believes that from the bottom of her heart." Milo took Tori's hand and led her from the sewing room, their feet padding softly past Rose's bedroom door. When they reached the tiny living room on the front side of the house, he stopped, his voice rising to a near-normal decibel. "I just hope she's right."

She heard herself gasp only to stifle it as quickly as it came. "Does that mean you think he stole Martha Jane's money?"

He shrugged. "Not necessarily. In all fairness, I don't know Kenny all that well. He tends to keep to himself. Even on the days he bags groceries at Leeson's Market he tends to say very little. In fact . . . the only time I've ever heard him say more than a sentence or two is whenever I see him with Rose." Bending at the waist, Milo pushed a sheer white panel from the window and glanced outside, downed limbs and sagging power lines greeting them in taunting fashion.

"Why?" she asked, the purported relationship between the elderly woman and her former pupil tugging at something deep inside her soul.

"You mean why does he talk to her when he doesn't talk to anyone else?"

She nodded.

"Because she believed in him from the start." Milo turned his head to the left and then the right, his gaze traveling down the road in either direction. "She believed in him when the kids on the playground teased him for being slow. She believed in him when prospective employers questioned his ability to work. She believed in him when his parents passed away when he was in his early twenties, leaving him to fend for himself for the first time in his life. And she believes in him now despite what sounds like damning evidence."

"Evidence?"

"Martha Jane Barker has stashed large sums of money in her house for years. Yet Kenny shows up to help her after the storm and it suddenly disappears?"

He was right. Things didn't bode well for Kenny Murdock's innocence. Then again, Tiffany Ann Gilbert—Sweet Briar's town sweetheart—had shown up dead in the library parking lot not long after Tori came to town. And while there were many who linked the two instances together, they couldn't have been more wrong. So didn't it stand to reason the same could be said for the situation with Kenny Murdock?

She said as much to Milo.

"I suppose. I mean, anything's possible. But you have to admit it's a heckuva coincidence."

A firm knock at Rose's front door brought an end to further discussion. Peeking out the window once again, Milo nodded at a man standing on the front porch. "Doesn't take them long to blow into town, does it?"

"Who is that?" she asked as she drank in the sight of the average-sized man with the dirty blond hair and sky blue eyes standing on Rose's front stoop.

"A drifter. Storms like these bring them by the dozens."

"Chasing work, I take it?" she asked as she noted the tool belt secured around the man's hips.

"That about sums it up." Milo shadowed her down the hall as she closed the gap between the window and the door with several quick strides. "If it goes as it usually does after these things, this guy won't be the last knock we hear."

Yanking open the door, Tori smiled at the man on the other side. "What can I do for you?"

Extending a calloused hand in her direction, the man, clad in a red and black flannel button-down over a white T-shirt, smiled back. "Good evenin', ma'am. My name is Doug. Hewitt."

"Doug," Milo repeated along with a slight nod of his head.

Gesturing toward the house, Doug continued, his left hand finding the top of his tool belt. "I can see the storm has turned your house topsy-turvy. Trees down, windows broke, shingles torn off your roof. Was wonderin' if you might need a little help. My prices are fair. I charge sixty dollars a day for labor, fifty if you can give me a roof over my head and food in my stomach while I'm workin'."

"Seriously?"

"Yes, ma'am."

Tori stared up at Milo. "He could get this place cleaned up faster than either of us could do after work. . . ."

"What kind of roof do you need?" Milo asked. "I mean, would a cot in the garage suffice?"

"Stayed in a lot worse 'n that before."

She looked back at Doug, studied the way his smile lit his face as his hand left his tool belt long enough to rake its way through his disheveled hair. "It's not like I'm lookin' to be real fancy or nothin'. Just need some work. Got myself a wife and two young-uns back home in Mississippi. Sooner I get some work lined up, sooner I can get it done and be on my way back home again."

"It must be hard to be away from them like this."

His eyes dulled as he nodded. "It is. But the souvenirs I bring back from each trip helps. Teaches them things, too."

"When could you start?" Milo asked.

"Don't see why I couldn't start this very moment."

Tori glanced at Milo over her shoulder, recognized the look of relief in his face. Turning back to the man on the porch once again, she stepped outside. "Then you're hired."

"Only instead of bunking here, you'll be staying at my place, about six blocks away." Milo, too, stepped onto the porch, his hand finding Doug's and shaking it firmly.

"And the food?" Doug asked.

"I'll take care of that." Tori motioned toward the downed trees that littered Rose's small yard. "In fact, if you start on some of these trees now, I'll head on home and be back with a pot of soup in about an hour or so. Will that work?"

Doug grinned. "Soup sounds mighty good, ma'am."

"Tori."

"Excuse me?"

"That's my name," Tori said as she turned and placed a hand on Milo's shoulder. "And this is Milo."

"It's mighty nice to meet you. And I sure appreciate the work."

"Do a good job and we'll appreciate you, too."

Surprised, Tori looked up at Milo, his gruff words catching her off guard. If Doug noticed though, he didn't let it show.

"I intend to do just that."

"Then everything will go just fine." Milo waved his

hand around the neighborhood, his gaze propelling hers to follow suit. "Seems you've got a lot of friends looking for work in this neighborhood. That's okay provided you understand that you will be watched."

"They may be lookin' for work same as me, but I don't know any of them. I travel alone. Just me, myself, and my conscience."

"Then we'll get along just fine."

She wasn't sure what made her do it, what propelled her to stop at Martha Jane Barker's house instead of going straight home. She didn't really know the woman beyond overlapping visits to Leeson's Market, and what she did know wasn't necessarily the stuff that inspired an overwhelming desire to strike up a friendship. Yet the pull to stop by and offer assistance had guided her feet from Rose's house to Martha's front door anyway.

There was a part of her that simply wanted to help someone through a rough patch. It had been part of her nature since she was old enough to know right from wrong. But there was also a part of her that recognized the glaring truth in a situation.

Tori raised her fist to the door and knocked, the staccato sound a near match to the beat of her heart. Hiring Doug to get Rose's place in order had been a smart decision, of that she had no doubt. Milo offering up his house as a bunkhouse for the man had removed any nagging worry about Rose's safety.

But something was still amiss. Something far bigger than shattered windows and downed trees, something more gut-wrenching than a tipped lamp and damaged sewing machine . . .

Rose was hurting, plain and simple.

And it wasn't the kind of hurt that would disappear with a few whacks of a hammer or the hum of a chain saw.

No, Rose's heartache would be erased by one thing and one thing only. . . .

She knocked again.

"She's sitting on the deck around back."

Tori glanced over her shoulder, her gaze falling on a solidly built man of about thirty, his high-and-tight military crew cut squaring a face that already leaned toward boxy. "Oh, hi. Are you Martha Jane's son?"

"No, ma'am." The man tipped his head to the right to avoid the last of the sun's rays. "I'm just here to get things back in order."

"Oh, like Doug?" she asked as she waved her hand in the direction of the house whose backyard abutted Martha Jane's.

He shot her a quizzical look. "Ma'am?"

"Doug . . . the man I just . . ." She stopped, realized she was speaking Greek to a man who was obviously one of the dozen or so drifters Milo had warned her about. "Do you think it's okay if I walk through her backyard?"

He raised his hands in the air. "Don't see why not. It ain't like you're walking on fine crystal or a bed of breakable diamonds."

"It could be." The second the words were out, she wished she could press Rewind. She didn't know Martha Jane Barker well enough to be passing judgment, her only real knowledge of the woman based on hearsay. "Thanks for your help. By the way, I'm Tori. Tori Sinclair."

"Ma'am."

And with that, he was gone, his muscular frame disappearing around the opposite side of Martha Jane's house.

Shrugging, she made her way toward the woman's deck, the steady sound of a rocking chair confirming her presence. "Martha Jane? It's Victoria Sinclair."

A lined face peeked through the torn and tattered screen that wrapped around three sides of the deck, the mesh material serving as a buffer for insects and other pests. "I know you . . . you're that new librarian that Rose is always talking about."

"I am." She motioned toward the screen door. "Would you mind if I come in?"

The woman stood and eyed her suspiciously. "Why?"

Why indeed.

"I noticed the damage to your home and just want to make sure you're okay . . . see if there's anything I can do to help."

"You mean the way Rose helped when she sent over that—that criminal?"

She felt her shoulders slump. "Martha Jane . . . are you *sure* Kenny stole your money?"

"Of course I'm sure," the woman snapped, the shrillness of her voice making Tori wince. "One minute my money was there . . . in my top dresser drawer. The next it was gone."

"Is it possible someone broke in? That *someone else* took your money?"

"No! That money was there for more years than you've been alive. And then suddenly, yesterday, it disappears right out of my drawer—poof! And you want to know what the only difference about yesterday was?"

She waited, knowing the answer would come whether she asked for it or not.

"I'll tell you what it was . . . it was Kenny."

The snap of a twig on the other side of the deck made her pause. "What about the other man you have working here?"

"You mean Curtis?"

She bobbed her head to the right, took in the man's muscular frame as he picked his way across the woman's backyard, his hands scooping up scattered tree limbs. "Curtis? Yeah . . . I guess."

Martha Jane propped her wrinkled hands on her hips. "I hired Curtis *after* Kenny stole my money."

Her shoulders slumped further. "Martha Jane, Rose is crushed by the news. Absolutely crushed." Glancing toward the man in the yard one last time, she willed her voice to take on a conspiratorial tone. "Would you mind if I saw the spot where Kenny found your money? So I can explain it to Rose in a way she'll understand?"

The elderly woman's eyes narrowed. "You want to come into my home?"

Tori held her breath and nodded.

"You want me to let you look inside my dresser drawers?"

Again, she nodded. "I know it seems odd, but I'm just trying to help Rose face reality sooner rather than later."

After what seemed like an eternity, the woman stepped backward, her hand tugging the screen door open. "Suit yourself. It's high time Rose faced facts about that good-for-nothin'. She's wasted enough time on that boy as far as I'm concerned."

Tori cringed at the woman's terminology. "Rose seems to think Kenny is a good guy. That he's honest and hard-working and—"

"Well she's obviously mistakin', isn't she?" Martha Jane stamped her slipper-clad foot on the wooden floor, her hands coming together in a clap as she peered through the screen beside the door. "They're all the same, I tell you. Rude and lazy to the core."

"All?" Confused, Tori followed the path of Martha Jane's gaze.

"See that one? He should have that yard cleared by now."

She looked past Curtis and into Rose's yard, the blond man she'd hired bending to retrieve sticks again and again, stopping occasionally to toss them into an ever-growing pile not far from the property line that separated the two homes. "It looks like he's working to me. . . ."

"Hogwash," Martha Jane argued. "He's pretending

'cause he knows we're watching. And look at *my* help. That man should be up on the roof patching holes instead of writing notes in that notebook of his. Writing doesn't fix things. A hammer and nails does."

Realizing the men were both within earshot of everything the elderly woman said, Tori lowered her voice to a near whisper. "When did Curtis start?"

"About thirty minutes ago."

"Thirty minutes?" she echoed in disbelief.

"That's right . . . thirty minutes."

"Maybe he's prioritizing the jobs, writing them down so he can refer to them as he goes along."

Stamping her foot once again, the woman gestured toward the yard. "He can do that in his head *while* he's fixing my home. That *is* what I'm paying for, isn't it?"

She considered arguing, contemplated defending the stranger on the other side of the screen enclosure who appeared to be working rather diligently in her view, but she opted in the end to let it go. She was there to help Rose, not to try and talk sense into someone who prided herself on arrogance and a sense of entitlement.

"Could I see that drawer now? The one where you kept your money until it disappeared?"

"You mean until it was *stolen*, don't you?"

Resisting the urge to roll her eyes, Tori simply nodded.

"Then follow me. My room's just inside this doorway." Martha Jane shuffled into her home via a door that led to the screened porch. One foot inside, she turned around, extending her finger within mere inches of Tori's nose. "Don't touch anything."

"I wouldn't think of it," she mumbled as she made a mental note to use Rose's neighbor as a local example the next time Leona took a dig at Chicago's big city dangers and paranoia.

Martha Jane beckoned her down the hall and around

a corner, the trek leading them to the back side of the house once again. Only this time, the screens separating the indoors from the outdoors were confined to a standard size window to the left of Martha Jane's canopied bed. "I keep my money in my top drawer. Have since my husband passed away twenty years ago."

Tori nodded absentmindedly, her attention thwarted by a wooden jewelry box in the center of the dresser, a beautifully handcrafted dark cherry box that begged to be noticed. She leaned closer only to feel a smack on her arm.

Startled, she met Martha Jane's defensive gaze. "I'm sorry. I guess your jewelry box caught my eye. It's exquisite."

The woman's stance softened ever so slightly. "My great-grandfather, Matthew Tucker Barker, made that box; his initials are even carved into the bottom. He made that picture frame over there"—she pointed from a framed black-and-white photograph to a dark cherry triangular wood and glass box on the opposite wall—"and that case, too."

Following the path made by the woman's outstretched finger, Tori stepped in for a closer look, her reflection disappearing as she focused on the pale blue material inside. "What's this?" she asked.

"Sweet Briar's first flag."

She leaned still closer, studied the trio of images that made up the town's crest. The flames were easy to understand, the image a reminder of the town's destruction during the Civil War. The pyramid of three bricks beside it symbolized the town's subsequent rebirth. But the third picture was one she didn't understand. Pointing at the image of a white picket fence bathed in sunlight, she peered over her shoulder at Martha Jane. "What does this one mean?"

"Warmth and friendliness."

"Warmth and friendliness," she repeated quietly, the

words bringing a smile to her lips. "I like that. I like that *a lot*."

"Hogwash is what it is," Martha Jane snapped as she folded her arms across her chest. "Except for the pile of bricks. That one, at least, is accurate. Or was for about three weeks . . . before the founders ordered a new one on account of their feeling that six bricks represented strength better than three."

"The flames are accurate, too. The town *did* burn to the ground."

"By derelicts."

Tori bit back the urge to smile. "And the warmth and friendliness part? What's wrong with that?"

"If Sweet Briar were still warm and friendly, good-for-nothins like Kenny Murdock wouldn't be robbing me blind."

Ahhh yes, the reason for this visit . . .

Pulling her gaze from the hand-sewn flag, Tori fixed it on the dresser once again. "Don't you think your money would have been safer in a bank? Where it's monitored by people and cameras?"

"I most certainly do not. Why would I want all those strangers handling my money when I could keep it here?"

"Because they're professionals and that's what they do?"

"Hogwash!" Yanking the top drawer open, the woman gestured inside. "See? I kept it right here. In the front corner by my socks where it's been for years."

"Oh, I see. . . ." Poking her head over the woman's shoulder, she took stock of a drawer that contained three thin stacks of pristinely folded shirts and sweaters. Confused, she looked back at Martha Jane. "Where are they?"

"*Kenny* took them. I told you that," the woman hissed.

"He took your socks?" She heard the sarcasm in her voice and rushed to soften its edges. "Why would he do that?"

"Good heavens, child, he didn't steal my socks. He wasn't after my socks. He was after my money. The socks are right here." With a push of one drawer and a firm pull on the one below it, Martha Jane pointed. "See? I switched drawers the other day and—"

A sharp intake of air escaped the woman's mouth as Tori's gaze picked through numerous piles of white ankle socks before coming to rest on more money than she'd ever seen in one place at one time.

She felt her mouth gape open. "Is that it? Is that your—"

"My money, my *money*! It's safe!"

Chapter 4

With a container of fried chicken in one hand and a bowl of fruit salad in the other, Tori stared at Rose's front door. Had she been thinking, she would have carried the various parts of Doug's lunch in one at a time, the availability of an empty hand making the entire process a whole lot easier.

But she hadn't.

And the door was closed.

Sighing, she looked from one full hand to the other, the ability to signal her presence with a knock all but gone. Then again, there was always a knee. . . .

"Afternoon, Tori. Need a hand?"

She set her foot back down on the front stoop, her shoulders slumping in relief as she turned. "A hand would be wonderful, Doug, thanks."

Doug's nose lifted into the air as his nostrils flared. "Do I smell chicken?"

Tori laughed. "Good nose."

He scaled the trio of steps that separated the sidewalk

from Rose's front door with one motion, his sky blue eyes shimmering with the sun's rays. "I can't tell you the last time I had fried chicken." Grabbing the container of chicken from her right hand, he inhaled once again. "Man, it's been months . . . at least."

"Good. I slaved over it all morning."

"Really?"

She knocked on the front door, then turned back to the man standing beside her, her gaze drinking in every detail of his average-sized frame. Twenty-four hours earlier, when she'd first laid eyes on him, she'd found the guy to be rather ordinary, his face fairly nondescript save for the sky blue eyes that seemed to dance in the light. Today, standing less than six inches apart, she could see she'd been mistaken.

Doug Hewitt was anything but ordinary. In fact, if she allowed herself to really *look*, he was downright hot. In a smoldering, sexy, rugged kind of way.

Forcing her gaze back to the door, she shifted from foot to foot, her left arm tightening around the bowl of fruit salad she'd whipped together before leaving for the library that morning.

"Tori? You okay?"

Say something . . . Say something . . .

"Sorry. I blanked there for a minute."

She knocked again, this time a bit louder in an attempt to drown out the sudden thumping of her heart.

You have Milo, dummy.

He moved the chicken container into the crook of his elbow and reached for the bowl of fruit salad, his tight gray T-shirt pulling all the more taut across his chest. "I guess you were probably affected by the storm, too, huh?"

The storm.

Seizing the opportunity to focus on something other than the way his faded blue jeans hugged his lower half, Tori nodded and then shrugged. "Yes and no."

"Excuse me?"

She rushed to explain as the click of the door's interior locking mechanism echoed through the air. "My cottage was fine. It's one of the newer structures in town so it fared wonderfully. But the library, where I work, suffered some damage. Nothing earth-shattering, but enough to shrink our collection temporarily."

The door swung open to reveal a Rose who looked much happier than she had the day before. Tori sighed with relief. "Rose, how are you?"

"Fine. Fine," the elderly woman said as she peered up at Tori and then Doug, her soft gray eyes magnified to nearly twice their size thanks to the wire-rimmed bifocals she wore. "Did you hear the good news?"

"About Kenny?"

Rose nodded. "I told you he didn't do it."

"And that was all I needed to hear." Tori pointed at the containers in Doug's hand. "I took a chance you might be free for lunch and packed a little extra fried chicken and fruit salad."

"A little? Looks like you have enough to feed a small army, Victoria."

She felt her face warm. "Okay, so I made a little more than I realized. Are you hungry?"

Pulling the flaps of her sweater closer to her body, Rose lowered her voice. "My stomach is a bit unsettled this afternoon. But, if you have the time, I would enjoy a little fresh air and some good conversation."

She studied her friend closely, her radar on alert. "Are you feeling sick?"

Rose waved off Tori's concern with her usual gruffness. "I'm not ready to kick the bucket if that's what you're asking, Victoria."

"I wasn't saying . . . I mean I . . ." She stopped when she heard Doug's chuckle of amusement. She made a face. "What?"

"My granddad used to say the same thing. He said he felt as if people were just waitin' around, holdin' chunks of dirt."

"Chunks of dirt?" she asked.

"To sprinkle on my coffin," Rose groused.

She grabbed the edge of Rose's screen door for support. "I wasn't saying you're going to . . . I mean, I was just concerned about what you said. About your stomach."

"Stomachs get upset, Victoria. They get upset from food that's gone bad, they get upset from viruses, they get upset from people who don't know when to stop. It happens."

"My mother-in-law gives me agita on a daily basis," Doug offered from his spot on the front stoop. "It's part of the reason I chase storms for a living. Gives me a chance to get away, rest my ears a little."

"See?" Rose wrapped her bony hand around Tori's upper arm and gently pulled her inside. "Let's get your food onto plates and then we can sit out back on the patio and catch up. Besides, I'd like you to meet Kenny." Turning to Doug, she moved the containers to Tori's hands. "Why don't you see if that man working next door would like something to eat as well."

"You mean Curtis?" Tori asked. "I met him last night when I stopped by Martha Jane's house. He struck me as being kind of quiet, like maybe he's the type who prefers to keep to himself."

"He's probably just learned to keep his mouth shut around the old biddy."

Tori snorted a laugh. "Old biddy?"

"Martha Jane, who else?" Rose snapped.

Tori closed her eyes as images of the previous evening flitted through her mind. Rose was right. Martha Jane would be a tough person to work for, her attitude bordering on cold and demanding. "You know what?

I think that sounds like a great idea." She looked at Doug. "Would you mind seeing if you can find Curtis? If you do, could you tell him we have some extra lunch if he's interested?"

"My pleasure."

She watched his lanky but defined back disappear across Rose's front lawn, her thoughts taking her to Mississippi and the family he left behind. "Seems like a nice man."

"He does. But I wish you'd have waited on hirin' him. Kenny does a fine job with his hands." Rose led the way down the hallway, her feet moving more slowly than Tori remembered. Was her friend simply tired? Or was it something more?

Setting the food containers on the nearest counter, Tori spun around to face Rose. "Milo and I were worried about you," she rushed to explain. "The storm did a lot of damage to your place and we didn't like the idea of you tripping over something and getting hurt. And as far as Kenny is concerned, hiring Doug wasn't a reflection on his ability. It was simply because we weren't sure when the whole robbery accusation would get cleared up."

"Robbery, schmobbery." Rose stamped her foot on the off-white linoleum floor. "I have a good mind to pay my neighbor a visit and let her know just what I think about her and her accusations."

Although it was a discussion Tori would enjoy watching, she knew it wasn't worth the inevitable elevation in Rose's blood pressure. She said as much to the woman.

"Perhaps you're right. But you should see how hurt Kenny is by this whole mess. I've never seen him so distraught," Rose said, her voice an unusual mix of despair and anger. "I wish people would stop judging by the exterior, seeing only the differences instead of the things that are the same."

Tori grabbed a plate from the stack Rose set out and began filling plates—one for Doug, one for Curtis, one for—

"You did say Kenny was here, didn't you?"

"He's out back, bundling up brush next to the patio." Rose shuffled over to the refrigerator. "I made a fresh pitcher of tea this morning so we'll serve that with dinner."

"You mean lunch . . ." Tori's voice trailed off as Rose rolled her eyes skyward. "Sorry. I forgot."

And she had.

As she always did.

Even with more than six months under her belt, there were still a number of southern expressions that threw her for a loop, much to the chagrin of Leona, her personal coach on all things southern. But she couldn't help it. *Dinner* was supposed to be served in the evening.

One by one she filled each plate with fried chicken and fruit salad, the strawberries she'd purchased from Leeson's Market bringing a vivid splash of color to a backdrop of banana slices and star-shaped kiwi. When she'd readied four plates, she looked up at Rose once again. "Are you sure you won't eat even a little? The fried chicken looks really good. Smells good, too."

Rose shook her head, the motion one of weariness. "Maybe later. After my visit with Kenny has settled."

"He's that upset, huh?" Tori looked around the tiny kitchenette, her gaze skimming across countertops and glass-fronted cabinets in search of the perfect carrying tray. When she found what she was looking for, she began shifting plates from the counter to the portable surface.

"He's . . . hurt. And understandably so in my opinion. He was there to help. But instead, he ended up down at the police station trying to explain away something he didn't do." Rose's voice lowered to a near whisper. "He's convinced it's because he's dumb."

Tori felt her throat tighten. "He thinks he's dumb?"

"Of course he does. It's how he's been treated since he was knee-high to a grasshopper."

"Do you really think that's why Martha Jane accused him so readily?"

"She wouldn't be the first," Rose mumbled as she preceded Tori down the hallway toward the back of her tiny cottage. "Even when he was in school, kids would blame him when things went missing from their book bags."

"But why?" Tori asked, her feet slowing as they reached the door separating them from the subject of their conversation.

"Because he was different. He moved different, spoke different, acted different. And *different* in our world means *wrong*." Rose grabbed hold of the doorknob, then stopped. "That's something you know firsthand, isn't it, Victoria."

And she did. When she moved to Sweet Briar she was different. She spoke differently, dressed differently, and acted differently in a town where everyone spoke, acted, and dressed the same.

Like Kenny, she had been the unknown in a sea of known and, hence, a perfect murder suspect when the town's former sweetheart turned up dead shortly after Tori's arrival.

She got it. She really did. And it made her heart ache for the mentally challenged man scooping up sticks on Rose's patio.

The mentally challenged *colored* man . . .

Shifting the tray to the opposite hand, Tori covered Rose's hand with her own. "Nina said something the other day that got to me. And after what just happened I have to wonder if maybe she's right."

"She thinks his color is the issue?" Rose waved a dismissive hand in the air then reached, again, for the door. "Martha Jane is racist, of that I have no doubt. But her racism isn't confined to the color of someone's skin. It's anything that makes a person different. Kenny just happens to have two strikes against him in her eyes."

A gust of warm air whooshed into the house as Rose opened the door, the sun's rays playing across the stone patio. "Look who's here, Kenny."

The thirtysomething man looked up, one hand clasped around a piece of rope while the other held tight to an unruly bundle of sticks.

Extending her free hand outward, Tori smiled. "Hi, Kenny. I'm Rose's friend, Victoria. It's a pleasure to finally meet you."

A shy smile tugged at the man's thin lips, sending his dark bushy eyebrows upward. "You're the book lady, aren't you?"

She set the tray down on Rose's picnic table. "I work at the library in town, yes. Do you like to read, Kenny?"

His smile disappeared. "I used to. When Ms. Winters was my teacher."

Rose reached out, rested a reassuring hand on Kenny's broad shoulders. "He's a good reader, he just lacks confidence. But we'll find it one of these days, won't we?"

Kenny kicked at a stick on the ground, his cheeks drooping as a piece of stonework lifted with his toe. "Ms. Winters, I'm s-sorry." Dropping to a squat, the man set the stone back in place, his hand shaking as he worked. "I didn't mean to—"

"It's fine, Kenny."

Sensing the sadness in Rose's guest, Tori gestured toward the table and the tray of dinner plates. "I brought lunch with me, Kenny. Enough for you and me and some of the workers. Would you like some?"

The man looked up, a hint of surprise evident in his eyes as he looked from Rose to Tori and back again.

"Of course he'd like some." Rose's voice, clear and firm, cut through the melody of chain saws and hammering in the distance. "Kenny has been keeping me company all morning and I'm sure he's worked up quite an appetite. Talking to old people can do that, I reckon."

Jumping to his feet, Kenny took hold of Rose's hand. "Ms. Winters t-takes g-good care of m-me."

Tori lifted a plate from the tray and handed it to Kenny. "From what I hear, you take good care of Ms. Winters, too."

A flush rose up in Kenny's cheeks as he reached for the food, Tori's words bringing a momentary smile to his face. "I try t-to. She be-believes in me. Even when—when . . . nobody else d-does." And like that, his smile was gone, his sweetly shy demeanor replaced by something resembling controlled rage. "Mizz Barker said I r-robbered her m-money. She c-called the police and . . . and t-told them I was b-bad. Very, very b-bad."

"Any food left? Or did you eat it already?" Doug strode around the corner of Rose's house, Curtis in tow. Flashing a smile that rivaled the light from the sun, Doug wagged a finger in Tori's direction. "You can't get a guy all excited about fried chicken and then eat it before he gets back."

"I couldn't eat all of that chicken if I tried," Tori said, her laugh temporarily stilling the tension that had descended over the patio like a smog-ridden cloud. Scooping up Doug's plate with her left hand and Curtis's plate with her right, she handed the food to the men.

Doug's gaze slid slowly down her body before returning to meet hers. She felt her cheeks flush as his lips spread outward in yet another face-lighting smile. "I suspect you're right. There's not a lot of room in that little body of yours to fit that kind of food. Us, on the other hand"—he smacked his empty hand against Curtis's chest—"could eat that entire bucket if we tried, couldn't we?"

Curtis simply nodded, his mouth already busy on a chicken leg.

"There's a place to sit right over there if you'd like."

Rose lifted a shaky hand in the direction of a wood-stained bench positioned halfway between her home and Martha Jane's, its proximity to the patio an indication she wanted a little breathing room. "Feel free to come back for seconds if you want."

Nodding, Curtis turned in the direction of the bench, his long legs making short work of the divide as he feasted on yet another piece of chicken. Doug followed the drifter with his eyes before setting off in the same direction, dimples carving holes in his cheeks as he looked over his shoulder at Tori and Rose. "Thanks for the chicken, ladies. It was right kind of you."

"You're welcome." Rose waited until Doug reached the bench before lowering herself to the patio's lone rocking chair. Hunching forward ever so slightly, the elderly woman resurrected their earlier conversation at the exact place it had been abandoned. "I don't want you worrying about what Martha Jane said. It's over now, Kenny. You hear me? It's over."

Tori's gaze swept across Rose's former student, an angry set to the man's jaw taking her by surprise.

"She told them I was b-bad," Kenny repeated, his words echoing across the lawn. "All I did was try to help. But she still told them I was b-bad . . . very, very b-bad."

"Kenny, it's over," Rose said, her voice patient yet firm. "Over."

"All I d-did was try to help." Dropping his head in line with his shoulders, Kenny stared down at his plate, his hands fisting into tight balls. "And her m-money was r-right there, r-right in her sock drawer like it was s'posed to be."

"Martha Jane made a mistake, Kenny. *I* know that. *Rose* knows that. And now, even *Martha Jane* knows that." Eager to soothe the worry from Rose's brow, Tori searched her arsenal of words for something, anything, that would soothe Kenny's agitation. "She probably feels just awful about her mistake. In fact, I'm betting she's probably sitting inside right now trying to figure out the best way to say she's sorry."

"Sorry?" Rose snorted. "That woman wouldn't say sorry if her life depended—"

Kenny's fist flew upward only to come crashing back to the table. "Mizz Barker won't s-say s-sorry to s-someone like m-me. I'm t-too d-dumb."

"I will not listen to that kind of talk, young man. I didn't listen to it when you were five and I won't listen to it now." Rose struggled to her feet, her voice doing little to disguise the anger she felt. "Victoria, I'm going inside for a spell. You stay out here and talk with Kenny for a bit, will you?"

She considered arguing but knew better than to go that route. Rose Winters was a sweet woman, her bristly personality nothing more than an outer covering for a soft interior. But if there was a time the claws stayed, it was when a demand was deliberately ignored. The key was differentiating between a Rose-issued demand and a true question.

The part about staying with Kenny was most definitely not a true question.

"I'd be happy to," she said as she, too, stood and planted a kiss on the woman's forehead. "I'll be in to check on you before I head back to work."

"No need. Just talk some sense into him before you leave," Rose mumbled as she shuffled her way up the steps and into her house.

When she was gone, Tori turned her attention to the man still sitting at the table, a man with hands still fisted and shoulders still tense. "Martha Jane's mistake doesn't reflect on your intelligence in any way, Kenny. Please know that."

"Don't m-matter w-what I know . . . or w-what Mizz Winters knows. Everyone else treats me like I'm d-dumb.

I'm used to that. Mizz Barker tried t-to m-make them think I w-was a c-crook, too."

Reclaiming her spot at the picnic table, she reached out and touched his forearm with a reassuring hand, the coldness of his flesh making her draw back in surprise. "But you're not a crook, Kenny. That's all that matters."

"She d-don't know what it's l-like to have p-people s-staring at you all the t-time. She don't know w-what it's like to have p-people sp-spit at you and m-make f-fun of you. But you w-wait . . ." Fisting his hands still tighter, Kenny continued on, his wooden rant drowning out Tori's reassurances. "You w-wait . . . you j-just w-wait and see."

A sharp chill shot down Tori's spine. "Wait and see what, Kenny?"

"You w-wait and see," Kenny repeated. "She m-might not s-say s-sorry to s-someone d-dumb like m-me . . . but—but someone d-dumb like m-me can—can m-make her sorry. *R-Real* sorry."

Chapter 5

She ran her left hand across the pale pink Polarfleece in her lap, the baby soft material warm and cozy
beneath her skin. From the moment Tori had decided on
hats and scarves as her contribution to the women's shelter in Chicago, she'd known it would be a labor of love.

On its own, a single hat and scarf set was the kind
of project that could be started and completed in a matter of an hour or two. But when you multiplied that set
by sixty as she intended, the time involved ballooned
significantly.

She'd known that. Had embraced it, even . . .

Until tropical storm Roger blew his way into Sweet
Briar, mandating more hours at the library, thinning out
her sewing troops, and leaving a general feeling of mal-
aise in his wake.

"If you don't mind, Roger, I think I'll pass on the
thank-you note," she mumbled as she grabbed her fabric scissors and began to cut, the blade gliding easily
through the fleece. Turn by turn she maneuvered around

the fabric, securing the 16 by 22 inch rectangular piece that would be the foundation for her second hat.

Dropping the scissors onto the sofa, she reached for the heart-shaped pincushion that had been her first sewing project as a child. One by one she removed pins from the red satin, depositing them, instead, into the pink fleece, temporarily adhering the two shorter sides together in preparation for the sewing phase.

Once the pins were set, she scooted forward on the sofa and unlatched the wooden sewing box she'd set on the coffee table. Spools of thread in varying shades and colors covered the bottom of the box, the perfect pink calling to her from its spot in the right corner.

Pulling the chosen thread from the box, Tori settled back against the seat cushions, her hands itching to sew for the first time all week. But like all good things in life, it came with a hurdle to cross—this one coming in the form of a knock at her front door.

She considered ignoring it, pretending the music in her ears had drowned out the sound. But that would be a double lie. Which would make the guilt twice as strong. . . .

Groaning outwardly, she shifted the strip of fleece to the coffee table and rose to her feet, a second knock propelling her steps forward. Somehow, someway, she'd get the hats and scarves done, even if it meant a week of sleepless nights.

"Good evenin', Victoria, look who I found on the porch." Margaret Louise stepped into the glow cast by the hallway light, her head tilting in the direction of a taller, leaner, younger shadow. "Apparently I'm not the only one lookin' to spend a little time with you."

Bobbing her head to the left, Tori felt the corners of her lips spread outward as Milo Wentworth stepped from the shadows of her front porch, a bouquet of fresh yellow daisies in his hand. "Hi there, Tori."

"Hi." It was amazing how shy she could still feel in the

teacher's presence, the excitement of their relationship still alive and well between them. There were times she actually pinched herself to make sure she was awake. Sure, she'd read romance novels with the perfect hero—the guy who held doors and lost himself in his companion's eyes, the guy who loved hour-long conversations and moonlit walks, the guy who knew how to make a woman feel special—but after the fiasco with Jeff she'd assumed that kind of stuff simply existed on the library's fiction shelf.

Milo, however, proved her wrong. Time and time again.

He leaned in through the open doorway, his hand holding the flowers in her direction. "I figured a splash of yellow might be cheerful."

Margaret Louise's laugh bellowed down the hall. "Yellow, red, pink, purple . . . or *wilted* . . . it don't matter none. Just rememberin' us in that way makes our hearts get downright mushy. Isn't that right, Victoria?"

Gazing down at the flowers in her hand, she had to agree. Though having them come from Milo upped the mushy factor tenfold. She peered up at him through thick lashes. "They're perfect, Milo. Thank you."

A flash of red appeared in his cheeks. "I'm glad."

"I brought somethin', too," Margaret Louise chimed in. "Only mine is brown, dark brown."

Her gaze ricocheted off Milo's face, pinning her friend's. *"Brown?"*

The woman nodded, her eyes taking on a mischievous gleam. "Perhaps it would be more accurate to say brown with a hint of white. Because there *is* some white. *Ribbons* of white."

Tori swallowed. "Ribbons? Of white?"

Milo clasped his arms across his chest and rolled his eyes skyward. "So much for my flowers now . . ."

"No. The flowers are beautiful," she said as she reached

out and pulled him in for a hug. "Really, they couldn't be more perfect."

"I agree." Margaret Louise swept her hand in the direction of the wicker furniture that graced Tori's front porch. "So let's get them in water and set them on the table out here with us while we have some brownies."

"Show off," Milo groused playfully, his chin bobbing against Tori's head.

She laughed, the sound a welcome respite to a day that had held more than its fair share of tension. "Quit it you two. I love them both." With one last squeeze she stepped back, the warmth of Milo's body lingering against her skin. "And I love both of you."

Clutching the flowers to her chest, she turned toward the kitchen only to stop halfway down the hall. "Can I get you something to drink? Some tea or wine?"

"Got milk?" Milo asked as he followed her down the hall, Margaret Louise two steps behind.

"Sure. That sounds perfect to me, too. Margaret Louise?"

"Wine works."

"Wine it is." She rounded the corner into her tiny kitchen, her hands instinctively seeking the cabinet that held her one and only vase—a gift from Milo when they hit their three-month dating anniversary. Looking over her shoulder, she flashed a grin at him. "We were so busy the other day with Rose that I forgot to ask how the school fared in the storm. Any major damage?"

"Nah." Milo crossed the room and plucked two glasses and a wine goblet from the cabinet to the left of the stove. "A few broken windows and some overturned playground equipment is all. None of which was big enough to keep the kids out longer than that first day."

"Thank heavens." Margaret Louise opened the refrigerator, studied Tori's meager wine selection, and extracted the best of the lot. "And the collection booth for the Autumn Harvest Festival? How'd that hold up?"

Tori paused in the middle of arranging daisies. "Collection booth?"

Raking a hand through his hair, Milo exhaled in frustration. "It's seen its last festival, that's for sure."

Margaret Louise clucked.

"What collection booth?" Tori repeated as she popped the last daisy into the vase and leaned against the sink. "You've lost me."

"Every year Sweet Briar hosts the Autumn Harvest Festival. It's held in early November, just after Halloween. In many ways it's not much different than Heritage Days and the Re-Founders Day Festival, which you've already seen," Milo explained.

"There's food, games, music, and rides," said Margaret Louise, taking the ball from Milo. "Only there are more than just carnival rides at Autumn Harvest. There're hayrides, tractor pulls, and pony rides, too."

"Okay . . ."

"Unlike the other festivals though, Autumn Harvest is a way to share our blessings with other people. The collection booth is where that happens."

She looked at Margaret Louise, then Milo, her mind working to fill in the gaps. "And the storm destroyed the booth?"

Milo nodded. "That it did. Though, really, it wasn't a surprise. That booth has been around since Debbie Calhoun was a little girl. It's been assembled and dismantled year after year and stored in a shed out on Colten Granger's property."

"And the shed was destroyed, too?"

Milo's nod turned to a shake. "No. I'd taken the various pieces of the booth out of the shed about a week ago. I wanted to assemble it and give it a fresh coat of paint before the festival." He poured milk into each glass and handed one to Tori. "I guess Roger wanted to save me a can of paint and a few paintbrushes."

"What do you collect in this booth?" she asked, her thoughts suddenly far from daisies and brownies.

"Canned food, old coats, gently used toys, you name it," said Margaret Louise. "Anything and everything people are willin' to part with."

"Where do the items go?"

"Some stay here in Sweet Briar, some get shipped around the county."

She studied Milo as his words took root in her head. "Are there needy folks in Sweet Briar?"

He took a long sip of milk, then wiped his mouth with the back of his hand. "You'd be surprised."

And he was right. She was.

She peeked into the living room, her gaze picking out the piece of pink fleece she'd left on the table. There was still so much to do, so much sewing that had to happen if she was going to make her goal for the shelter. But there were always enough hours to help, weren't there?

"Can we rebuild the booth?"

Closing the gap between them in two long strides, Milo cupped the back of her head with his hand and tilted her face up to his. "Yes, and I will. But I don't want you worrying about it. Get those hats and scarves done. Help is help no matter where the people who receive it happen to be living. I'll get a new booth built between now and the festival."

"But I—"

"Listen to the man, Victoria." Margaret Louise replaced her sip of wine with another, then tossed the empty bottle in the recycling bin. "In the meantime, I'd like to help with the hats and scarves. Count on me for ten by the end of the week. Dixie for another five."

"Dixie?" She knew her voice was bordering on shrill but she couldn't help it. *Dixie?*

Margaret Louise nodded. "You're winnin' her over, Victoria."

Sliding an arm around her waist, Milo pulled her close. "I knew she'd cave in time. No sane person could ever have a lasting issue with you."

She considered his words. Maybe he was right. Maybe people could soften over time, their edges smoothed by the power of reality to win out over the fear of change.

"Do you think Martha Jane Barker might finally cave where Kenny Murdock is concerned?" The question surprised her, the words leaving her lips before they were fully formed in her conscious thought.

"Stranger things have happened so I s'pose it's possible," Margaret Louise mused as she lifted her wine goblet to her lips and took another sip. "But Dixie loves the library, it's her passion. The two of you have that in common. So every time you do something to benefit that shared passion, she takes notice and appreciates it. Martha Jane, on the other hand, doesn't have any outside passions."

It made sense. But still . . .

"And I'm not sure Kenny can handle the tension with the same grace you have. That makes a difference, too."

She looked at Milo. "But she accused him of a crime he didn't commit. He has a right to be—" She stopped, shook her head against the memory of Kenny's chilling words earlier that day. "He has a right to be hurt. Even a little angry."

"A lot depends on how he handles that anger," Milo explained. "He has a reputation for having a temper when he's wronged. If he exercises that temper too much, sympathy will fall toward Martha Jane, not Kenny."

Margaret Louise set her glass on the countertop and peeled the cover from the brownie tin. "It don't matter what Kenny does. Martha Jane will never change. I suspect she was born ornery and I'm right sure she'll die ornery as well. Those types usually do."

Eyeing the brownies as Margaret Louise began to cut, Tori shrugged. "Seems kind of silly to live your life being so paranoid about people, don't you think?"

"I agree." Milo pulled three plates from the cabinet and placed them beside Margaret Louise's right elbow. As each plate was graced with a brownie, he handed them around. "I guess there's always a chance she'll change but I wouldn't put any money down on it."

She laughed. Even if it *was* a sure thing, Milo wouldn't gamble. He was a stand-up kind of guy, one who played life by the book.

"Maybe Doug or Curtis could help you with the collection booth. I don't think either will be at their job long based on how thoroughly they work." She closed her eyes as she bit into the brownie, the white chocolate drizzle making her moan in delight. "Oh, Margaret Louise, these are amazing."

The woman grinned. "Why thank you, Victoria. You're always a pleasure to bake for. As long as it's chocolate, I can be fairly certain you'll like it."

"Hey! I'm not that easy, am I?" She looked from Margaret Louise to Milo and back again, their playful jabs at one another's sides making her laugh out loud. "Okay, so I am. Is that really such a bad thing?"

When the laughing subsided, Milo's eyebrow arched. "Who's this Curtis fellow you just mentioned? The one you said might be able to help with the booth?"

"The man working over at Martha Jane's. He's not nearly as friendly as Doug but he is a hard worker."

"I wonder how much the two of them would charge to help me make a new booth."

"You can always ask." Margaret Louise popped her entire brownie into her mouth, her cheeks puffing momentarily, only to shrink down to size as she chewed and swallowed. "And I'm sure there'd be more than a few of us in town who'd be willing to help foot the bill to get that booth up and runnin' in time for Autumn Harvest."

"Okay. I'll look into it. . . ." His words trailed off as a police siren echoed its way through the windows, the sudden and unexpected sound making them jump. "I wonder what's going on."

"There's only one way to find out." Margaret Louise pulled her cell phone from her pants pocket and flipped it open, her finger pushing a few buttons before bringing the contraption to her ear. "Georgina? It's me. Everything okay?"

Tori took the opportunity her friend's phone call afforded to sidle up alongside Milo for a hug, the feel of his lips on her forehead warming her from the inside out. "Thank you for the flowers, they really are beautiful."

"Like you," he mumbled against her skin.

"I'm glad you stopped by."

"So am I." He reached down, hooked a finger beneath her chin, and lifted it until their eyes met. "How's the sewing going?"

She exhaled a whoosh of air from her lungs. "It's not. But it'll be okay. Having help from Margaret Louise and Dixie will make a big difference."

"I'd help if I knew how to sew."

"I know you would. But you need to concentrate on this booth. It's every bit as important as what I'm doing."

A gasp from Margaret Louise brought them up short. "Margaret Louise? Are you okay?" Tori asked.

The woman lowered the phone to her side, her face ashen.

In an instant Tori was at her side, pulling the phone from her friend's hand and snapping it closed. "Margaret Louise? What is it? Are Jake and Melissa okay? The kids? Leona?"

Margaret Louise nodded, her hand waving off the notion. "Fine. They're all fine. But Martha Jane . . ."

"What about Martha Jane?" Milo asked, his deep voice cutting through the hushed tones.

"She's . . . she's been strangled."

Chapter 6

It was official. The library had replaced the backyard fence when it came to the members of the Sweet
Briar Ladies Society Sewing Circle and their penchant
for gossip. And it made sense.

Unlike its clichéd counterpart, the library was far less
prone to weather constraints, was void of flying insects
and their constant competition for attention, and sported
a more favorable proximity to bathroom facilities—all
plusses when half the members were looking at sixty-five
in their rearview mirror.

The only snafu, really, was the presence of other
people—people who came to the library looking for
quiet only to find five women huddled around the information desk shaking their heads, clutching their throats,
and peppering their not-so-quiet conversation with loud
gasps of shock.

"Ladies, we really need to keep this down. My patrons
are trying to read," Tori pleaded as she caught not one

but two disapproving looks from the research corner of the library.

"Perhaps they should find somewhere else to read, dear," Leona drawled as she brought a freshly manicured hand to rest at the base of her throat. "We have things to discuss."

Rubbing her eyes free of the sleep that threatened to overtake them, she lowered her voice still further. "This is a library, Leona. Its main purpose is reading."

"And research," Dixie said. "Just as many people come to the library to research as they do to read for pleasure."

Tori considered spouting a few statistics for discussion purposes but opted, instead, to let the former librarian have her moment in the sun. Besides, in many cases, she was right.

"Research," Leona repeated in a quieter-than-normal voice.

Leaning forward, Margaret Louise rested her forearms on the counter and grinned. "Here we go . . ."

"Go? Go where?" Tori asked.

"Not me . . . her," Margaret Louise said as she pointed at her sister on the other side of the counter.

Tori turned to find Leona's eyebrows furrowed together in a dramatic show of confusion. Removing her hand from her throat, the woman—who had taken Tori under her bossy and somewhat ornery wing from the start—gestured toward the circular counter that housed a computer, a pencil holder, and several stacks of books waiting to be shelved. "This is the information desk, isn't it?"

"Yes . . ."

"Well, that's why we're here, dear. To get information."

Tori's mouth gaped open as Margaret Louise snorted with pleasure. "Good one, Twin."

"Consider it, dear," Leona continued, her voice a study

in poise and perfect articulation. "We're here to gather information. Information that can only be gleaned by asking questions."

"Who strangled Martha Jane Barker and why aren't really the kinds of questions I can answer."

"Then let's try another question, shall we?"

Tori, too, leaned against the counter, amusement over her friend's persistence temporarily winning out over sense of duty. "Okay, shoot."

Leona gasped. "Shoot? Shoot what?"

"It's an expression. It means go ahead."

Closing her eyes, Leona shook her head, a soft *tsking* sound emerging through closed lips. When she finally opened them again, she threw her hands skyward. "I had hoped, by now, that you'd have abandoned your big city ways, dear."

"Big city ways?" Tori repeated.

"I realize living in Chicago is akin to residing in a war zone, but we don't liken words to dangerous objects or their actions here in the south."

"War zone? What are you talking about?"

"Could Chicago function with a police department the size of Sweet Briar's, dear?"

"No, but it's Chicago . . . it's bigger. Much, much bigger."

"And much more dangerous."

"Maybe in comparison, I suppose. But, really, it's a safe city, Leona."

The woman rolled her eyes. "They have alleys, dear."

"So does Paris."

"Oooh, she's got you there, Twin." Margaret Louise pushed off the counter, her smile stretching her face to a near breaking point. "But as fun as this is, I'd rather get back to the questions on everyone's tongue right now."

"Which are what?" Beatrice piped up, her charge momentarily distracted by a picture book on fire engines. "What else is there besides who killed Rose's neighbor?"

"What *else*?" Leona asked, her eyes narrowed on the British nanny.

"Yes, Leona, what else?" Dixie echoed.

"Well, there's the matter of whether Martha Jane's killing was an act of revenge." Leona jutted her chin upward and sniffed.

"Revenge?"

Tori swallowed back the bile that rose in her throat. She knew, without a doubt, where Leona was headed. It was the same place she, herself, had visited again and again over the past fifteen hours or so. And it was the same place that had caused the normally stoic Rose Winters to burst into tears in front of Tori and Milo just hours after the murder was discovered.

"Yes, revenge." Resting her hands on their opposite upper arms, Leona peered at Dixie over the top of her glasses. "Kenny was furious with her. Everyone knows that."

"Kenny?" Beatrice yelled, her voice drawing more than a few raised eyebrows from around the library.

Leona rolled her eyes.

"Kenny *Murdock*," Margaret Louise corrected, making Beatrice's shoulders slump downward.

"You think Kenny Murdock murdered Martha Jane?" Dixie brought her hand to her mouth, her eyes large and luminous. "He wouldn't harm . . ." The elderly woman's voice trailed off as she closed her eyes tightly.

"He has a horrific temper," Leona reminded.

"He's been known to snap things in two." Margaret Louise pushed off the counter only to lean against it once again. "Do you remember that time he busted the

Heritage Days sign in half a few years ago? He was angry because no one let him work a booth."

"And don't forget that time he came into my shop and knocked one of my antiques onto the floor by accident." Leona looked from one member of the sewing circle to the next, her bent toward the dramatic heightened tenfold in the presence of a captive audience. "He flew into a rage because of something *he* did. Can you imagine what he would do if *someone else* triggered that rage?"

Dixie nodded.

Margaret Louise shook her head.

Beatrice grew paler.

Tori held up her hand. "Wait a minute. So the guy has a temper . . . big deal. You have a temper, Leona. And so do you, Dixie."

"I most certainly do not," Leona argued, followed by a sniff of indignation.

"Yes, you do. Your claws come out every time Rose calls you old."

"Because *I'm* not old. *She's* old," Leona hissed through clenched teeth.

"If you don't have a temper, Twin, why are you turnin' beet red?" Margaret Louise took a few steps in her sister's direction, only to halt when she was given the stare down. "I rest Victoria's case."

"You're right about Leona, Victoria, but *I* certainly don't have a temper."

Tori turned her attention on her former predecessor-turned-nemesis. "You don't? Then what would you call all those nasty barbs you hurled at me during my first meeting with the library board?"

Dixie's cheeks turned crimson.

"Look, I'm not trying to make anyone feel bad. Everyone has a temper sometimes. And Kenny Murdock is no exception." Exhaling an errant strand of light brown hair from her forehead, she continued, her voice still quiet yet firm. "Branding him a killer because of it is simply ludicrous."

Problem was, she wasn't buying what she was selling. She'd seen Kenny's face the previous afternoon. She'd heard the blatant threat he'd hurled in Martha Jane's direction. She'd felt the rage simmering inside him.

And now the woman was dead. Strangled by a piece of rope that sounded a lot like the kind he'd been using that very day to bundle sticks in Rose's backyard.

"Victoria is right," Beatrice said, her accent and her innate shyness making them all lean closer to hear. "What's that expression? Just because it looks like a duck and acts like a duck, it doesn't mean it's a duck."

Margaret Louise laughed, her hand slipping around the nanny's shoulders in a conspiratorial fashion. "They may say it like that across the pond . . . but here, in the States . . . if it looks like a duck and quacks like a duck it *is*, in fact, a duck."

"Oh." Beatrice flashed a look of apology in Victoria's direction. "I'm sorry. I was only trying to help."

She reached out, patted the girl's hand. "I know. But don't worry. It will be okay. Martha Jane's killer will be found."

What that would do to Rose when it happened, though, was anyone's guess.

Squaring her shoulders, she grabbed hold of a stack of books and began thumbing through them, her hands sorting them into smaller piles based on where they were shelved around the library. "So what do you think? Can you tell we were semiflooded just two days ago?"

Four heads turned to scan the main room of the Sweet Briar Public Library.

"You mean other than the fact that the bottom shelf of every section is empty?"

She ignored Leona and grabbed a second stack, sorting those books into the correct piles. "I was referring to the carpets and the walls . . . though right now all I have on the wall is a special paint that covers water marks. If all goes well, I'm hoping we'll get a fresh coat of paint up in the next few weeks."

"Did you take pictures of the damaged books?" Dixie asked.

"I did. I dried them out the best I could and then boxed them up and put them in the basement until a claims specialist can make it in."

"Very good, Victoria, you're on the ball. And the carpet looks good."

She smiled at the woman. "You picked a good one, Dixie. It held up well. Just needed a few power fans to dry it out."

Dixie beamed at the praise.

"How is Rose's place doin'?" Margaret Louise asked.

"Better." And it was. In just the first twenty-four hours since his arrival, Doug had made rapid progress, repairing damaged shingles, removing downed trees, and boarding broken windows. Despite his efforts though, Tori was still worried about her elderly friend.

"And how is *Rose*?" Leona asked, her ornery streak of earlier gone.

Tori shrugged.

"How many times must I tell you not to shrug like that, dear? Your forehead has this nasty little habit of wrinkling when you do and wrinkles are most unattractive."

Leave it to Leona to bring any topic back to beauty tips. Men would be next . . .

"In fact, if you keep doing that, your forehead will prematurely wrinkle," Leona continued as she pulled out a chair from a nearby table and sat down, her ankles crossing in regal style. "And if there's one thing men don't like, dear, it's a face that looks like a wrinkly old elephant."

"I'll keep that in mind," she mumbled.

Margaret Louise looked at the ceiling and shook her head. "Ignore my twin, Victoria. You're lovely just the way you are. Milo thinks so, too."

Just the mere mention of Milo's name turned the corners of her lips upward.

"The wrinkles aren't permanent yet. We'll see if he still thinks so when they are."

"Leona!"

All eyes turned to Dixie Dunn.

"Good heavens, did I just hear you defend Victoria?" Margaret Louise teased.

Dixie blushed but said nothing.

Tori laughed and mouthed a thank-you in her predecessor's direction before turning back to Leona. "In a *verbal* reply to your question, Leona, Rose is having a tough time right now."

"Oh?"

She nodded at Dixie. "She's heartsick over the notion Kenny"—she shot a look at Beatrice—"*Murdock* might be responsible for Martha Jane's murder."

"Have you seen her?"

She nodded once again. "When Margaret Louise left to pick up Jake Junior from football practice, Milo and I headed over to check on Rose. We were worried about her when we heard what had happened. But she had very little to say to either of us."

"What *did* she say?" Leona asked.

"Just that she couldn't believe Martha Jane was gone . . . that she was afraid for Kenny . . . and that she would talk to him first thing this morning to see if he was responsible."

Margaret Louise grabbed hold of the counter. "She was goin' to talk to him?"

"If he hasn't been arrested, yes."

"We have to stop her."

"Why? Kenny wouldn't hurt Rose," she protested even as her heart began to pound. "He—he worships her."

"That may be true, Victoria. But when backed into a corner, rage can be mighty blindin' I reckon."

Chapter 7

"Are you sure this is okay?" Tori asked as she led the way through the employee entrance and into the back parking lot. "The Johnsons won't mind you driving the three of us over to Rose's house?"

Beatrice reached into her purse, extracted a set of keys, and aimed it at the navy blue minivan closest to the door, a series of lights and sounds responding in kind. "Luke will be just fine during story time with Dixie looking after him."

"Did you see Dixie's face when you asked if she could hold down the fort for a little while, Victoria? She was glowin' like a firefly on a warm summer night." Margaret Louise fell in step beside her sister, her mouth moving a mile a minute. "I don't think it matters no more whether she's runnin' the place or not. I think she likes the changes you've made even if she'll no more utter that aloud than Leona will admit she's old."

"I'm not old."

Margaret Louise waved her sister's protest aside.

"Dixie just likes feelin' like she's still needed once in a while."

"And she is. With Nina being off today, there's no way I could be going to Rose's right now without Dixie." Tori slowed as she approached Beatrice's van. "Leona, why don't you ride up front? Margaret Louise and I can sit in back."

Feeling a hand on her arm, she looked up, Margaret Louise's smile wide as the woman tugged on the handle of the sliding door and motioned Tori inside. "Consider yourself warned."

"Warned?" Tori echoed.

"Warned."

"Okay . . ." Her voice trailed off as she slid across the middle bench, her mouth frozen in the open position. Everywhere she looked there were images of Kenny Rogers. Pictures, drawings, album covers, internet printouts, an assortment of buttons, and even a dashboard bobblehead came together to create a shrine-on-wheels to Beatrice's favorite country crooner. "I—I . . ."

"I warned you, didn't I?" Margaret Louise elbowed Tori in the side. "It's a sight, ain't it?"

"That's one word," mumbled Leona from the front seat as Beatrice took her spot behind the wheel.

"Is everyone buckled in?" Beatrice reached up, adjusted the rearview mirror, and slowly backed from their parking spot. "Even though I think Luke will be just fine with Dixie, we mustn't dillydally at Rose's home."

"Of course not." Margaret Louise leaned forward between the seats, her seat belt digging into her middle. "I see you got a bobblehead since the last time I was in your car."

Beatrice's face lit up. "I did! Don't you just love it? I found it at a flea market a few weekends ago. It was on a shelf between Dr. Phil and Julie Andrews."

Leona leaned her head against the seat back and closed her eyes, her mouth twisted into a grimace.

"I found a lunch box, too! But that's on my dresser in my room at the Johnsons'."

"That's wonderful, Beatrice." Tori peered out the window as the trees surrounding the eastern side of Sweet Briar zoomed past. There was a part of her that wanted to explore her friend's over-the-top obsession, to fire off a set of questions that might provide a better window into the girl who sat so quietly at their circle meetings. But she couldn't. Not when Rose's safety was foremost in her mind.

She understood Margaret Louise's concern for the retired schoolteacher, but it still seemed inconceivable. Kenny adored Rose. One only needed to watch them for all of about five seconds to know that.

Sure, anger was a powerful emotion, propelling people into committing horrific crimes across the world on a daily basis. But did those people turn on elderly women who had steadfastly stood by them for nearly three decades?

She said as much to Margaret Louise.

Leona lifted her head and turned to establish eye contact with Tori. "People in rages don't think clearly, dear. They simply act."

Margaret Louise nodded. "No one is saying Kenny would strike out at Rose with forethought. I don't think he has it in him to think like that. But if he's spittin' mad and seein' colors the way he does sometimes . . . who knows? I'm not convinced his feelin's for Rose would be enough to stop him."

Tori glanced back out the window, the urge to beg Beatrice to drive faster bordering on overwhelming.

"We're almost there," Beatrice said as she turned right onto Confederate Street and left onto Battlefield Road. Letting up on the gas pedal, she glided to a stop in front of Rose's one-story cottage home.

"Who is *that* handsome soul?" Leona purred from the front seat as she stared out the passenger side window, condensation forming on the glass.

Tori leaned forward for a better look. "Oh, that's Doug. Milo and I hired him to help get Rose's place back in order. He's been an absolute godsend."

"Mmmm . . ."

"Good heavens, Twin, he's half your age," protested Margaret Louise, her mouth torn between horror and amusement.

"And he'd be lucky to have me," Leona huffed as she grabbed hold of the visor and pulled, an autographed photograph of Kenny Rogers covering the lit mirror. "What on earth . . ."

Beatrice pulled the key from the ignition and clapped her hands. "I just got that one . . . for my birthday. I joined his fan club when I came to the States and every year he takes time out of his schedule to autograph a birthday picture for me."

Leona looked from Beatrice to the photograph and back again, her perfectly waxed eyebrows rising ever so slightly. "Would you mind if I move Kenny long enough to check my eyes?"

"Your eyes are beautiful, Leona. Truly luminous." Tori glanced at Margaret Louise and grinned. "But I have to tell you . . . Doug is married. Has kids, too. A boy and a girl if I remember correctly."

Leona pushed the visor back into place, her shoulders slumping momentarily.

"What about *him*?" Margaret Louise asked as her finger extended across her sister's shoulder. "Is *he* married?"

"He? Who? Where?" Leona's head lifted like a periscope, her gaze moving side to side.

"Over there." Margaret Louise leaned forward once again, her finger providing a better route for Leona to follow. "The hunk with the bulging muscles and military style crew cut."

"Military style crew cut?" Leona repeated. "Where? Wh—Ohhh, there he is."

Tori laughed. "That's Curtis. He's working for Martha—" The sentence stalled on her tongue, her mind still struggling with the notion that Rose's ornery neighbor was dead.

"It's a shame to see someone so strong and in shape out of work. Perhaps I can find something for him to do around the shop."

"Your shop is fine," Margaret Louise offered. "What on earth could you possibly find for him to do?"

Leona pulled the visor down once again, her hand removing Beatrice's autographed picture in one motion. Peering at her reflection, she whipped a tube of lipstick from her purse and applied it to her lips. "Perhaps around my house, then."

"What needs fixin' there?"

"I could use a shed."

"For what? You have no children. You have no grand-children. You live in a three-bedroom house all by your—"

"Oh shut up, Twin." Leona dropped the lipstick back into her purse and extracted a tissue instead. Quickly, she pursed her lips together once, twice, three times before dabbing the excess color onto the tissue. "It's not his fault he's suddenly without a job. Isn't it my civic duty, as a human being, to provide work to someone who needs it?"

"Your civic duty?" Margaret Louise repeated with a teasing lilt. "Since when have you ever been worried about civic duty?"

Leona pushed the visor back into place and tugged on the door handle. "Since now."

Tori reached across the seat and grabbed hold of Leona's shoulder. "Wait. He's not in a uniform."

Beatrice's giggle was drowned out by Margaret Louise's snort of laughter.

Leona pulled the handle toward her body, her stocking-clad legs swiveling toward the street. "Snug jeans . . . a T-shirt that hugs his biceps . . . and a tool belt armed with any number of enticing objects . . . I'd say he's most certainly a man in uniform."

"And the fact he, too, is about half your age?"

"That just means he's still teachable." Leona stepped onto the sidewalk, her narrow black skirt showcasing a pair of legs women half her age would envy.

Shaking her head, Margaret Louise followed suit, her plump body a stark contrast to her twin's. Tori and Beatrice joined them on the sidewalk.

"Tori, hi!" Doug strode across Rose's front lawn, sunlit highlights shimmering through his dirty blond hair. "What brings you by at this time of day?"

"My friends and I just wanted to check in on Rose real quick." She gestured to each of the women standing alongside her. "Doug, I'd like you to meet some of Rose's friends—this is Beatrice, Margaret Louise, and L—"

"Leona . . . Leona Elkin," the sixtysomething woman supplied as she extended her hand in pristine fashion while batting her eyelashes at Mach speed.

Grabbing hold of her fingers, Doug lifted her hand to his lips and kissed it gently. "Leona, what a beautiful name."

The woman sighed, the enamored sound a mere backdrop to Margaret Louise's guffaw.

Leona glared at her sister.

Margaret Louise motioned toward Leona. "Leona and I are twins. On the outside, we're fraternal. But underneath our clothes we look exactly the same. Though I think I might have just a *wee* bit more cellulite than she does."

"Cellulite?" Leona hissed through clenched teeth. "Cellulite? I don't have cellulite anywhere."

"Oh. I'm sorry. My mistake," Margaret Louise said before bestowing a wicked grin in Tori's direction.

Shaking off her friends' antics, Tori nodded toward the house. "How is she today?"

The smile that had lit Doug's face just seconds earlier slipped from his face. "Terribly distracted. I tried talking to her when I arrived this morning but she just doesn't have the heart for it right now. I tried to encourage her to sit out on the patio while I worked on a few patches of siding but she wasn't interested."

Tori glanced at her friends briefly. "Has she had any visitors this morning?"

Doug hooked his thumb across the hammer in his tool belt and nodded. "Milo dropped me off this morning and he went in to check on her first thing. Then, not more than an hour ago, that one fella stopped by."

Margaret Louise's head jerked upward. "You mean Kenny?"

"Kenny?" Beatrice asked.

"Murdock. Murdock, Murdock, Murdock," recited Leona with an eye roll.

"Oh."

Ignoring Beatrice's obvious disappointment, Margaret Louise addressed Doug once again. "Kenny Murdock?"

"I guess," Doug said with a shrug. "The colored fella with the big nose."

"That's Kenny." Leona clasped her hands together, her eyes still intent on Doug's face. "Did he leave?"

"Been about fifteen minutes or so since he trotted out. Slammed the door so hard it made my teeth rattle. I thought about saying something but opted not to when I saw his face."

Tori reached out, grabbed hold of Margaret Louise's

arm for support as Doug's words filtered their way into her heart. "His face?"

"It was dark with the kind of anger I've not seen in my life terribly often. Figured he got a phone call that sent him off in a tizzy."

She swallowed against the lump that threatened to close off her throat in panic. "Have—have you checked on Rose since he left?"

He shook his head, his sky blue eyes narrowing on her face. "Not yet, no. Figured I'd do that when it gets a little closer to lunch."

"Did you . . . did you see her standing at the door when he left? Or maybe looking out the window since?" Beatrice asked, her voice a mere whisper.

Again, he shook his head. "Can't say that I did. Why? Is there something wrong?"

"Let's hope not," Tori muttered as she turned and ran toward Rose's front steps, Margaret Louise, Leona, and Beatrice in tow.

Chapter 8

The classic signs were all there—clammy fore-head, pounding heart, and mumbled pleas fleeing her lips. But the click clack of Leona's heels and the warmth of Margaret Louise's breath on the back of her neck as they ran up the steps was enough to push the present moment from potential nightmare into frightening reality.

Kenny had been inside Rose's house. He'd slammed the door when he left. He'd been angry enough to keep Doug from engaging him in conversation. . . .

And there hadn't been a Rose sighting since.

Grabbing hold of the door, Tori pushed it open, her heart beating still louder in her ears. Had Rose confronted Kenny? Had she backed him against a wall?

"Rose?" she shouted as she zigzagged her way through the elderly woman's home, her three friends hot on her heels. "Rose? Where are you?"

"Check her bedroom, Victoria . . . I'll check the sew-ing room." Margaret Louise veered off as the rest of them continued to search. Seconds later she reported in with a yell. "She's not in here."

"Please, please, please be okay," Tori mumbled under her breath, her ankle boots clanking on the wood floor as Rose's bedroom door loomed closer. Stopping long enough to catch her breath, she looked back over her shoulder, Beatrice's frightened eyes and Leona's pursed lips reinforcing the fear in her heart.

Since the very moment she'd stepped into her first sewing circle meeting, Rose had been ever present. Their first encounter had started out strained, with Rose making her loyalty to Dixie known loud and clear, evidence of any thawing coming only when Tori shared her plans for a children's room at the library. Then, during the days and months that followed, a full-fledged friendship and mutual admiration society had blossomed between them, creating a relationship that meant the world to both of them.

She wasn't ready to lose that. Not yet.

Yanking her hand to the right, Tori pushed her way into Rose's room, her stomach lurching at the sight of the white-haired woman lying sprawled—facedown—across her bed, her body still clothed in a housecoat, her feet still sporting her favorite slippers.

Beatrice stopped in the doorway, her gasp crystal clear in the absence of Tori's pounding heart. Or any discernable heartbeat at all, for that matter.

"Rose?" she whispered as her voice began to shake along with her hands.

"Rose?" echoed Beatrice.

"Wake up, you old bat!" Leona shoved her way between Tori and Beatrice, the fear in her eyes at war with her words and tone.

They stared at the bed, waiting for a reaction Tori prayed would come.

"Sounds to me like you're already awake, Leona."

The breath she didn't realize she was holding burst

through her lungs as unshed tears seared the corners of her eyes. "Rose!"

Slowly but surely, the woman rolled over, her puffy eyes swollen with sleep. "Who else did you expect to find? You are, after all, standing in my bedroom."

Tori laughed, a sound echoed by Beatrice.

"I thought I heard your voice," Margaret Louise said as she strode through the door and over to Rose's bed. "Which is a good thing considering the fact we thought you had gone the way of Martha Jane."

Uh-oh.

"Gone the way of—" Rose stopped, slowly pushed her way up onto her elbow. "You thought I was dead?"

Jutting her chin upward, Leona crossed her arms. "We'd rather hoped."

"Leona!"

"What? Did you hear what she said to me when she woke up?"

"What? What'd I miss?" Margaret Louise looked from her sister to Rose and back again before settling a questioning eye on Tori. "What'd she say?"

"She basically called your sister an old bat." Tori waggled a finger in Leona's direction. "Not that that's an excuse for what *you* just said, Leona."

Rose struggled to her feet, her slippers making soft sounds on the floor beside her bed. "Don't mind Leona. She's just jealous is all."

"Jealous?" Leona sniffed.

"Are you deaf?" Rose hollered back. "Yes, jealous."

"Why on earth would I be jealous of you, Old Woman?"

Rose stood and walked over to the window that overlooked her side yard. Lifting the curtain, she pointed outside. "Because you don't have *him*."

They crowded around the window, Leona's sigh ricocheting its way around the room.

"I *could* have him."

They looked at Leona.

"But he's married," she said with a wave. "And I don't feel the need to encroach on someone else's territory." She pointed just beyond Doug, to the muscular man standing not more than ten feet away. "He, on the other hand, is a different story."

Rose snorted. "Since when did you start plucking books off the children's shelf, Leona?"

"Plucking? What are you—" Leona stopped, pulled her hand back, and used it as a fan against her reddening face. "He's not *that* much younger."

"And he's not wearing a uniform either." Rose spun around, hands on hips. "Isn't that a prerequisite?"

Beatrice shook her head. "Apparently he is. Leona says his jeans and tool belt qualify."

"As a *uniform*?" Rose asked, her thin white eyebrows inching upward.

"The uniform of a man who is proficient with his hands." Leona stepped away from the pack surrounding the window and made her way over to the door. "I'll catch up with the rest of you outside."

"Makin' your move, Twin?" Margaret Louise bellowed.

Leona made a face. "I don't make *moves*, dear sister of mine. I *meet*—you know, say hello and welcome to Sweet Briar. Then I simply wait."

"For?" Tori prompted.

"Moves, dear . . . *his* moves."

If anyone had something to say, it went unspoken as they watched their poised-to-perfection friend head out the door in search of a temporary male companion. A male companion she'd no doubt land if her track record was any indication.

Margaret Louise broke the silence. "I think we came from different folks."

Rose rolled her eyes. "You're twins, aren't you?"

Throwing her hands into the air, Margaret Louise shook her head. "Well *somethin'* went wrong. Somethin' catastrophic."

"Catastrophic?"

Leona's twin nodded. "How else could you explain her?"

"How indeed." Rose shuffled her way into the hall, her slippers making pitter-patter sounds on the floor. "So you thought I was dead?"

Tori followed, Beatrice and Margaret Louise in her wake. "I don't know that we thought you—"

"We sure did. Figured he did you in, too." Margaret Louise continued on despite Tori's frantic hand-waving attempts to thwart further discussion of the subject. "Especially after Doug said he left here spittin' mad."

Rose's eyes narrowed behind her bifocals. "The three of you thought *Kenny* had killed me?"

"I, uh . . ." Tori's mouth clamped shut as Rose's teeth clenched behind open lips.

"I, uh . . ." echoed Beatrice as she stepped behind a nodding Margaret Louise.

"Sure as shootin' we did."

Tori laid a hand on Rose's shoulder. "It's not that we came here thinking he hurt you. We didn't. I just knew you'd planned to talk to him this morning and I was worried he might get angry."

Rose turned her less than happy gaze on Tori. "And people can't just get angry without murdering someone?"

"No. I mean, it's just that—"

Margaret Louise muscled her way to the front of the group. "We don't know what to think, Rose. We all like Kenny, we really do. But he has a history of a violent temper. You know that."

"I knew you were going to talk to him today and I was afraid it would be a hard conversation for you. I just wanted to make sure you were okay." Tori pulled her hand from Rose's shoulder and shifted from foot to foot. "Then, when we got here, Doug was out front. He said Kenny was furious when he left here. So furious in fact that Doug wasn't comfortable engaging him in conversation. So we were worried."

"I see."

"I'm sorry." She looked down at her hands, then back up at Rose. "If you believe in Kenny's innocence, that's good enough for me."

For a long moment, the woman said nothing. She simply stood there, looking from Tori to Margaret Louise to Beatrice and back again, the fight in her eyes dissipating only to be replaced by something Tori couldn't quite read.

Rose's words filled in the blanks. "I want to. I thought I did. But now . . . I just don't know anymore."

Tori felt her mouth gape and closed it quickly. "You mean you're questioning Kenny's innocence now?"

"I don't know," Rose said sadly, her voice garbled.

"Why?" Margaret Louise asked as she leaned against the wall. "What's changed?"

Taking a few steps, Rose lowered herself onto a kitchen chair, her pale white legs visible as the flaps of her housecoat parted. "I don't know. Maybe *I* have."

Tori, too, claimed a chair. "What do you mean, Rose?"

"I've heard that people grow suspicious of the world when they get old. Convinced that everyone is out to get them . . . to prey on their vulnerabilities."

"You're not like that!"

"Beatrice is right, Rose. You're not like that. You're very levelheaded."

"I happen to find you rather ornery, but not in a paranoid kind of way," Margaret Louise chimed in as she hoisted herself off the wall to claim the side of the counter instead.

Rose bent her arms at the elbows and rested them on

the table, her chin finding the tops of her fingers. "But I've always believed in Kenny. I knew he could learn his alphabet even though it took him an entire year of near constant after-school tutoring to get it done. I knew he would make it all the way through school, provided each new set of teachers believed in him, too. When his folks died, I knew he could live on his own, that he could find a job that would fit his abilities. And he did."

The rest of them remained silent as the elderly woman continued, her words alternating between raspy and broken. "And when Martha Jane accused him of stealing her money, I knew he hadn't. Money doesn't hold the same meaning for Kenny that it does for other people. He's simple and innocent. Completely untainted by a materialistic world."

"Sometimes people make bad choices," Margaret Louise stated in a matter-of-fact tone.

Rose nodded gently against her fingers, her eyes—magnified by her bifocals—fixed on some faraway spot. "And, in some cases, I suppose that's true. But not in this one."

"Then what's different about Martha Jane's murder?" Tori asked as she reached out and smoothed a strand of hair behind Rose's ear.

Forcing her gaze onto Tori, Rose shrugged, her bony shoulders rising beneath her ill-fitting housecoat. "The one thing Kenny struggled with, that I couldn't fix, was his temper. He was suspended from school for starting fights with classmates, he lost his first job for screaming at a customer, and he's been picked up by Chief Dallas on a number of occasions for breaking things."

"But those were just fights."

"Fights that happened in reaction to something," Rose explained, her voice assuming the faraway quality her eyes had held just moments earlier. "Kids teasing him over a mistake he made, a customer complaining he'd packed her groceries poorly, neighbors who took issue with the way he painted his house . . ."

Margaret Louise nodded her assent.

"But they were fights. I knew a kid who picked fights all the time in school." Tori looked from Rose to Margaret Louise and back again, their train of thought escaping her.

"They were always violent fits of rage on people who had wronged him in one way or the other." Rose pulled her gaze from Tori's face and planted it on a still nodding Margaret Louise. "Then Martha Jane wronged him. And now she's *dead*."

Chapter 9

When she needed a little space, music was the best medicine—preferably blasting from her car radio as she maneuvered narrow country roads. When she was scared or unhappy, Milo's warm arms and soothing kiss made everything a million times better. When she was stressed about money or an unforeseen issue at work, sewing calmed her soul and brought clarity to her thoughts. But when it came to feeling thoroughly helpless, chocolate was her therapy of choice.

Fortunately for Tori, Debbie Calhoun's bakery was less than a block from the library, its endless supply of decadent treats a sight for sleep-deprived eyes. Peeking into the glass case closest to the register, she scanned its contents closely—brownies, cupcakes, tarts, mousse cups, donuts, cookies . . .

"Good morning, Victoria. Emma told me you were here." Debbie wiped her hands on her apron and leaned against the counter, her dirty blonde hair swept off her face in a French braid. "And while you haven't been in Sweet

Briar all that long, it's been enough time to know that a prework visit from you means something's wrong."

Her head snapped up. "Am I really that transparent?"

"Yes."

"Seriously?"

"I'm right, aren't I?"

She looked back at the case, her gaze lingering on a chocolate-dipped donut drizzled with caramel, and swallowed. Hard.

"You can deny it if you want to, but I'll know you're lying. You look as if you haven't slept in days. Maybe even months." Debbie reached in through the back of the case, extracted the object of Tori's affection, and placed it on a doily-covered plate. "So what's wrong? Is there anything I can do to help?"

Reaching for the plate Debbie held in her direction, Tori closed her eyes briefly, the aroma of warm chocolate wafting its way into her nose. "Mmmm. You just did."

Debbie folded her arms across her flour-dusted chest. "While the business woman in me is happy with your answer, the friend side isn't."

She stared at the plate.

"Everything okay with you and Milo?"

The corners of her mouth tugged upward. "Milo is great."

"Is there more damage at the library than you thought?"

"Nothing I didn't know about on Monday." Setting the plate on the counter, she pulled her backpack purse from her shoulder and unzipped the top compartment. "How much do I owe you for the donut . . . oh, and for a hot chocolate in a to-go cup, too?"

"Nothing," Debbie said as she set about the task of making the hot beverage.

"Debbie, I can't take this."

The woman waved her off. "You're not. I'm giving it."

"Thank you," she whispered as she took the cup and looked down at the plate. "And you're right. There *is* something wrong."

In an instant, Debbie was out from behind the counter, her hand taking hold of Tori's upper arm and leading her to a table in the corner of the bakery. "Tell me."

Exhaling a piece of hair from her forehead, she dropped onto a wire-backed chair and reached for her donut. "It's Rose. I'm worried about her."

Debbie paused, her hand on top of a chair. "Why? Is she sick?"

"No. Nothing like that." Tori slumped her shoulders as she leaned back, the allure of the donut dissipating in record time. "It's just this whole thing with her former student and Martha Jane's murder. It's affecting her deeply and I don't know how to help her."

"Affecting her how?"

She sat forward, her elbows resting on the table as her hands sought the warmth from her to-go cup. "I'm not sure, exactly. Near as I can figure it's a horrible case of disappointment . . . maybe even denial. Either way, she's spent nearly three decades championing this guy—helping him, nudging him, teaching him, and believing in him. In that time she's celebrated his successes and taken him under her wing whenever a challenge came up. Now, all of a sudden, he's a very real suspect in a murder. Try as she might to discount the possibility as hogwash—

Hogwash . . .

Debbie sat down. "Tori? You okay?"

Hogwash . . .

"Huh? What?" Pulling her focus from some distant place, she forced herself to get back on task, to explain Rose's situation to someone she respected for the ability to be levelheaded. "Oh. Sorry. I guess I kind of zoned out there for a minute. Anyway, try as she might to discount the possibility that Kenny was involved in Martha Jane's death, Rose is realizing there are a few facts that simply can't be explained away."

"Like what?" Debbie prompted.

She raised her cup to her lips and took a sip, the warm liquid barely registering in her mind. When she set it down, she met Debbie's gaze head-on. "First and foremost? The fact that Martha Jane wrongly accused Kenny of robbery."

"She made a mistake."

"You know that, and I know that. But neither of us experienced the humiliation Kenny must have felt when he was hauled down to the station for questioning in a crime he knew darn well he didn't commit."

"Ahhh, I get it now. Rose is concerned what that humiliation may have set off inside Kenny in terms of anger, right?"

Tori nodded, then reached out for her donut. Breaking off a piece, she popped it in her mouth, the donut's former allure suddenly restored to its full glory. "Mmmm . . . wow. This is delicious."

"I'm glad. But keep going. I miss so much being here all day long."

She popped a second bite into her mouth and swallowed quickly. "Kenny was mad—spittin' mad, as Margaret Louise would say. And to listen to everyone talk, he has a habit of getting nasty when upset."

Debbie nodded her agreement.

"In fact, I saw him earlier that day at Rose's house. Not only was he angry, he also—" She stopped and stared down at her food, her mouth unwilling to share what her mind knew to be true.

"He also what?" Debbie asked, her louder-than-normal voice causing more than a few customers to look in their direction. Forcing a smile to her lips, she waved them off before turning back to Tori. "It's not fair to take me so far and then leave me hanging . . . So spill it, Victoria."

Leaning forward across the table, she lowered her voice to a near whisper. "He threatened Martha Jane."

"What? Are you sure?"

"Absolutely, positively sure."

"When?"

"The day she was murdered."

Debbie's face paled. "Wait a minute . . ." She poked her head up and looked around the bakery, her pale blue eyes widening with relief when she spotted her youngest employee. "Emma? Victoria and I have some catching up to do. Can you handle things for a little while on your own?"

"Sure thing, Mrs. Calhoun. Take all the time you need."

Tori watched as Debbie mouthed a thank-you in Emma's direction before resuming their conversation. "Did Martha Jane tell the police?"

"No." She wrapped her hands around her to-go cup once again, the lingering warmth doing little to dispel the chill that had plagued her all morning. "She—she didn't know."

"Didn't know?"

"He didn't threaten her to her face."

"Then how . . . Oh, wait. I get it." Debbie scooted a crumb across the table and into her hand. "He threatened her in front of other people, right?"

Her shoulders rose and fell. "Nope. Just me."

"Did *you* tell the police?"

She closed her eyes against the sudden onslaught of tears that threatened to inundate the mental barricade she'd erected against them, Debbie's wording a near-perfect match to the question she'd asked herself again and again throughout the night. Unfortunately, the light of day hadn't changed the answer. "No."

"Oh."

Slowly, she opened her eyes, her gaze fixed on her friend's face. "Honestly, Debbie, I thought it was just an idle threat. You know, something said in the heat of anger. I had no idea he meant it literally."

"Maybe he didn't."

It was the same argument she'd considered while lying in bed staring at the ceiling. "Then how do you explain the fact that she was murdered not more than seven hours later?"

Debbie shrugged. "I don't know.

"He told me she'd be sorry . . . for making people think he was a crook."

"Wow."

Reaching out, she picked up the rest of her donut only to drop it back onto the plate. "*Wow* is right."

"Will you tell them now?" Debbie asked.

Her stomach lurched. "Who? The police?"

"Who else?"

It was a thought she hadn't wanted to visit—her mind wrapped up in what she should have done, not what she still had to do. "But what about Rose? She'll be even more crushed than she is now."

For a moment, Debbie said nothing, her silence hovering above them like a thick cloud. When she finally spoke, her words were to the point. "Rose is one of the most honest people I've ever known. Sure, she loves Kenny. A person would have to be blind not to know that. But she wouldn't want a murderer to walk free simply because he was a sweet and misunderstood kid thirty years ago."

Tori thought back to her visit with Rose the day before, recalled the way the elderly woman had begun to see the possibility that Kenny was, indeed, involved. But what Tori couldn't convey to Debbie with any justice was the look of deep-rooted sadness that had swept across Rose's face as the visit progressed.

Did she really want to be the person who eliminated any remaining hope her friend still had in Kenny's innocence? Couldn't she just leave it to the cops to figure it out all on their own?

Sure, Rose would still be crushed when Kenny was carted off to jail for Martha Jane's murder, but *Tori* wouldn't be the one who delivered the final blow.

"Mrs. Calhoun? Mayor Hayes is on the phone."

Pushing back her chair, Debbie stood up. "I'll be right back, Victoria."

Looking at the plate in front of her, she forced herself to pick up the donut, to take a bite or two in an effort to calm the butterflies in her stomach. It would be okay. It had to be. The truth would come out on its own. Rose would be crushed, but she'd get over it. Tori and the rest of the sewing circle would make sure of that. . . .

"Victoria?"

She glanced up, saw the worry in Debbie's eyes. "Is everything okay?"

"There's going to be an emergency sewing circle meeting at Georgina's house tonight."

"An emergency meeting? Why?"

"To brainstorm ways to help Rose."

"There's proof?" she whispered past the lump in her throat.

"There's proof," Debbie repeated as her gaze locked on Tori's. "The rope that was used to strangle Martha Jane is the same rope Kenny was using to bundle limbs in Rose's yard."

Chapter 10

They'd had them before, last-minute sew-athons designed as a way to get together, to help each other through personal crisis or even to sample one of Margaret Louise's latest culinary concoctions. Emergency meetings, as they were fondly called, were usually held at the home of the member who requested the gathering, while regular weekly meetings cycled their way through the circle's roster.

Since Georgina Hayes, in her official capacity, had her finger on the goings-on in the Sweet Briar Police Department, it made sense that she'd call the group together in light of the latest development in Martha Jane's murder. One by one the dominoes were beginning to fall, each subsequent tile leading the way to Kenny Murdock's front door.

Which meant one thing. Rose Winters's heart was about to be broken. There was really no stopping it. But if the group banded together, perhaps they could find a way to help their friend pick up the pieces.

Tori said as much to Leona as they waited for

Georgina's housekeeper to answer the door. "And maybe, if we can find something to distract her, she can get through this faster."

Wrapping her fingers around the chocolate-colored clutch in her hand, Leona tilted her head downward and peered at Tori over the top of her glasses. "What do you propose, dear?"

She slid one of her tote straps down her arm and motioned inside the bag. "I could really use some help making hats and scarves."

"I thought Margaret Louise had already offered to help." Leona shot an impatient glare at the door and then rolled her eyes. "It's almost impossible to find good help these days."

The words were barely through the woman's lips when Maria, Georgina's longtime housekeeper, opened the door and welcomed them inside. Quickly and efficiently, the woman took the plate of homemade marbled brownies from Tori's hand before addressing Leona. "May I get your plate from the car, Ms. Elkin?"

"The bakery was closed by the time I heard about the meeting," Leona said as she brushed past Maria and into the foyer. "So I don't have anything."

"The *bakery*, Leona?" Tori said with a grin as she followed her friend inside. "I thought you told me so long ago that only homemade treats were allowed at these meetings."

"They *would* be homemade if I bought them from the bakery, dear." Leona pulled her latest travel magazine from under her elbow and then looked around, her gaze skirting across the freshly waxed wooden entryway flooring and down the long chandelier-lit hallway that eventually led to the study.

"How do you figure that?"

"Debbie would have made them. So, therefore, they'd be homemade, yes?"

She considered arguing but opted, instead, to let it go. Some battles just weren't meant to be won, especially those that had her questioning Leona's personal rulebook on southern etiquette. "So how's Paris?"

In an instant, the aloof and slightly irritated demeanor Leona seemed to wear like a badge of honor disappeared, in its place a smile that rivaled the sun on a warm summer day. "He is getting to be such a big boy. I have a picture . . ." The woman tucked her magazine back under her arm, opened her clutch, and extracted a three by five print of Paris, the garden-variety bunny she'd pilfered from former Sweet Briar resident Ella May Vetter. "See? Isn't he just the most handsome little thing you've ever seen?"

"Handsome?"

"Yes, handsome." Looking down at the picture in her hand, Leona's smile widened. "His little nose is just so well proportioned on his face and his eyes could melt a block of ice in a matter of seconds. And do you see his ears? They have such a perfect shape . . . so sleek and long."

"A perfect shape?" Tori stared at the picture, the rabbit's ears no different than those on any other bunny she'd ever seen before. "Well, I guess that means you won't be having to worry about expensive cosmetic surgery on the little guy, huh?"

Leona pulled the photograph to her chest while raising an eyebrow at Tori. "Are you mocking me, dear?"

Tori tugged her tote higher on her arm and leaned forward, planting a kiss on her friend's cheek. "Of course not. He's precious. Really."

The woman held the picture out once again. "He is, isn't he?"

Footsteps in the foyer made them both turn. Georgina Hayes's tall, slender form filled the open archway that separated the foyer from the hallway. "Leona . . . Victoria, I'm so glad you could make it." Waving off her housekeeper, the mayor looped her arms through theirs and led them toward the study and the near constant background chatter. "Did you bring anything to work on, Victoria?"

"I did. I brought material for hats and scarves. If I don't get moving, I won't have enough to send to the shelter in Chicago before winter sets in." She patted the tote with her free hand. "Margaret Louise has committed to making some, as has Dixie. Between them, that's fifteen. That still leaves me with forty-five."

"*Forty-five* hats and scarves?" Leona asked as her nostril rose along with her lip.

She nodded. "And the shelter can use every last one of them, I'm sure."

"So you're hoping to find some reinforcements?" Georgina teased.

"How did you guess?" Tori looked past Georgina to Leona, a grin tugging her lips upward. "Leona? Any chance?"

"Will they be silk scarves, dear?"

"No."

"Cashmere?"

"No."

"Egyptian cotton?"

"No. Why?"

"Just trying to gauge how big my donation check should be."

She rolled her eyes in time with Georgina. "We're making the scarves, Leona, not buying them."

"Making? As in sewing?"

"Land sakes, Leona, why do you think we get together for these meetings as often as we do?" Georgina asked as they stopped outside the study.

"To talk."

"And?" Georgina released her grip on their arms and crossed her own.

"To critique one another's baking ability."

"You don't bake, Leona. You buy, remember?" Tori teased.

"I buy what Debbie bakes."

Georgina extended her right index finger and pointed. "Do you see that machine in front of Beatrice? Do you know what that is, Leona?"

"A sewing machine, of course."

The mayor's finger shifted left. "And those objects in Debbie's lap?"

"Thread." Leona straightened her shoulders with pride. "*Stools* of thread."

"Spools," Tori corrected.

"And that?" Georgina asked as she pointed to a table on the other side of the room.

"A table?"

"I was referring to the pile on top of the table, Leona."

"Fabric."

Georgina nodded. "So let's see . . . we have women in a room with a sewing machine, spools of thread, and a pile of fabric. What do you suppose we do here?"

"Waste your time," Leona huffed as she marched into the study in pursuit of the leather armchair to the right of the massive stone fireplace that graced the entire back wall.

"Waste our time?" Georgina repeated.

Whirling around, Leona lowered herself onto the chair and crossed her stocking-clad legs daintily. "That's right. *Plastic* is for clothes."

Tori shot a look at Georgina before furrowing her brows at Leona. "Plastic?"

"That's right, dear. Plastic. Clothes should be *purchased*, not made. Unless your name is Armani or Vera Wang."

Margaret Louise glided up behind Georgina and Tori, her breath short and labored. "I'm sorry I'm late. Jake Junior had a late soccer game this evening. I tried to slip out a few minutes early but Lulu had a little problem she wanted to discuss."

The fourth of Margaret Louise's seven grandchildren, Lulu held a special place in Tori's heart thanks to her sweetly innocent outlook on life and her deep passion for books and reading. One mention of the little girl in conjunction with a problem sent her internal radar pinging. "Is Lulu okay?" Tori asked as Georgina excused herself to join the others in the study.

Tugging Tori to her side, Margaret Louise chuckled. "Yes, Victoria, your Lulu is fine. She just wanted to know if I could help her with a little project."

"What kind of project?"

"She asked me not to tell anyone . . . especially you." Margaret Louise motioned toward the study with her left hand, her right holding tight to a large sack. "Shall we?"

Nodding, Tori fell in step behind Leona's twin sister, the woman's words replaying in her thoughts. "Especially *me*? Wait. I don't understand. . . ."

Ignoring Tori, Margaret Louise strode across the room and claimed a spot on the sofa beside Dixie Dunn. "So what did I miss? Is someone trying to replicate a Vera Wang design?"

Leona snorted.

Georgina rolled her eyes.

Tori un-pouted her lip. "When you say a surprise, Margaret Louise . . . what kind of surprise are you talking about?"

"I got a wonderful surprise in the mail today." Beatrice looked up from the sewing machine she'd been hunched over and beamed.

"Something from your folks in England?" Dixie asked.

Beatrice shook her head, the hum of the machine coming to a halt as she paused all progress on her vest. "No . . ."

"Tickets to go home for a visit?" Georgina guessed.

The nanny's grin grew still wider. "No . . . But I'll give you a hint. It's something people receive when they celebrate an anniversary or a birth—"

Leona peered over her glasses. "That really doesn't help because, depending on the anniversary, it could cover a wide range. Frankly it doesn't get good until the twelfth . . . and then it depends on the quality of the silk."

Beatrice's eyebrows furrowed.

"And even at that, I'd bypass silk at the twelfth and gold at the fiftieth. Diamonds don't come into play until the sixtieth."

Margaret Louise's trademark hearty laugh echoed around the room. "That would mean you'd have to get *married*, Twin."

"For the rest of you . . . yes. For me"—Leona lowered her travel magazine to her lap and brought her hand to the base of her neck—"exquisite grooming and a well-timed bat of my eyelashes brings treasures my way."

Slapping a hand to her forehead, Margaret Louise shook her head.

"I can almost hear Rose's retort right now," Debbie drawled.

Rose.

Settling into a chair beneath the bay window, Tori set her bag on the floor at her feet as Beatrice's machine resumed its quiet hum. "I'm worried about her."

"Make that two of us," Dixie stated as she looped her needle and thread underneath the shirt collar she was working on and pulled it through the fabric. "I called her about tonight's meeting but she said she was tired."

"Maybe she was," Leona offered as she picked her magazine back off her lap and started flipping the pages once again. "She's old . . . and she's ornery. She *needs* her sleep."

"Leona!" Margaret Louise admonished through clenched teeth.

"It's not good to clench your teeth like that, dear sweet sister of mine. First and foremost, it's not good for your teeth. Second, it lends a masculine quality to your face that is most unbecoming."

One by one, five sets of eyes trained on Leona while Tori simply laughed. Leave it to Leona to defuse—or create—tension in a room.

"Margaret Louise's face is just fine, Leona. In fact, it's when she clenches her teeth like that that she looks most like you," Dixie quipped as she continued to work on the collar of her latest project.

Leona's mouth gaped open. "Like *me*?"

Margaret Louise nodded, a mischievous glint to her eyes. "That's what the woman said, Twin."

Leona's mouth snapped shut.

"That was very good, Dixie," Georgina said as her throaty laugh rang out. "Rose would be so very proud."

Seizing the opportunity to get the conversation back on track, Tori leaned forward. "From what I've seen, Rose took Kenny—"

Beatrice's machine stopped. "Kenny?"

"*Murdock*!" Dixie and Georgina hissed in unison.

Tori cast a look of amusement in Leona's direction before resuming her train of thought. "From what I've seen, Rose took Kenny on as a pet project a long, long time ago."

"And he flourished in a way he never would have had it not been for her."

Acknowledging Dixie's loyalty with a smile, Tori continued. "She believed in him. She encouraged him. She nudged him when she had to, sat back and celebrated his successes when they happened. Having him accused of murder—"

"Technically he's not been accused yet, though it won't be long," Georgina interjected from her spot beside Debbie.

"Either way, having something you've believed in for that long suddenly blow up in your face has to be rather defeating." Tori met Dixie's avid gaze once again. "Don't you agree?"

"*Devastating* would be a better choice of words." Dixie grabbed a pincushion from the end table beside her seat and poked the tip of her needle inside. "It's like what happened to me with the library. I spent the bulk of my adult life nurturing it only to have it ripped away because three men, sitting on a board, decided I was old."

"Walked right into that one, dear," Leona murmured from behind her magazine.

"Not now, Dixie."

"Why not, Georgina?" Dixie asked, her face flushed with indignation. "Maybe it makes you uncomfortable to hear. And maybe retiring me was the right thing to do."

A hush fell over the room as six pairs of eyes focused on the town's former librarian.

"Did . . . did you just say Victoria's hiring may have been a good thing?" Margaret Louise asked in disbelief, her words echoing the ones firing through Tori's head.

Dixie's shoulders rose and fell beneath her thin white button-down sweater. "In hindsight, yes . . . now that I've seen the wonderful things she's done there." The elderly woman inhaled deeply, her gaze resting briefly on Tori before resuming their journey around the room. "But, at the time, it was as if the ground was ripped out from beneath my feet. Everything I counted on . . . and even lived for at times . . . was gone."

"And Rose has spent her life fighting for Kenny . . ." Georgina said, her words trailing off.

"Fighting for him to be valued and seen and treasured." Dixie pulled her needle from the pincushion and returned to her collar, the meaning behind her words leaving them all in silence.

It was Debbie who finally spoke. "Then what do we do? What do we do to pick Rose up off the ground again?"

"I could bring her a few dinners. She loves my sweet potato pie and my beef stew."

"And I could add to Margaret Louise's contribution with a few desserts. Rose has a thing for chocolate." Debbie placed a strip of red fleece on top of a strip of navy blue fleece and starting cutting. "In fact, I think she's most partial to chocolate mousse."

"That's what happens when you get old. You prefer to eat soft things." Leona turned the page of her magazine and then looked out at the group as a gasp spread around the room like fire. "Oh, lighten up, would you?"

Georgina bristled in her chair. "And you, Leona? What will *you* do for Rose?"

Leona tapped her chin with a pearl-colored fingertip. "Well . . . I suppose I could—I know! I could try to find her a man."

Dixie rolled her eyes.

"I could bring Luke by for a visit. He'll be going to kindergarten next year. Maybe she'd enjoy coaching him on what to expect." Beatrice's soft British accent restored a sense of calm to the room. "It might help her feel needed."

"At least someone is on the right track." Laying her project on her lap, Dixie looked from one circle member to the next. "Rose needs a sense of purpose, something to help keep her mind off the thing she *can't* change in favor of something she *can*. Like talking to Luke, as Beatrice said . . ."

A flush of pleasure spread across the nanny's face before she ducked behind her sewing machine once again.

"We could get her involved in your project, Victoria," Margaret Louise suggested. "It would lessen the number of hats and scarves you have to make and give her something to do at the same time.

Dixie nodded. "She's certainly a beautiful seamstress."

"I do need help," Tori said as she looked down at the latest hat she was working on. "Lots of it."

"And there's the collection bin, too," Debbie said, only to shake her head as the last word left her lips. "Then again, I'm not sure how she'd do with a hammer and nails."

"Curtis has that covered."

Tori turned her attention to Leona. "Curtis?"

The woman peered over her glasses. "Didn't I tell you, dear? Age doesn't make a difference."

Tori felt her mouth beginning to open and stopped it midway. "You're not saying . . ."

Leona dropped her magazine into her lap. "That's exactly what I'm saying."

She stared at her friend.

"What? What did I miss?" Georgina asked, her voice taking on the gossip pitch they all knew well. "Who is Curtis?"

Without taking her eyes off Leona's unreadable face, Tori addressed Georgina's questions. "Curtis is the drifter who was hired by Martha Jane. He's what? Maybe thirty-five at best? And, if I'm hearing Leona correctly, she's captured him in her lair."

Five sets of eyes joined Tori's.

After a long pause, Leona lifted her magazine once again. "He has excellent taste, what can I say?"

"He's thirty-five?" Georgina repeated, her voice one of shock and awe mixed together.

The right corner of Leona's mouth quivered.

"Is he good-looking?" Beatrice asked.

"Exquisite." Leona flipped a page.

"And you've—" Dixie cut herself short. "Actually, I don't want to know. I really don't."

"Imagination is usually better anyway," Margaret Louise offered as she gazed up at the ceiling.

"Not in this case." Leona flipped another page and then another. "Imagination can only go so far."

Six mouths dropped open.

Tori's was the first to recover. "So what does *May* have to do with the collection booth, Ms. *December*?"

Leona lowered her magazine and pinned Tori with a stare while Margaret Louise snorted back a laugh.

"December?"

"December," Dixie repeated with a grin.

Laughter ballooned around the room, only to be cut short by Leona's audible huff of displeasure. "My dear sweet sister told me about what happened to the collection booth in the storm and how Milo was looking for someone to help him rebuild it. I asked *Curtis* if he'd consider helping."

"And?"

Leona turned her stare on Georgina. "He said yes."

"At least the carpetbaggers are making themselves useful this time around."

"Carpetbaggers?" Beatrice asked. "That's not a term I'm familiar with, Dixie."

"It's what we called northerners who traveled south to exploit our misfortune following the Civil War," the elderly woman explained. "They made their wealth from our suffering."

"And this Curtis bloke is one of these . . . these carpetbaggers?"

Tori stepped off the sidelines and joined the conversation. "No. They're simply here to—"

"Take advantage of people who are suffering," Dixie quipped. "They come with little and leave with our money."

"And, in some cases, our possessions." Georgina

compared spool colors before deciding on the perfect yellow for the piece of fleece she'd quietly taken from Tori's bag. "I remember about five years ago, after Gus, a parade of carpetbaggers swept into town, fixing roofs, replacing shingles, cutting trees, and stealing car parts."

"Stealing car parts?" Tori asked.

Georgina nodded. "Car after car around town stopped working. Eventually we figured it out . . . but not before that particular band of drifters was long gone."

"Well, I don't know about Curtis for sure, but Doug— the guy who is helping out at Rose's house—is from Mississippi, not the north."

"Curtis is from Tennessee." Leona set her magazine on the chair and folded her hands in her lap. "But, really, the term *carpetbagger* has become a catchall for drifter types more than it is a commentary on where a person is from."

Beatrice paused as she seemed to consider the explanation she'd been given. "What is this Curtis fellow doing now that Martha Jane is dead?"

The nanny's question resonated throughout the room, causing six sets of eyes to cast their way onto Leona once again.

"Adelaide Walker hired him on."

"Who's Adelaide Walker?" Tori asked.

"The elderly woman who lives on the other side of Martha Jane." Leona picked at a piece of lint on her black slacks before looking up. "She thought he was a hard worker."

Georgina set her fabric and thread on the table beside her and stood. "Sounds like it if he's willing to volunteer his time and expertise in helping restore our collection booth." She strode toward the archway that led into the hallway and then stopped. "Dessert, anyone?"

Debbie, Dixie, Beatrice, and Margaret Louise rose to their feet and headed in the direction Georgina had gone, their hushed conversation peppered with laughter and happiness.

Tori eyed Leona. "Aren't you going to have dessert?"

Looking down at her sterling silver link watch, Leona waved Tori off. "You go ahead, dear. I'm meeting my dessert in forty-five minutes."

Chapter 11

Tori peered at her reflection in the driver's side window. Tendrils of light brown hair escaped her ponytail, thanks to the warmer than normal temperatures that had prompted her to open the windows for the short drive to Milo's house. The effect wasn't her first choice, but it would do.

Making her way around the car, she stepped onto the sidewalk and headed toward the hammering that punctuated the otherwise quiet day. With the storm and Martha Jane's murder, the two of them had barely had more than five minutes alone all week—a fact she was eager to change.

The hammering ceased only to be replaced by the rumble of a male voice that didn't belong to Milo Wentworth.

"So much for being alone," she murmured as she rounded a moss tree and continued in the direction of the Man Shed behind Milo's home. The first time he'd shown it to her, he'd pointed out every tool and contraption in its arsenal, painstakingly explaining the purpose of each.

When she'd complimented him on his work shed, he'd puffed out his chest and gently corrected her terminology to incorporate the structure's many uses—which included a spot to play darts and watch football.

Milo spotted her and waved. "Well aren't you a sight for sore eyes." Popping his hammer into his tool belt, he closed the gap between them in two long strides and pulled her into his arms. "Mmmm . . . you smell good."

"Too good for the Man Shed?" she teased.

"Never." He released his hug just enough to guide her lips upward to meet his. "I've missed you these past few days."

She closed her eyes briefly, savored the feel of his lips as they moved to her forehead. "Ditto." Stepping back still farther, she waved at the wooden shell to the side of the shed. "Is that the collection booth?"

"It sure is. And it's really starting to come along, thanks to—" He stopped, looked around, and then shrugged. "Well, they were here just a minute ago."

"They?" she asked, as she, too, did a visual scan of their surroundings.

"Curtis and Doug." Milo took a few steps forward, then turned back to Tori. "Curtis showed up at eight this morning. Then, before I knew it, Doug was stumbling out of the garage saying he wanted to help, too."

"Things going okay with him staying in the garage while he's working at Rose's place?" She lifted her hand to her brow line to block the noon sun. "It's not getting to be too much?

His shoulders rose and fell once again. "Nah. He's a good guy. Gets himself to work in the morning and gets himself back in the evening." He turned back to the booth. "Curtis? Doug? Where'd you two go?"

"Right here, boss." Doug stepped out of the Man Shed, his muscular body filling his navy blue T-shirt out nicely. His face lit up when he noticed Tori.

She swallowed.

"Why if it isn't my scrumptious meal maker. How are you this mornin', darlin'?"

"I'm fine. How are you?"

Tucking his thumbs inside his waistband, he flashed a knee-melting smile in her direction. "Better now. All this male bonding is great and all but it don't hold a candle to the sight of a pretty lady."

She flashed a look at Milo, felt her shoulders relax at the sight of his easygoing smile. "Hands off, chum. She's taken."

Doug laughed. "I know. And so am I. But I ain't blind."

"It must be hard being away from your wife and kids like this," Tori said, her gaze diverted from Doug by the appearance of Curtis in a black and white ball cap. "Oh. Hi there, Curtis. I'm not sure if you remember me but I met you at—"

The man brought his fingers to the bill of his hat and tipped his head forward a hairbreadth. "Mizz Barker's house. I remember. Nice to see you again." He released his grip on his hat and toed the ground with his work boot. "I'm mighty sorry to hear about your friend, miss."

She stepped closer, extending her hand to the man. "Thank you. And I'm Tori, by the way."

"Tori," he repeated quietly. Her name was no sooner past his lips before a shy smile spread its way across his face. "Leona's mentioned your name to me."

"Don't believe a word that woman says," Milo said with mock seriousness. "Tori is truly far from a lost cause when it comes to the ways of the south."

Curtis looked from Tori to Milo and back again, his brows furrowed in confusion. "She didn't mention that. Just said Tori was real sweet."

"Sweet?" Tori echoed.

"Actually I think her word was *refreshin'*. Yeah, that's it. I remember because it's a word my grandmammy used to use." Curtis stretched his arms above his head only to bring them back down to his sides.

"She said I was refreshing?"

"Yes, ma'am."

"Did you happen to get it on tape?"

He looked a question at her.

She stifled back the urge to laugh, instead opting for an explanation for her silly response. "Don't mind me. Leona is one of my dearest friends. It's just that—"

"Ladies talk a whole 'nother language, Curtis, my boy. A whole 'nother language." Doug pointed at the booth. "So what'cha think?"

Eager to see their work up close, Tori maneuvered her way around the wooden two-by-fours they'd nailed together to form the booth's shell. A crossbeam, about chest high, denoted what she assumed was the front. "Will that be a counter?"

Milo nodded. "Very good." He took point, leading her around the shell. "This booth is going to be better than the last one. It's size will enable several people to work inside it at any given time, and its depth will allow for the presence of bins that can hold some of the items we hand out most—cans of food, diapers, those sorts of things."

She listened, her mind digesting everything he said. "Where did you keep those things before?"

"In the basement of town hall. Folks would come to the booth, tell us what they needed, and we'd give them a ticket to redeem at town hall as well as the next date someone would be manning the station." He glided his hand along the crossbeam. "And it's a system that works for the most part. But sometimes, when someone comes with a more immediate need . . . like they can't feed their family that night . . . you feel kinda helpless telling them to come back in a week. Having these bins in the booth will cut down on that somewhat."

"It's a good thing you folks are doin' with this here booth," Doug said as he grabbed a piece of plywood and positioned it along the back of the booth. Curtis stepped up beside him and pulled a hammer from his tool belt. "It's nice to be helpin' out in a town where people look out for one 'nother."

Curtis nodded but said nothing, his right hand finding its grip on the hammer as his left steadied the nail.

"It is, isn't it?" Tori asked as she glanced at Milo. Like clockwork, the butterflies that often took flight when she looked at him soared into action. "But you can't lump me in with Milo. In fact, I didn't even know there *was* a collection booth like this until just the other day—*after* it was destroyed in the storm."

Milo pulled his hand from the beam and slipped it around Tori's waist, pulling her close. "Don't listen to this woman. Hammering a booth together is like child's play compared to what she's done since she's come to town."

Curtis poked his head around the portion of wall he'd hammered into place. "Come to town?"

"I'm not from here," she explained, turning her head to avoid the direct rays of the sun. "Not originally, anyway. I spent the past few years living up north . . . in Chicago."

"Hey, I've been there!" Doug stepped out from behind the booth. "Brought my kids back a jar of water from the lake."

"A jar of water?" Milo asked.

Doug nodded. "Didn't work so well. My son and my daughter each want something different. They don't want to share. So I thought about buyin' them a stone in that Millennium Park place but then decided not to. There'd have been nothin' to bring back to show them 'cept some papers with my name on it."

"I've been to Chicago, too." Curtis walked around the

booth, stopping to tap a few nails in harder. "Only I left with nothing."

"Nothin'?"

He nodded, his gaze focused on a distant point over Doug's shoulder. "Been barely scraping by ever since. It's why I'm here . . . chasing storms. Keeps me from having to come to a place"—he pointed at the booth in front of him—"like this with my pride all but ripped from my heart."

Leaning against the Man Shed, Milo raked a hand through his hair. "That's the problem. I'm betting there are far more families in the area who could use the kind of help this booth symbolizes but they're too afraid—or too proud—to tell anyone."

"Sometimes, when times are tough, pride is all a man has left." Curtis dropped his hammer into his tool belt. "Asking for help destroys pride. And when it's the last thing you have left, it's mighty hard to part with it. Trust me on that."

"But if a person needs help, he should ask," Tori whispered.

Curtis met her gaze before looking away, his own voice barely discernable. "Easier said than done, sometimes. That's why figuring it out yourself, and on your own terms, is often the better way to go."

A cracking noise broke through the silence that followed, Doug's grin softening the transition made by his knuckles. "Sorry 'bout that. But talkin' about things like this ruins a mood. And when we're surrounded by a day like this"—he held his arms outward—"that's not the kinda mood I'm lookin' for."

"Sorry, man, my mistake." Curtis bent over and picked up a second piece of plywood. "Let's get back to it then."

"Do you guys mind if I take five?" Milo asked

"Not at all." Doug pointed his hammer from Milo to Tori and back again. "You take some time. We've got things covered here, don't we, Curtis?"

Curtis simply nodded, his attention focused on positioning the second piece of wood alongside the first.

With his back still against the Man Shed, Milo pulled her close. "So how was your emergency meeting the other night? The one at Georgina's?"

"It was good. Everyone is willing to chip in and help with the hats and scarves."

"See? I knew they'd help you."

She closed her eyes at the feel of his finger as it traced its way down her jawline. When she opened them, he was studying her with nothing short of love in his eyes.

Which started the butterfly brigade all over again.

Determined to keep things light in the presence of the other men, she continued on, her gaze locked on his. "And everyone has agreed to reach out to Rose . . . nudge her into different projects to keep her mind off things."

Milo's shoulders dipped. "Yeah, I heard about Kenny. Seems the entire faculty of Sweet Briar Elementary knew about the rope."

She nodded but said nothing.

"And it won't be long before they release the contents of the house."

"To whom?"

"Seems Martha Jane has a sister in a nursing home in Georgia. Rose knows who she is. Anyway, she'll need someone to gather up Martha Jane's things and ship them to her unless she hires a company." Milo's finger moved to her cheek, cupping her face in his hand. "But even with that, I'm sure she'll want someone watching over to make sure nothing is taken. The elderly are favorite targets for scam artists."

She considered his words. "Maybe I could help."

"You mean during those five seconds you have between working, sewing, making hats and scarves for the shelter, and everything else you do?"

She shrugged. "How hard could it be? Besides, maybe

that's something Rose and I could do together." As she spoke, the idea became more and more appealing. "It might make her feel a little less helpless and—"

Nudging her face upward, he squelched her words with a kiss to end all kisses, leaving her more than a little weak-kneed. When he released her, he smiled, dimples carving holes into his cheeks. "You are a special woman, Tori Sinclair. You do realize that, don't you?"

Unaccustomed to such heartfelt sentiment from a man who tended to lean toward sweet actions rather than tender words to convey his emotions, she simply stared up at him, unsure of what to say. When she finally spoke, her words were little more than a whisper. "It's nothing my friends wouldn't do for me."

"Ahhh. Paying it forward, huh?"

"Paying it *back* . . . to a woman who stood by me through some of my own dark days." She rose up onto her tiptoes and kissed the tip of Milo's chin before turning toward the street and her awaiting car.

"Lucky Rose," Milo mumbled just loud enough for her to hear.

She turned back, waving farewell to Doug and Curtis in the process. "No. Lucky *me*." Raising her palm beneath her bottom lip, she blew Milo a final kiss, his humorous attempt to catch it making her laugh out loud. "Now get back to work. All of you."

Chapter 12

Tori paused her hands over the keyboard and looked up, the bright afternoon sun reflecting off the counter and temporarily blinding her for the umpteenth time. She could make out a shape—relatively slim, and an approximate height of about six foot two—but beyond that, she was at a loss as she waited for the door to close behind her latest patron.

Traffic had steadily increased throughout the day, with students working on last-minute school projects, youngsters selecting their latest round of storybooks, and parents ready to dispose of the previous week's choices.

While there was a part of her that wished she had the day off to sew or catch up on her own reading, she couldn't deny the fact that this was when she loved the library most. Sure, quiet mornings with barely more than a few toddlers and their moms were nice, but so were busy days that underscored the power of books.

"Excuse me. I keep getting an error message on my computer and I can't figure out how to make it go away."

Pulling her focus from the shadowed figure in the door, Tori scooted off the stool and made her way around the information desk. "Let me see what I can do."

"Thanks." A look of relief passed across the teenager's face as he pointed toward the row of computers on the far side of the room. "I don't know what happened. One minute I was typing up my report for science and the next—wham!"

She walked around the computer bank and stopped beside the machine the boy indicated. Sure enough, a box had popped up in the bottom right corner, thwarting his progress.

"Do you think I'm gonna lose my report?" He rubbed a hand over his buzz cut, his voice growing more panicked with each passing word. "Mr. Bogan is gonna flunk me if I blow another one of his assign—whoa . . . you fixed it. . . ."

Slowly, she backed away from the computer, the corners of her mouth lifting upward in a smile. "We can't have Mr. Bogan flunking you when you've been working so hard all day, now can we?"

A matching smile lit the teenager's face. "No, we can't." Plunking himself into the chair, he grabbed hold of the mouse. "Thanks. You saved my life."

"That's what librarians are for." She patted him on the shoulder, then gestured toward the screen. "You might want to hit Save now . . . just to make sure you don't lose what you've written so far."

"I'll do that. Thanks."

Looping back around the computer bank, Tori headed toward the information desk, her stride quickening at the sight of a waiting patron. "I'm sorry, I was attending to a computer issue. How can I help—oh, Curtis . . . hi. I didn't see you come in."

Tipping his head forward, the man shrugged. "No worries. I can see it's busy in here today." He thrust a stack of books onto the counter and looked around, his gaze skimming its way around the room. "Looks like a nice library you've got here."

"Thank you. We certainly try."

When his visual inventory was complete, he gestured toward the books in front of him. "I read a lot when I'm on the road. Helps pass the time. But when I'm done, I don't really have much room in my duffle bag for things I don't need anymore."

She pulled the books toward her, her hand running across the top one on the pile. "These are in great shape. Are you sure you even read them?"

A cloud passed across the man's face. "I just said I read them, didn't I?"

Caught off guard by his tone, she rushed to explain her statement. "Oh, I didn't mean to imply you were lying. It's just that they"—she glanced down at the books— "look so good."

His posture relaxed. "Oh. Well, they're books. You read them once, you're done. No reason to abuse them."

"I agree. Though you'd be shocked to see the condition of some of the books we get." One by one she went through the pile, her mind registering each and every title. "You have some great choices here."

"Yes, ma'am."

She glanced up. "Did you enjoy them?"

"Yes, ma'am."

"Call me, Tori. Please." She ripped a sticky note from the pad beside her computer and wrote herself a note to check the titles with those in the system. "That was awfully nice of you to think of us for your books."

His broad shoulders rose and fell once again. "I donate my books everywhere I go. My favorite aunt used to work at a library and I know how limited funds can be."

"You're right. And thank you."

He leaned against the counter. "She used to take me

to work with her sometimes when my mamma was too hung over to wake up in the mornings . . ." His voice trailed off momentarily only to return with the shake of his head. "I loved those days. I loved exploring all those books and visiting all those places the writers described in such vivid detail."

Surprised by his willingness to say more than two words, she pulled her stool closer and sat down.

"I remember the steps . . . they had blue carpet. And there were three of them," he said, as he motioned his hand upward.

"Steps?"

"For kids to sit on while they looked at books." He glanced around the room, his brows furrowing.

"Is there something wrong?" she asked as she followed his gaze across shelves and over tables and chairs.

"Don't you have books for kids? You know, picture books and stuff like that?"

She felt the smile before it crossed her face, the familiar pride over her greatest accomplishment to date surfacing with a vengeance. "We do."

He bobbed his head left and then right. "Where?"

"Come with me." Stepping off the stool, she motioned the man to follow as she led the way down the hall located off the back of the main room. "Like you, I remember spending hours upon hours in the library as a kid. Mine didn't have steps, though. We had miniature rocking chairs."

"What did you like to read?"

She looked over her shoulder as she continued walking, the memories his question evoked bringing a smile to her lips. "I could get lost in the pages of a Little House on the Prairie book by the time I was eight. Then, when I'd devoured all of those, I moved on to Nancy Drew. How about you?"

"I liked Hardy Boys novels myself. I got a kick out

of trying to figure out the mystery before they did. I did okay most times."

Nodding, she stopped just inside the door of the children's room, her gaze fixed on his. "Did you ever pretend to be them?"

Shrugging as if embarrassed, Curtis glanced down at the floor, then back up at Tori. "Sometimes. But the story I liked to act out most was Robin Hood. I liked what he stood for even then."

"Then I think you would have loved this even more than the blue-carpeted steps." Tori took a step backward and motioned him inside. "I know I sure would have."

Barely two feet into the room he stopped and simply stared.

"The murals on the wall are enlarged renditions of drawings some of our local schoolchildren did. They represent some of their favorite books," she said as she worked her away around Curtis and into the middle of the room. Pointing to the back wall, she began naming some of the books that had prompted the illustrations. "That's Cinderella's castle . . . and Mr. McGregor's Garden . . . and—"

"Nottingham Forest . . . and the log cabin from the Little House books . . ." His gaze ricocheted around the room. When he'd completed his fourth or fifth pass of each and every picture, he looked back at her, awe evident in his eyes. "Who did this?"

"The kids did. It's their drawings."

"I get that, but who put them on the wall?"

"I did. I used a projector. Once their drawing was on the wall, I simply traced and then painted."

Nodding, he stepped further into the room, his hand grazing across a row of book spines. "The kids must love this."

"They do." And it was true. From the moment they'd opened the new children's room, it had become a favorite destination among the children of Sweet Briar. Suddenly, those youngsters who had resisted reading were slowly but surely giving books a try, eager to learn about the tale that went with the various pictures. "But the highlight of the room is the dress-up trunk."

"Dress-up trunk?"

Rather than explain, she simply beckoned him to follow once again, her feet traveling a favorite and well-worn path. When she reached the trunk she'd found at a local flea market, she bent over and lifted the lid. "Red Riding Hood, Laura Ingalls, Cinderella"—sifting her hand through the trunk, she pulled out a green hat affixed with a feather—"Robin Hood . . . you name it, they can be it."

His hand brushed against hers as he reached for the hat. "Where did you get these?"

"We made them."

He looked from the hat to Tori and back again, turning the green material over in his hand. "We?"

"The Sweet Briar Ladies Society Sewing Circle." She dug around in the box once again until she found the vest that went along with the hat. Holding it against her chest, she made a silly face. "I was a real girly-girl when I was little so I'm not sure what kind of Robin Hood I would have been, but it probably would have looked great on you."

"Are you part of this sewing circle, too?" he asked as he took hold of the vest and stared down at it as if it were made of gold.

"I am. It's how I met Rose Winters and Leona's sister, Margaret Louise." She walked over to the stage area and sat down, her feet dangling over the edge of the wooden platform. "I'm not sure what I would do without them."

Setting the Robin Hood costume on the platform beside Tori, Curtis ran his hand along the stage overhang. "Who made this?"

"A man from the town. He heard what I wanted to do

in this room and he volunteered to help. Just like you're doing with Milo and the collection booth." She pointed to the wooden two-by-four that denoted the top of the stage. "One of these days I'm going to put some brackets up so we can hang a curtain. I think the kids would love that."

He pulled his hand back. "This room was your idea?"

She nodded. "It was used as a storage room when I started working here. The moment I saw it, my mind started dreaming up ways to make it something special for the kids—something that would ignite their interest in reading. The only problem was what to do with the boxes of old books that were piled in nearly every corner. Once I started opening them it didn't take long to realize we were wasting space. Some of the books were in good enough condition we could sell them in the spring at the library's annual sale, but some were in terrible shape. I moved the good ones to the basement and pitched the bad ones. And, well, the space that was created was simply too hard to ignore."

Retrieving the costume from the platform, he folded it carefully in his hands. "I'm glad you didn't."

"Didn't what?" she asked as she watched him place the hat and vest back into the trunk and close the lid.

"Didn't ignore it." He gestured to the pictures, the trunk, and the stage with his chin. "You've done something mighty special here."

She followed his gaze, a familiar sense of pride rearing its head. "And you know what? It cost us less than two hundred dollars to get this room up and running."

He snorted in disbelief.

"No, really, it did," she said. "We already had the shelves and the books, the local hardware store donated the paint, I painted the pictures onto the wall myself, I found that trunk at a flea market for twenty-five bucks, my friends and I made the costumes to put in it, and Nina, my assistant, donated the bean bag chairs. All I needed to purchase was the lumber for the stage and a few additional seating options.

"Though now that we're in here and using the room all the time I see some things I'd still like to do."

"Like what?" he asked with true interest in his voice.

She gestured toward the stage once again. "I'd put up those brackets I just mentioned, I'd order the curtain Leona found for me on some site somewhere, and I'd get two or three . . . ideally four . . . reading chairs—kid-sized ones—and a table to go with them . . ."

"And you did all this because . . ." His words trailed off as he waited for her to fill in the blank.

"Because I love books. Because they were such a huge part of my childhood—such a huge and wonderful part."

For several long moments he simply studied her as if he were trying to see past her eyes and into her soul. And for some reason, it didn't bother her or make her uncomfortable. There was something about Curtis that made her feel as if he understood. Understood the drive, understood the passion, understood the desire to make a dream come true.

When he finally spoke, his voice was little more than a raspy whisper. "I wish I'd known you when I was a kid."

"Why is that?"

"Because I think you would have gotten me in a way no one else did."

Chapter 13

It never ceased to amaze Tori how fast life could change. One minute you could be down for the count, and the next you could be standing on a mountaintop basking in the sun. The problem was not always trusting that the mountaintop was out there.

The last few months in Chicago had been awful, the devastation over her broken engagement to Jeff making it hard to get out of bed every morning let alone find a reason to smile and laugh.

But now, living here in Sweet Briar, she was happy—completely, utterly happy. Sure, her ever-deepening relationship with Milo was a factor. He was loving, caring, genuine, honest, and romantic—a rare combination she recognized as nothing short of a gift. Yet it was more than just Milo. Her mountaintop was being bathed in sunlight from *multiple* directions, the majority of which were sitting right there in her living room.

Looking around, she couldn't help but feel blessed.

Margaret Louise was the epitome of loyalty and warmth. Her twin sister, Leona, was the kind of friend that kept you on your toes, anxious to see what the next adventure would bring. Debbie was thoughtful and good, her inability to be mean to anyone a quality to be respected and emulated. Melissa, Margaret Louise's daughter-in-law, was the picture of motherhood, reminding Tori of what she, too, wanted . . . one day. Georgina was an example of strength and grace in the face of tragedy, her ex-husband's embarrassing incarceration on murder charges doing little to stop her spirit. Beatrice's quiet nature was a gentle reminder to always listen with two ears. And Dixie . . . well, her aloof façade where Tori was concerned was crumbling more and more each day.

But no matter how many rays were streaming down in her direction, one was noticeably missing. One who combined many of the qualities the others exuded and hid them under a prickly shell.

"Has anyone talked to—"

"You won't believe what happened today," Georgina interrupted from her spot beside Dixie on the wicker settee Tori had dragged in from the porch. Switching off one of the circle's portable sewing machines, the mayor of Sweet Briar waited for someone to bite.

Dixie took the bait in record time. "Tell us."

"Yes, please do," drawled Leona as she rolled her eyes skyward. "Because it's not like Victoria was trying to say something."

Suddenly flustered, Georgina shot a look of apology in Tori's direction. "Victoria . . . I'm sorry . . . I guess I wasn't listening."

Tori held her hands up in the air. "There will be plenty of time to ask my question, Georgina. Tell us what happened."

"Well . . ." The woman's voice trailed off in a moment

of hesitancy, only to return with an undeniable excitement. "Someone left a very nice donation— with instructions on how it was to be used—in an envelope at town hall." Georgina sat up tall as all eyes in the room focused on her. Including Leona's.

"How large?" Leona asked.

"Three thousand dollars."

A long, low whistle escaped Margaret Louise's lips as she leaned back in the kitchen chair she'd commandeered. "Three thousand dollars? That's some mighty generous givin'."

Heads nodded around the room. Tori swallowed and shifted on the sofa beside Debbie.

"Whom did it come from?" Beatrice poised her hand above the soft yellow scarf she was working on for the women's shelter in Chicago and waited, with everyone else, for the answer.

Georgina didn't disappoint. "We don't know. The envelope was empty except for the cash and the instructions."

"You mean the three thousand dollars was in *cash*?" Debbie asked.

"So was the fifteen hundred we got at the library." Tori felt every eye in the room leave Georgina to flock in her direction.

"You got a donation, too?"

She nodded, her mind traveling back to the moment her assistant brought in the mail, a look of stunned belief etched across her face. "Our envelope was in with the rest of the mail but didn't have a stamp. Nina said it was sitting on top."

"That's the way ours showed up, too." Georgina scooted forward on her chair. "Was there a note specifying what it was to be used for?"

Again she nodded. "Any library projects I've been

wanting to tackle yet haven't had the funds to undertake to this point."

Dixie lowered her chin and peered over the top of her glasses in much the way Leona did. "Do you have any ideas?"

A smile stretched across her face as the list she'd compiled in her thoughts that morning sprang to the foreground once again. "First and foremost I want to find brackets to mount a curtain above the stage. I think the kids would get a kick out of opening and closing a curtain at the start and close of their little shows. Then there's the curtain itself—something thick and hard to see through. And then, I'd like to buy a few kid-sized chairs to go along with the beanbag chairs Nina donated."

"That sounds lovely, Victoria."

"Thank you, Dixie." Looking across at Georgina, she posed the question begging to be asked. "What was your donation for?"

All eyes returned to Georgina.

"Would you believe the collection booth?"

Margaret Louise clapped her hands together as Beatrice gave a little squeal of pleasure.

"For the building phase?"

Georgina shook her head at Tori. "No . . . to buy the items that go in the booth. And the letter specified that he or she wanted all of the items that are purchased with the money to be available in the booth during the Autumn Harvest Festival."

"Can the booth hold that kind of inventory?" Melissa asked as she glanced up from her strip of fleece. "Three thousand dollars is going to buy a *lot* of food."

"We'll make it fit." Margaret Louise reached into her sewing box and extracted a spool of turquoise-colored thread, then held it against the fleece she'd chosen to work with that night. "There have been so many times I've wished we had the food on hand rather than a coupon to redeem during a specific weekend."

"Maybe you could use some of the money to buy a storage chest for all of the items and store it behind the booth during the festival," Dixie suggested.

"That's a good idea except the note said it had to be used on items that would help the less fortunate." Popping the spool back into her box, Margaret Louise pulled out a slightly different shade of blue and, again, held it to the fleece. "Although helpful for the volunteers at the festival, a chest wouldn't benefit the needy in a direct way."

"I agree," Georgina said.

"Colby has a chest in the garage for paint cans and various tools he never uses. Perhaps that would work."

"Three thousand dollars is going to buy a *lot* of food," Melissa repeated.

"I think Rose has a chest like Debbie just described, too." Dixie rested her hands on her thighs and released a sigh. "It might be another way to help her feel needed right now."

Rose.

Seizing the opportunity to pose her earlier question in its entirety, Tori jumped back into the conversation. "Has anyone heard from her today?"

Seven heads shook from side to side.

"She's taking this Kenny situation very hard."

Beatrice sat upright. "Ken—"

"*Murdock*," Dixie hissed. "Kenny Murdock. The same Kenny we've been talking about for the past week. You know . . . the one who strangled Martha Jane Barker to death in her bedroom?"

Tori closed her eyes against the image spawned by her predecessor's words. It still seemed so surreal, so foreign.

Seven days ago she'd stood in the very same room where Rose's lifeless neighbor would be found, the grouchy woman alive and well right beside her, pontificating on everything from the laziness of her newest employee to the inadequacies of the banking system.

"I stopped by her place this morning to bring her some fleece."

"And how was she?" Leona asked of her sister.

The woman's plump shoulders rose only to fall back down to their normal position. "Quiet. Distracted. Sad. I tried my best to cheer her up . . . even told her a few stories about you, Twin . . . but nothing perked her up."

"Stories about me?"

"Did they involve her being old?" Dixie asked with a mischievous tone to her voice.

"I'm not old." Leona tossed her magazine onto the end table beside the green and blue plaid armchair that was a favorite among the circle when meetings were held at Tori's house.

"And I don't breathe," snapped Dixie.

"If only we could be so lucky."

A chorus of gasps rang out around the room.

"What?" Jutting her chin upward, Leona crossed her arms in front of her chest. "She started it."

"I think it's time we head into the kitchen and try out the treats everyone brought . . . what do you say?" Tori looked around the room in a desperate attempt to give Leona time to pull her foot out of her mouth. "Margaret Louise brought chocolate chess pie, Debbie brought those mini cheesecakes everyone adores, and that's just the beginning."

Slowly but surely, the members of the circle left their chairs in favor of the kitchen, whispered outrage still passing between their lips as they shot daggered looks in Leona's direction. When they were gone, Tori turned to her friend. "Must you antagonize Rose and Dixie the way you do?"

"Must *I*?" Leona balked as she brought her hand to the base of her neck. "Surely you mean, must *they*?"

"No, not really."

Pulling back, Leona dropped her hand to her side. "They live to antagonize me."

"I don't think that's true."

"They're jealous, that's all. Rose might be able to catch a peek at Curtis from her window during the day but I"— Leona spun on her stylish pumps and marched toward the kitchen—"I get to see him all night—"

Tori held her hands up in the air. "Too much information, Leona. Too much information." Turning to follow, she stopped in her tracks as her gaze skirted across the end table. "Um, Leona?"

The woman turned, a look of disgust on her face. "*Um*? *Um*? Have I not taught you how to speak in true southern fashion yet?"

"What are you doing with that?"

"Doing with what, dear?"

"That!" She pointed at the magazine.

A pinkish hue blossomed across Leona's cheeks. "I left my travel magazine at home. And that's all you had."

"That's all I—" She stopped and shook her head. "My subscription ran out a few months ago. I've been meaning to extend it but I haven't gotten around to it yet." Leaning over, she lifted the magazine from the table and turned it over in her hands, her gaze seeking and finding the mailing label.

Leona Elkin
15 Heritage Way
Sweet Briar, South Carolina

"Leona Elkin?" she whispered. Feeling the corners of her mouth tug upward, she glanced in her friend's direction, the woman's cheeks still redder. "You subscribe to a *sewing* magazine?"

"It's a gift. For Margaret Louise."

"Then why doesn't it have her name and address on the label?"

Stamping her foot on the hardwood, Leona narrowed her eyes at Tori. "Okay, yes . . . I get a sewing magazine. Must we place more importance on it than is truly necessary?"

"It's a sewing magazine," Tori repeated. "And you don't sew, Leona."

"I do, too. I sewed that handkerchief that was supposed to be for that—that crazy Vetter woman."

Tori raised her left eyebrow.

"You know I did."

She raised her right eyebrow. "You pushed a button on the machine, Leona."

"Oh give me that." Leona strode across the room, pulled the magazine from Tori's hands, ripped the mailing label from the back cover, and stuffed it behind the envelope pillow that graced the armchair she'd abandoned in lieu of dessert. "You have better things to think about, dear."

"Such as?"

"Milo, for one. Really, dear, you need to be constantly reinventing yourself to keep him interested."

"Milo and I are just fine."

"And then there's these hats and scarves you're hurrying to make for that shelter in that dreaded city."

She opted to ignore that one.

"And last, but not least, there's the little matter of how to spend that donation you got today."

Cocking her head, she studied her friend. "Leona? Did you give those donations?"

"No, dear. Donations like those tend to come from people who have come into money they weren't expecting. If that were me, I'd go to London."

"London," she repeated under her breath as Leona waltzed out of the living room and into the kitchen.

Leona was right. People who had money to burn tended to do one of three things. They spent it—traveling to exotic places and/or adding to their list of possessions, donated it to a favorite charity or cause near and dear to their heart, or tucked it aside in a bank.

Unless your name was Martha Jane Barker. Then you stuffed it in a sock drawer. . . .

A sock drawer.

In a second she was across the room, rounding the corner into the kitchen, seven backs hunched over the table as their owners discussed the merits of one another's desserts. "Georgina?"

"Yes, Victoria?"

"What happened to Martha Jane's money?"

Brushing a strand of hair from her forehead, the town's top elected official shook her head sadly. "It's gone."

"Gone?" she echoed.

"Gone."

"You mean—"

"Whoever killed her stole her money, too."

For the first time in days she felt a sense of hope, hope that maybe Rose was right. Maybe Kenny wasn't involved. "So maybe it was nothing more than a robbery gone bad. Maybe Martha Jane walked in on the thief."

The woman tapped her chin with the index finger of her right hand. "Perhaps. But there was nothing else amiss."

Tori narrowed her eyes on Georgina's face. "What do you mean there was nothing else amiss?"

"There was only one drawer open in the entire house."

The mayor's words filtered their way through her mind. "Only one drawer . . . So whoever did it knew where to find the money, is that right?"

"It certainly looks that way."

"And Kenny knew?"

Georgina nodded. "Martha Jane said it loud and clear when she accused him of stealing it the first time."

Chapter 14

No matter how hard she tried, she simply couldn't sleep. And the reason wasn't hard to figure out.

She hated to see people hurting, plain and simple.

It had been that way since she was a little girl, her instinct to help the underdog propelling her in front of more than a few schoolyard bullies in elementary school and again with locker room mean girls in high school.

Even then she'd known the difference between the kind of hurt that was patchable and the kind of hurt that wasn't. When Colby Calhoun went missing, that was a patchable hurt. At least in the sense that she could do whatever it took to find answers for Debbie. And she had.

The death of her great-grandmother, on the other hand, had been the kind of hurt that lasted . . . until Rose came into her life and softened the pain.

Not being able to help her in return was nothing short of crushing.

Rolling onto her side, she shifted the alarm clock into view.

11:00 p.m.

She couldn't call Milo now. It was too late. He had to get up early to teach in the morning.

Then again, he'd be upset if he knew she'd needed him and hadn't called.

For nearly five minutes she wrestled with what to do, her hand inching toward—and then away—from the phone over and over again.

Finally need won out.

Punching in his number, she held the handset to her ear and waited as it began to ring.

One.

Two.

Three.

She was about to give up when he answered, his sleepy voice bringing a lump of guilt to her throat. "Hello?"

"Milo?"

"Tori? Are you okay?"

His obvious worry only increased the size of the lump.

"I'm sorry. I shouldn't be calling so late . . . it's just that—well, it's just that I can't sleep."

"Talk to me."

Closing her eyes, she held the phone still closer. "Are you sure?"

"Absolutely. What's on your mind?"

"Rose."

A long sigh filled her ear. "I figured as much."

"Look, I'm sorry, I really am. Let's just talk tomorrow . . . after school."

"Wait! I didn't mean that in a bad way. I just know you. I know how you are about the people in your life. So I figured the situation with Rose was keeping you awake."

She breathed a sigh of relief. "I feel awful, Milo. Because there's nothing I can do to help her . . . short of keeping her busy with projects. But you and I both know that's only a Band-Aid. When it comes off it's still going to hurt."

"I know."

"For just a few minutes during our circle meeting I actually had some hope."

"Hope? How?"

"Martha Jane's money is missing. And I figured that maybe her death was from a robbery gone wrong."

A sound on the other end of the phone made her envision Milo propping himself up on a pillow. "And you figured Kenny might not be that person?"

She shrugged, then realized the gesture was futile. "Rose said in the beginning that Kenny had no use for mon—" She stopped as yet another nail was hammered into the coffin.

"Tori? You still there?"

"Yeah, I'm still here." Pressing her fingers to her forehead, she began to knead her skin in an attempt to combat the pain that was pressing down just above her eyebrow. "It's just that I think I figured it out."

"Figured what out?"

"Who left an envelope with fifteen hundred dollars inside it as a donation to the library along with instructions on how it's to be spent."

"Fifteen hundred dollars?"

"Fifteen hundred dollars," she confirmed. "And who left an envelope with three thousand dollars inside it as a donation to the collections booth . . . along with instructions on how it's to be—"

"Someone donated three thousand dollars for the collections booth?"

She nodded, then remembered to replace the action with words. "Don't get too excited. I don't think either of us can really use it."

"Why not?"

"I think it's from someone who really has no use for money."

"Kenny?"

"Kenny." But even as she said his name aloud, doubts still flitted through her mind. Doubts that pulled at her heart every bit as much as resignation.

"I'm hearing something in your voice. There's more, isn't there?"

It was funny how some people could be part of your life since the beginning and never know you as well as someone you've only known for a matter of months. Milo was definitely one of the latter. As was Margaret Louise and Rose.

"I know the evidence points to Kenny. I know he was using the rope earlier that day. I know he was furious at Martha Jane for falsely accusing him of stealing her money. And I know it's because of that accusation he knew where she kept it."

"Martha Jane said it loud and clear. . . ."

Georgina's voice filled her ears as she recalled their earlier conversation, the woman's words leaving her with an unsettling feeling she simply couldn't put her finger on.

"You want to do a little checking, don't you?"

Did she?

She did. Somewhere deep inside she'd known it all the while she was trying desperately to fall asleep. It didn't mean she'd find anything that would help Rose. But she wouldn't know if she didn't try.

"I guess I do."

"You do realize it's probably futile, right?"

"I do."

"And you know that getting involved in this is only going to further fill an already full plate, right?"

"I do."

"Then count me in for whatever you need. Chocolate

for energy, hugs for motivation, late night phone calls for reassurance . . ."

She blinked against the sudden moisture in her eyes. "Thank you, Milo. For everything."

"Thank *you*. For being the kind of person I never really believed existed except for in the fairy tales I read my students."

Chapter 15

Casting one final glance around the office, Tori grabbed her keys and her purse and headed for the door. She knew she should feel some guilt over leaving Nina shorthanded on a Tuesday of all days, but she didn't. Not really, anyway.

Besides, she'd managed to lure Dixie into covering toddler story time with nothing more than an early morning phone call and a relatively short ego-patting session. Between the two of them, they could surely handle the day's busiest hour without her assistance, freeing her up to do a little sleuthing.

She just hadn't counted on two—scratch that, *three* partners in crime.

Once she was in the hall that ran from the front to the back of the library, she turned left. Five steps later and she was out the door, the late morning sun nearly blinding her as she jogged down the stairs and over to the pale blue station wagon parked just beyond the Dumpster.

"We all set?" Margaret Louise asked as she popped her head out the driver's side window.

"All set. Nina and Dixie have everything covered for the next few hours." She crossed behind the wagon and slid into the passenger seat, tossing her purse onto the floor before scanning the backseat and coming up empty. "I thought we were going to have reinforcements."

"We were and we are." Drumming her pudgy fingers on the steering wheel, Tori's friend gestured toward one of the hundred-year-old moss trees with her chin. "Paris just needed a dab of privacy. You know how those bunny rabbits can be and all."

Tori shook her head, then leaned against the seat back. "If you would have told me four months ago that your sister would be fawning over a garden-variety bunny, I'd have told you you were crazy."

"Ain't nothin' I ain't heard before." Margaret Louise swiped a hand across her brow. "But I know what you mean. I didn't think Leona was fittin' to care for anything—man or beast."

"She's got the man thing down pat from what I can see," Tori mused as the subject of their conversation emerged from behind the tree, a small brown rabbit nestled against a classy autumn brown suit. "I mean, really, how many sixtysomethings can land a thirtysomething as fast as Leona did Curtis? She should be in the record books quite frankly."

The driver rolled her eyes. "Good Lord, Victoria, whatever you do don't go tellin' my sister something like that. You do and she'll be crowin' mornin', noon, and night."

"And that would be different because . . ." She winked a smile at the woman, then turned to acknowledge the latest addition to their crew. "Good morning, Leona. Love that suit."

"It's a Donna Karan original. Curtis bought it for me

yesterday." Yanking the car door open, Leona tucked Paris under her arm and lowered herself into the backseat. "He really has spectacular taste for someone who spends his days wearing little more than a tool belt."

"He bought it for you?" Margaret Louise echoed.

"He sure did. I've trained him well." Raising Paris to eye level, Leona released a series of air-kisses in the direction of the bunny until Margaret Louise turned the key in the ignition and peeled out of the library parking lot en route to their final destination. "Must you drive so recklessly? Bunnies die in senseless car accidents every day."

Tori glanced over her shoulder, raising an eyebrow at the occupant in the backseat. "Every day, Leona?"

"Okay, maybe not every day but—"

Margaret Louise extended her neck and peered into the rearview mirror. "Twin, I'm bettin' most folks aren't drivin' bunnies around in their cars. In fact, I reckon you're probably the first."

"Good sense must start somewhere." Leona brushed her free hand down the length of her skirt, stopping every few inches to remove a speck of invisible lint from the fabric. "Anyway, I really must ask . . . where are we off to this afternoon?"

She snuck a sidelong glance at the driver. "You didn't tell her?"

"No."

Swiveling in her seat, she met Leona's gaze once again. "If you didn't know where we were going, why did you come?"

Margaret Louise's trademark laugh burst from her mouth, drowning out all road sounds as they turned onto Grove Street and headed east toward Rose's neighborhood. "Haven't you figured that out yet, Victoria?"

"What?"

"My twin, here, is as nosy as they come."

Leona gasped. "Nosy? Me?"

"Yes, you. You've been that way since we were no bigger 'n Granddaddy's knee. But somehow I always got blamed for your curiosity."

The sole human occupant of the backseat sat up tall. "That's because I was a pure angel. Granddaddy and everyone else knew it."

"'Cept me, of course."

"Are you implying I was anything less?" Leona drawled. Lifting a finger into the air, she began pointing out various sights for Paris as they sped through town. "And that's where Investigator Daniel McGuire and I first . . ." Her explanation trailed off, a giggle bursting forth in its place. "I suspect it's best to skip that snippet of information." Lifting the bunny back to eye level, she pouted her lips momentarily as she wiggled her finger mere inches from the animal's twitching nose. "Mamma wouldn't want to corrupt her precious little Paris, now would she?"

"No. She wouldn't." Tori flashed a grin in Margaret Louise's direction before addressing Leona once again. "As for your earlier question, we're doing a little . . . checking."

"Checking?"

"Investigatin'."

"Of what?" Leona asked, leaning forward in her seat.

"I don't know, exactly." And she didn't. Not really.

"*Of course*, that makes perfect sense."

Tori worried her lip. Leona was right. None of this made any sense. The rope, the stolen money, and a pretty sound motive all pointed to one person.

Kenny Murdock.

Resting her forehead on the side window, she moaned softly. "What am I doing? This is dumb."

Margaret Louise swerved onto the gravel shoulder and slammed on the brakes, a string of very unladylike mutterings springing forth from the backseat. Shifting the car into Park, she turned a disapproving eye on Tori. "Why did you call me this morning?"

Tori stared at her friend for a moment, confusion clouding any semblance of intelligent thought. "Uh, well . . ."

"You had something stuck in your craw, didn't you?"

"My craw?"

"Something eatin' at you, twistin' your innards into knots . . . that sorta thing, didn't you?"

Slowly, she nodded, images of her restless night replaying their way through her thoughts.

"Well, what was it?"

"This thing with Kenny."

"What 'bout it?"

She thumped her head against the back of the seat, raking a hand through her hair as she did. "Did you know Martha Jane's money was missing when they found her body?"

Margaret Louise nodded. "Heard it at our circle meetin' just like you did."

"Well then you know that fact just points an even stronger finger in Kenny's direction, right?"

Again, the woman nodded, her gaze never leaving Tori's face.

"Ugh. I sound like an idiot. None of this makes any sense."

"You won't get any argument from Paris or me," Leona interjected from the backseat.

"Hush, Twin." Margaret Louise leaned across the front seat and patted Tori's knee. "Something is buggin' you, so talk it out. We're listenin'."

She exhaled an errant strand of hair from her forehead, then watched as it floated back to its exact same spot. "You're right, there is. Unfortunately I have absolutely no idea what's nagging at my thoughts so hard."

"What's your gut tellin' you?"

"That I'm just trying to protect Rose."

Margaret Louise seemed to mull over her answer, her head nodding ever so slightly as she closed her eyes momentarily. When she opened them again, her focus traveled to some distant place well beyond the confines of her station wagon. "Even someone as carin' and sweet as you, Victoria, wouldn't go runnin' off on some wild-goose chase unless there was a reason."

Shrugging, Tori, too, closed her eyes. Margaret Louise was right. "But what happens if I can't put a finger on what that reason is? Or where the goose chase is leading me?"

"You go with it."

"You do?" Leona asked.

Margaret Louise rolled her eyes in a mixture of amusement and disgust. "Sometimes that not-knowin' part of your brain knows more than you realize. All we have to do is find a way to coax it out."

"And how do you propose we do that?"

"By investigatin', Twin. Just like Victoria planned."

"But what, exactly, do we investigate?" Tori asked as she looked from one sister to the other.

"I don't rightly know. But I reckon we'll find out. 'Specially with Leona's nose leadin' the way."

An audible sniff rang out from the backseat.

Shifting back into drive, Margaret Louise pressed her foot on the gas pedal and peeled back onto the road, gravel spewing upward in their wake. "So that's what we're gonna do."

Tori couldn't help but smile as they sped down one road after the other.

"Are we going anywhere dangerous?"

"For us? No. For you? Possibly." Margaret Louise bit back a grin as her words generated a rustling in the backseat.

"For me?"

"Well, technically that depends on whether Rose is actually home."

Leona gasped for the second time that day. "Rose? We're going to Rose's house? No one ever said anything about visiting that old biddy."

"Land sakes, Twin, would it kill you to extend a little empathy in Rose's direction just this one time?" Margaret Louise asked as she slowed the car in preparation for their final turn. "She is sufferin', you know."

"Suffering, schmuffering." Leona extended her index finger into the air and pointed it smack down the middle of the front seat, Rose's home springing into view. "Tell her to look out her window every day after breakfast. Maybe that will keep her mind off things."

"Look out her window?" Tori followed Leona's hand. What she was pointing out was anyone's . . .

Ahhh. Now she got it.

Doug, clad in a tight white T-shirt and a pair of faded blue jeans, was squatting on Rose's roof, hammering shingles into place.

"Let me guess," Tori said as she continued to observe Rose's temporary employee as he repaired yet another souvenir from Roger's visit to Sweet Briar. "You think looking at Doug would be enough to eliminate Rose's hurt and frustration over Kenny's part in Martha Jane's murder?"

"He's a man, isn't he? A well-built, hardworking one to boot if I might add."

"He's a *married* man, Twin," Margaret Louise reminded as she shifted the car into Park and turned off the ignition. "And you've got your hands full as it is with that one"— the woman pointed farther down the street—"over there, don't you?"

"And he buys you clothes." Tori opened the door and stepped out onto the sidewalk. "You can't get much better than that."

Clutching Paris to her bosom, Leona, too, stepped from the car, her lip slightly curled. "I could if he were a bit more attentive."

Margaret Louise stopped midstep. "You've found a man who isn't fallin' all over you? Why, Twin, this young man of yours is gettin' better all the time, ain't he, Victoria?"

"He's just preoccupied is all," Leona insisted before peering up at Doug and elevating her voice a touch. "That roof never looked finer."

"Why thank you, ma'am." Doug tipped his ball cap forward, then repositioned it on his head, a grin stretching across his face as he set his hammer down beside him. "Tori, Ms. Davis . . . what brings you by?"

It was a hard question to answer, since she didn't really know herself. But, fortunately for her, Margaret Louise fielded the question with ease.

"Martha Jane's sister, bless her heart, has asked us to keep an eye on the place until she knows what's happenin'."

"Seems to me she's got nothin' to worry about now."

Tori studied the man. "Nothing to worry about?"

He shrugged, then picked up his hammer once again. "That Kenny fella is sittin' in lockup right now, ain't he? Which stands to reason any threat to Mizz Martha Jane's place is gone."

Unless Kenny didn't do it . . .

Turning to Margaret Louise, she motioned toward the victim's home, her voice punctuated by the hammering from above. "Shall we care for the plants?"

"That sounds like a good place to start to me." Leona's twin waved at Doug and set off in the direction of Martha Jane's home, Tori bringing up the rear.

"Tori?"

She looked over her shoulder.

"I'd be happy to turn a hose on those plants durin' the

day. Seems kinda silly for you to drive a country mile for somethin' I can do just as easy from right here." Doug ran his hand over the shingle he'd just attached and grabbed another from the pile at his feet. "Might help me feel less . . . helpless, y'know?"

She did. "That would be nice, thank you, Doug." She motioned toward Margaret Louise. "I better head on over now before she starts hollering for me and disturbing the neighborhood."

"Not sure how much disturbin' she can do with all the hammerin' and sawin' going on here. Drowns out pretty much everything in the vicinity, includin' my thoughts."

"I know what you mean. Though, for me, it's not hammering and sawing and those kinds of noises that are making it hard for me to think."

He laughed. "Crazy kids running around the library?"

She shook her head. "I wish it were that simple. They actually listen—most of the time—to a good old-fashioned shushing."

"Crazy boss?"

Again, she shook her head only to change it to a nod. "Actually yes, that's exactly what it is."

"Why the change?" he asked as dimples appeared beside his mouth.

"I was going to correct you and point out the fact that *I'm* the boss. But, with the incessant chatter going on in my head these days, the *crazy* tag applies just fine."

"What's it sayin'?"

"Saying?"

"The chatter in your head. What's it sayin'?"

"Victoria, you gettin' to the short rows yet?" Margaret Louise bellowed from somewhere out of sight.

She drew back. "Short rows?"

Doug's laugh rained down from the roof, his eyes getting into the action. "You're not from the south, are you?"

"How could you tell?"

"Besides the fact you talk funny?"

"*I* talk funny?"

"To me you do. And to folks in this town you do, too, I imagine." He set the next shingle in place and grabbed hold of his hammer. "But I like it. It's nice."

"Thanks." She waved up at him, her own genuine smile quieting the voices in her head for the first time in days. "I'm going to let you get back to work. I've taken enough of your time already."

"You never answered my question."

"About the chatter?"

He slipped a nail between his lips and nodded.

She looked toward Martha Jane's house, the momentary calm their conversation had created disappearing as quickly as it had come. "It's saying the opposite of what everyone else is saying."

When he raised his eyebrow in lieu of using his mouth, she continued, her words serving as the reassurance she needed to be where she was at that exact moment. "Kenny didn't do it."

The man pulled the nail from his mouth. "You're kiddin' me, right?"

"I don't know why and I have absolutely no proof to back it up . . . but I don't think he did it. Call it a gut feeling."

For a long moment he said nothing, his eyes squinting against the sun. Finally, though, he spoke, his southern drawl slow and lazy. "I played Clue when I was a kid, Tori. Wasn't much good at it back then. But I know this . . . when that Mustard guy was in the kitchen with the gun and the blood, it didn't take much to figure out he did it."

"Meaning?"

"Meanin' that guy was just waitin' to explode. Add the rope and his runnin' from back there"—he pointed toward the grove of trees behind Martha Jane's house—"not more 'n two hours before they found her facedown and, well, I wouldn't need to be openin' no little yellow envelope to see who did it."

Doug was right. She wasn't playing a smart game. The evidence was there—right in front of her face.

Yet, still, she couldn't accept it as truth.

Chapter 16

She was staring at the nearly completed scarf in her hand when he showed up, his presence the reprieve she hadn't realized she needed. But interruptions were the best form of procrastination known to mankind, and right now, she'd take anything she could get.

Especially when it came carrying chocolate . . .

"Ohhh, I love these." Ripping the corner edge open, she lifted the candy bar to her lips only to stop when he made a face. "I'm sorry, do you want some?"

He shook his head.

Lowering the candy bar to her side, she bobbed her head left then right, peering at her reflection in the window beside the door. "Do I have something on my face?"

Again, he shook his head.

"Then what?"

"I was hoping for a kiss."

A kiss, how could she have forgotten?

She rose up on tiptoes and brushed a kiss across his lips. "Do you forgive me?"

"I suppose." With a shy yet playful smile, Milo slid his hand to the back of her head and tipped it slightly, planting a second kiss on the very top of her forehead. "You okay? You seem distracted."

Stopping the candy mere inches from her mouth once again, she shrugged, then led the way into the living room. "Let's talk about something else for a little while, okay? I think my brain needs a break from its current obsession."

He dropped onto the sofa beside her, his eyes pinning hers with a hint of worry. "You sure?"

"I'm sure." She pointed at the scarf she'd set on the coffee table. "We're getting there. Dixie told me she's completed six so far. Hats, too. And Debbie, she's at ten on both."

"So they'll be done by your goal date?"

"With any luck, hopefully." Swinging them to the opposite side, she pulled her legs onto the couch and nestled her head against Milo's shoulder. "How's the collection booth coming?"

"It's almost done, thanks to Curtis and Doug. Those two have made this whole project a kabillion times easier."

She nodded.

"And with the work ethic Curtis has, and the woodworking talent Doug possesses, the finished project will be dynamite."

"I'm glad." And she was. It was nice to see people stepping up to the plate and helping each other out regardless of how long they had or hadn't lived in a particular area. "The festival is Saturday, right?"

"That's right." He turned his head toward hers, the feel of his breath on her hair making her feel more at peace. "You don't have to keep holding that candy bar. You *can* eat it, you know."

She stared at it, its former appeal missing in action. "Maybe later."

"Did you start your personal crusade yet?"

"Sort of."

"And?"

"And . . . a big fat nothing." She leaned forward, set the uneaten candy bar on the coffee table, and then grabbed the throw pillow from the corner of the couch and hugged it to her chest. "But Martha Jane's plants look good."

He hooked his finger under her chin and turned it ever so slightly until their eyes met. "I'm sorry, Tori, I really am. I was hoping that the simple act of getting out there and looking around would give you a sense of peace about all of this."

A sense of peace . . .

"We got all excited at first."

"We?" he asked.

"Margaret Louise was with me." She looked down at the pillow in her arms, her mind traveling back through the day, a day that had yielded nothing more than a headache and a few bug bites. "Leona was, too, though she was hanging around Curtis most of the time, making it nearly impossible for him to make much headway on the Walker place."

"No need to worry. Curtis is a machine. You should see how fast he is—in and out in a flash." He picked his feet off the floor and stretched them across the coffee table. "Probably because he doesn't say much."

"He's an observer."

Milo peered down at her. "Where did that come from?"

She released her hold on the pillow, his words taking root as it fell forward onto her thighs. "I don't know. I guess maybe from the library the other day. He stopped by to donate some books he'd finished reading and we started talking. About our memories of the libraries we visited as kids."

"Did you show him the children's room?"

The smile in his voice made her look up. "I did. And he loved it."

"You'd be hard-pressed to find someone who doesn't." Milo scooted into the far corner of the couch, his hands pulling her with him. "Hey . . . guess what? I've got my first career lined up for the kids."

"First career? What are you talking about?"

He pulled her back to his chest and wrapped his arms around her shoulders, his breath against her ear making everything in the world as close to right as possible. At least temporarily. "Every fall I invite people from different careers into my classroom to talk to the students about what they do. And every time I do it, I tend to have the same people—Georgina Hayes, Robert Dallas, Colby Calhoun, Carter Johnson, and Harrison James."

"The mayor, the police chief, a published novelist, a restaurant owner, and an attorney sound like a pretty good lineup to me."

"It does. But this year I'm going to get to showcase a trade."

She looped her hands around his arms and closed her eyes, his nearness relaxing her body for the first time all day. "Oh yeah?"

"Yeah. Doug does a little woodworking when he's home for an extended period of time."

"What kind of stuff does he make?" she asked.

"Well, all I've seen so far is a cane, a doll, and a bird-house, but it's really good. He said he'd bring more when he comes to talk to the kids."

"That's good. It'll be nice for the kids who struggle with schoolwork to see that there are lots of options in life." She felt her breath changing to match his, the rise and fall of his chest behind her much steadier than hers had been before he arrived. "I think I'll have that candy bar now."

He let his arms fall to his sides as she sat up and

reached for the chocolate, her hand brushing the dark green scarf she'd nearly completed. "So, did Georgina tell you about the money yet?"

She offered him a piece of chocolate and he opened his mouth in response. "What about it? Do we get to spend it?"

"Don't know that yet. But, apparently, Martha Jane's sister has said that if it is her money, she'd like to keep the donation in place. The one for the library, too."

It was news she knew should make her happy. Yet, for some reason it didn't, not really anyway.

"What's wrong?" Milo asked.

She glanced back at him, her shoulders rising and falling beneath her Chicago sweatshirt. "I don't know. I guess it all comes back to the same thing."

"Kenny?"

"Yeah. Kenny." She set the candy bar back on the table and grabbed the pillow once again. "I guess it's all this talk about the money. It's the one place where things don't add up."

Milo sat up. "How so?"

"Well . . ." She stopped only to start again, previous conversations with Rose guiding her words. "From what I gather, Kenny has some learning issues, yes?"

He nodded. "I believe that's putting it mildly."

"He has trouble reading, trouble processing, and trouble with the value of items."

Again, he nodded.

"But what sticks in my mind most from everything Rose has ever said is the fact that he doesn't have a concept of money. It's why she helped him with his bills. He didn't seem to know the difference between a dollar and a thousand dollars."

"Okay . . ."

She pulled her right knee onto the couch and swiveled her body to face him. "If those donations are from him, why wouldn't there be smaller amounts? You know . . . a few dollar bills, maybe a couple of tens?"

"I don't know."

"See? That's what I'm talking about. The amounts don't make sense. If he was as money-challenged as Rose said, how come the amounts were so good?"

"He just grabbed a handful and stuffed it inside? I don't know."

"You guys got three thousand, right? That's a lot of stuffing for one envelope."

Milo bobbed his head slowly, as if he was considering her statement from various angles. "But in what form was Martha Jane's money? Do you know?"

She closed her eyes tightly, willed her mind to recall the various wads of money that had left little room for socks in the woman's drawer. "Hundreds, I think."

"Well, that makes it easier to understand how he got to such high amounts."

Damn.

"But doesn't it stand to reason, he'd have put one or two into each envelope . . . or the same amount in both?"

"I don't know, Tori, I really don't. I don't know if we'll ever know how or why he did the things he did. His cognitive ability isn't where it should be."

Exhaling loudly, she slumped against the back of the couch, the peaceful feeling she'd welcomed disappearing as quickly as it had come, leaving a sense of defeat in its place.

"It's hopeless, isn't it?"

He studied her for a long moment, his gaze fixing on hers with an apologetic expression. "I'm afraid it might be. The evidence they have makes it virtually a slam dunk."

"Because of the rope?"

"That's one."

"His anger at her public accusation?"

"That's two. With a capital *T.*"

"And the fact that he came running out from behind her house not long before she was found?"

He cocked his head to the left. "I hadn't heard that, but it certainly doesn't help." Pulling her close once again, he cupped the side of her face with his hand and touched his nose to hers. "I think it's time to focus your efforts in another direction."

"What direction is that?" she whispered.

"Helping Rose accept the truth."

Chapter 17

She looked up from her desk as Nina walked into the room, a shy smile lighting the woman's dark face.

"You should have seen little Tommy Davis just now. He was wearing the Paul Bunyon costume and singing some silly song. He had his sisters in stitches."

"Are they here with Melissa or Margaret Louise?"

"Their Mee-Maw."

"Are they still here?"

Nina nodded.

"I'll be right out. I'm just looking through this catalogue to see how much the kid-sized chairs are going to run us. See if we can get two or three like I've been thinking. If we can score a table, too, even better."

"The kids will love that. They like the bean bag chairs, but I think the little guys would do better in real chairs."

"I agree." She flipped back to the index page, her finger trailing its way down the list of items sorted by page number. When she reached the line for juvenile furniture, she turned back to the proper page, little wooden chairs and tables showcased in various configurations and sizes.

"That one would be perfect," Nina said, peeking over Tori's shoulder. "It wouldn't take up too much space."

Her assistant was right. The set was perfect. But four chairs and a table? On top of the brackets and the curtain she'd already written down on her sheet? She matched the item number to the cost on the left and plugged it into the calculator after pressing the Plus sign.

$1,498.50.

Nina clapped her hands. "We can do it!"

Tori stared at the calculator, then pressed Clear. "It's got to be wrong." Looking at the paper she'd slid to the side, she plugged in the cost of the brackets and the stage curtain once again, then added the cost of the furniture from the catalogue.

$1,498.50.

"How on earth?"

"It's called an angel, Miss Sinclair. And she's sitting on your shoulder right now."

"An angel with an uncanny sense for money . . ." The words trailed from her mouth as her thoughts traveled back to Kenny for the umpteenth time that week. Shaking her head, she willed herself to let it go. Coincidences happened. They happened all the time. This was just one of those times.

A swell of giggling filled the hallway, only to be hushed away within seconds.

Setting the calculator atop the catalogue and pushing them both to the side of her desk, Tori glanced up at the door and waited, her lips ready with the smile that was synonymous with the Davis kids.

First came Lulu, the dark-haired eight-year-old who had captured her heart the moment they met. A former student of Milo's, Lulu adored books in much the same way Tori had at that age. She was sweet and shy, clever and creative, and sharp as a tack just like a modern and more pint-sized version of Nancy Drew.

Next came Jake Junior, the oldest of Jake and Melissa's brood. A natural with his six siblings, he was a teacher in the making Milo once said . . . unless Jake Senior had plans to hijack his son to help in the garage he owned in the center of Sweet Briar.

Hot on their heels came three more—Julia, Tommy, and Kate—followed by Margaret Louise and Sally.

"Hi, Miss Sinclair!" Lulu ran around the desk and wrapped her arms around Tori, her smile brighter than the sun streaming through the plate glass window. "When Mee-Maw said we could go anywhere we wanted today I said the library!"

"No, I did." Sally hopped up and down and danced in a little circle.

"No, I did," protested Tommy.

Margaret Louise cleared her throat in her trade-mark way of getting order among the troops, and like clockwork, all arguing stopped. The woman grinned at Tori.

"To what do I owe this happy honor . . . on a school day no less?" she asked, tapping Lulu's nose. "Are you playing hooky? In my library?"

The four oldest giggled while the two youngest stared at Tori. "What's hooky?" Lulu finally asked, looking from Margaret Louise to Tori and back again. "Mee-Maw?"

"Hooky means to skip school, sweetheart."

"I can skip!" Sally announced. "Wanna see me, Miss Sinclair? Huh? Watch this!" In a flash the little bundle of four-year-old energy skipped across Tori's office, pigtails flying. When she reached the opposite end of the tiny room, she turned around and skipped back to her spot beside her grandmother. "Did you see? Did you?"

She rose from her chair and came around the desk, Lulu at her side. Squatting down, she got to Sally's eye level and offered the biggest smile she could muster. "I did. And it was very, very, very good."

Sally spun around on her pink sneakers and grabbed her grandmother's hand. "Mee-Maw . . . did you hear that? Miss Sinclair said my skipping is very, very, very good. That's three whole *very*'s!"

"I heard that." Margaret Louise placed her hands on the child's shoulders and backed her up against her own plump form, the gesture as much about love as it was to gain order. "To answer your question, Victoria, the children have off today because of parent-teacher conferences."

"Oh, that's right. Milo mentioned that the other day. I guess it slipped my mind."

"Jake and Melissa are meetin' with Jake Junior, Julia, Tommy, Kate, and Lulu's teachers. I offered to take Molly, too, but Melissa said six was enough." Waving Jake Junior to her side, the woman met his gaze with a no-nonsense one of her own. "If I let you take everyone outside, can I trust you to keep an eye on them for ten minutes while I visit with Miss Sinclair?"

Jake nodded.

"That means keeping every last one of 'em with you and not lettin' 'em wander off willy-nilly."

The boy grinned. "I know, Mee-Maw."

To the others, Margaret Louise cocked an eyebrow and adopted her best warning face. "Jake Junior is in charge. What he says . . . goes. Is that understood?"

"Yes, Mee-Maw," five little voices said in unison."

"Lulu?"

"Yes, Mee-Maw."

"Tommy?"

"Yes, Mee-Maw."

"Kate?"

"Okey dokey spa-mokey."

Tori bit back a laugh.

"Julia?"

The child nodded, eyes wide.

"Sally?"

"Can I skip?" she asked.

"If your brother says it's okay, yes . . . but *only* if you skip where he says you can skip. Do you understand?"

"Yes, Mee-Maw."

Bending at the waist, Tori watched as her friend kissed each and every grandchild as they fell in line behind their appointed leader, her back straightening more with each child. When she reached Jake Junior, she gave him a kiss followed by a stern eye.

"I've got it covered, Mee-Maw."

And then they were gone, six heads trailing out the door and toward the back steps. When they were safely outside, Margaret Louise slumped in one of two rattan chairs grouped together in the corner of Tori's office, her body hitting the yellow cushion with an audible *oomph*. "I tell you, as good as those children are, I just don't get how their mamma does it, bless her heart."

She joined her friend, claiming the seat with the lavender cushion for her own. "Melissa is amazing, that's for certain. But so, too, are you."

Margaret Louise studied her for a moment, the expression on the woman's face hard to discern.

"What? Did I say something wrong?"

The woman shook her head. "It's what you're not sayin' that's got my beehive in an uproar."

"Hmmm, I wasn't aware beehives had uproars," she teased.

"Oh, they have uproars all right. Have 'em all the time." Waving her hand in the air, Margaret Louise leaned forward. "But let's not get sidetracked."

"From . . ."

"From what it is that's botherin' you."

She stared at her friend. "Is it that obvious?"

"To someone other than me, probably not. But I'm sharp, Victoria, you know that. In fact, if I was any better I'd have to be twins."

Tori laughed. "You are."

"I am?"

"Remember Leona?"

The woman made a face. "Oh. Yes. Well, she's her own entity entirely. I believe she's what they call a fluke of nature."

She knew she should protest, defend her absent friend in some way, but she couldn't do anything other than laugh. When she finally got herself under control she pulled her hair into a ponytail only to set it free once again. "You have a way of snapping me out of a funk, you know that?"

"So I *was* right."

"Well, technically it wasn't a funk. It was more a case of that pesky voice chattering away in my head once again."

"The Kenny voice?"

She nodded.

"What got it started this time?"

"The eerily perfect donation that covers exactly what I wanted with less than two dollars to spare."

Margaret Louise's mouth gaped open. "What are you talking about?"

She told her about all of it. The donation amount, her gut feeling that something didn't fit, Rose's claim that Kenny had no concept of money, and finally the total of the items she wanted in comparison to the anonymous donation everyone seemed to be tying to Kenny.

"Can I see?"

Tori retrieved the catalogue, scratch pad, and calculator

from the top of her desk and brought them back to Margaret Louise. "Here you go."

One by one, the woman set each item on her lap, her hand pausing above the catalogue. "Dixie gets this, too. I saw it in her hand the other day at the post office."

"That's not a surprise. Once you're on this company's list—as a library and/or a librarian—you're on it forever. I get a copy at home, too."

"For Leona, it's men and trips. For Beatrice, it's Kenny Rogers. For Dixie, it's libraries. Land sakes, I swear she spends her days decoratin' one of those—those"—the woman snapped her fingers in frustration—"oh, good heavens, what do they call it when they make it on the computer so you can see it plain as the nose on your face?"

"Virtual?"

"Yes, that's it! She spends her days decoratin' a virtual library with all the things she'd do if she had the funds. Funny thing is, it has a children's room very much like the one you created in reality."

The news made her smile. So Dixie really did approve . . .

"Anyway, you'll have to ask her 'bout it next time we have circle at her place. She'll drag you over to that computer faster 'n you can say barbecue. Heck, she'll tell you 'bout it whether she's got her computer nearby or not. I don't think she was out of that post office more 'n five feet and she was stoppin' and showin' the first body she could find all the things she'd buy and why. Least he was a good sport 'bout it. My Jake would have likened it to torture no doubt."

Margaret Louise flipped to the dog-eared page and found the circled item number. "Oh, Victoria, this is perfect. The kids are goin' to love it."

"I hope so. But"—she reached over and pressed the calculator's On switch—"add it up. You'll see what I mean."

The woman slowly plugged the cost in, her head bobbing between the catalogue and the calculator and back again. When she was done, she looked up. "What else?"

Tori retrieved the catalogue and replaced it with the pad of paper containing the costs associated with the brackets and curtain. "Add this in, too."

"Where'd you find the curtain?" Margaret Louise inquired as she plugged in the additional numbers.

"Leona found it online one day while she was placing an order for her shop."

When the numbers were all inserted into the calculator, Tori's friend pressed the equal sign.

$1,498.50

A long, low whistle escaped the woman's mouth. "Wow. I see what you mean."

Tori stared down at the calculator, the reaffirmation of what she already knew nagging her all over again. "So, either Kenny has an uncanny knack for shoving just the right amount of bills into an envelope, or he's a psychic mind reader who not only knew everything I wanted to buy for the children's room but also how much they'd cost down to almost the penny."

"Ah-ha! He forgot the taxes."

"No, he didn't. Libraries are not for profit, therefore they're tax exempt."

"Oh." Margaret Louise looked at the calculator one last time, then swung her gaze upward to meet Tori's. "You're right, Victoria. Something smells mighty funny. Unless . . ."

"Unless what?"

"Unless the donation has nothin' to do with Martha Jane's money whatsoever."

Damn.

She hadn't really thought of that angle. Not since the

notion it was tied to the missing money came into play to start with. But even now, hearing the possibility Margaret Louise laid out, she knew her friend's suggestion was wrong.

"You ever have a gut about something, Margaret Louise?"

Her friend nodded. "I had one 'bout you, for starters."

Her throat tightened with the memory, the woman's loyalty at a time she desperately needed it making all the difference in the world when she'd been a suspect in the murder of Tiffany Ann Gilbert. Without it, she wasn't sure what she would have done.

"Well, I have one now. About this money . . . and Kenny."

"Then we'll follow it until we know, one way or the other, whether it's right."

Chapter 18

It was as much a tradition as the sweet tea in their glasses and the barbecue on their plates. In fact, if push came to shove, she'd almost bet the people of Sweet Briar would give up their southern fare in a head to head toss-up with one of their prized festivals.

Heritage Day, Re-Founders Day, and Autumn Harvest all had their chance to shine in the town square each year. And shine they did with all the trappings that made them popular—rides, game booths, car shows, entertainment, and every kind of southern delicacy known to mankind.

"You like fish, right?" Milo asked as he slipped his hand into hers amid the jostling crowd.

"I like shrimp best."

"Have you had Calabash style yet?"

She sneaked a look at him as they maneuvered their way around a line of teenagers waiting for the opportunity to board a ride billed as the human slingshot.

"Calabash style? What does that mean?"

"Calabash is a place just north of Myrtle Beach. And they have this little restaurant that people come from miles to visit and the lines are long. They have boats to bring in the seafood and you can get just about anything you want. Their specialty, though, is in how they prepare the fish—drenched in flour and deep-fried. It's known far and wide as Calabash style."

"Sounds yummy." She felt his hand propelling her forward through the crowd, a small yellow tent in the distance growing closer and closer. "I take it we're going to try some?"

"Absolutely. Gotta get something real in you before you catch sight of a treat booth."

"As if food drenched in flour and then deep-fried is considered *real*."

"It's real good. That's all that matters." He stopped at the end of the line, his nostrils pinching inward with an inhale. "Mmmm, do you smell that?"

She nodded.

"That, my lovely Tori, is Calabash-style cooking."

Her tummy grumbled.

"Hi, Victoria."

She looked up, her mouth stretching outward in a face-splitting smile. "Hi, Debbie, hi, Colby. How are you?"

"We're good. The kids are on the mini roller coaster and we're taking advantage of the momentary lull in the can-we's."

"Can-we's?"

"Can we do this, can we do that," Milo explained. "I get it in the classroom all the time."

"Though, in all fairness, it's still better than what we heard at the Re-Founders Day Festival a few months ago." Colby nuzzled his wife's ear with his chin, the temporary pain that flitted across her face squelched by the tenderness of his touch.

"You can say that again." Milo pulled Tori closer. "But Colby . . . in the future . . . it might be wise to let sleeping dogs sleep."

"But what if they're sleeping off a moonshine hangover?"

Debbie rolled her eyes while Tori laughed out loud. "Come on now, Colby. It's onward and upward, right?"

"If onward means all lingering talk about me will finally die out in favor of the next Sweet Briar crisis, I'm all for it."

The next Sweet Briar crisis . . . like Martha Jane's murder and Kenny's likely guilt . . .

As if reading her mind, Debbie tucked her hand inside Tori's arm and tugged her off to the side. "Any news on Rose? I haven't seen her in the bakery in days."

"No. She's staying close to home, claiming she's tired." She exhaled a sigh from deep in her chest. "But it's more than that. I know it is. She's heartbroken. She doesn't want to face the inevitable scuttlebutt she'll hear about Kenny and the case if she's out and about like normal."

"Poor Rose," Debbie clucked. "We have to do something."

"I'm trying."

Debbie patted her arm as they rejoined the men. "I'm sure you are. She's lucky to have you as a friend, Victoria. We all are."

"Trust me, the lucky part goes both ways." And it did. She was confident of that.

As the roller coaster Suzanna and Jackson were riding came to a stop, Debbie and Colby bid their farewell, their backs disappearing into the swarm of parents clamoring to claim their children.

Tori looked up at Milo. "Could we skip the Calabash stuff for just a little while? Maybe just take a walk and look around first?"

"Uh, okay. Yeah, sure." He glanced toward the booth and then back again, any sign of disappointment well hidden. "So, which way do you want to go? The rides are pretty much in this area, the game booths are more that way"—he pointed to the east, his finger traveling around as he continued listing off various areas—"and then the car heads are that way . . . and the food booths are scattered all over the place."

"How did parent-teacher conferences go?"

"Okay."

"And that career week is starting up soon, right?"

He stopped, midstep, turning her to face him. "Look, I appreciate the interest in my job, I really do. And yes, career week starts up Monday. But what's this about? You seem . . . I don't know. Troubled or preoccupied or . . . I don't know. Are you okay?"

She shrugged. "I'm not conscious of anything. If there *is* anything, I guess it's just this feeling of having way too many loose ends."

A smattering of applause rang up around them as a local band took the floor of the pavilion. "Like what?"

"I still have about thirty more hats and scarves to get done in the next week, I'm meeting with the insurance adjuster about the storm-damaged books later in the week, I'm trying everything I can think of to coax Rose out of her home to no avail, and then there's that nagging feeling that something is very wrong where Kenny Murdock is concerned."

He guided her toward a bench off to the side and pulled her down beside him, his hand finding and then kneading her shoulder. "One at a time, Tori, one at a time. Can anyone else from the circle contribute some more hats and scarves?"

"Dixie hasn't turned hers in yet and neither has Beatrice. So that should help that number I just gave you decrease somewhat."

"See? That's good." Waving at a student who came running up only to stop about ten feet shy of the bench, Milo continued. "The visit with the insurance guy should go smoothly. You documented everything with your camera and even saved the damaged books, right?"

She nodded.

"Okay, one less thing to stress about. As for Rose, all you can do is try, Tori. Maybe you could slow it down a little more."

She looked a question at him.

"Instead of trying to coax her out, why don't you just spend some time with her there, instead?" He sat up. "That's it! Why don't you bring some of the fabric for the hats and scarves *to* Rose? Spend a couple of hours together sewing and talking. Baby steps, you know?"

Bring the fabric to Rose. . . .

She had to admit, it was a good idea, a very good idea. And maybe, just maybe, during the course of the conversation, she could pump Rose for some more information about Kenny's many challenges in life. Specifically those relating to his knowledge of money and research . . .

Cuddling close, she couldn't help but marvel at her good fortune in finding this man. While Jeff had been selfish and arrogant, Milo was sensitive and humble. Where Jeff had often put her at the bottom of his list of priorities, Milo put her at the top. Where Jeff had seemed to belittle her interest in sewing, Milo had not only encouraged it but also accepted its place in her life, asking real questions about her projects and seeming truly interested. "Thank you, Milo. You're such a blessing."

"Not nearly as much as you are." He kissed her head, then stood, offering his hand to her. "Want to check on the booth with me? See how things are going?"

"Absolutely." She'd been so busy the past few days worrying about things that weren't hers to worry about she'd not gotten to see the final product. "So you got it done with time to spare?" she asked as they turned left and made their way through the crowd.

"We sure did, thanks to Curtis and Doug. I'm not sure we would have if it hadn't been for them." He gestured right as they reached a tent featuring dozens and dozens of homemade pies. "Curtis is such a hard worker, fast yet thorough. And Doug, his detail work is really amazing. The kids are going to be so excited when he shows up later in the week to talk about what he does for a living. He made me a chest for some of my dad's stuff . . . a case for the flag they placed on his coffin, a case for his saber, and even a case for his medals."

She squeezed his hand as his voice faltered a smidge, the relatively unexpected loss of his father surely compounding the grief over losing his wife to cancer. But if Milo was still hurting from Celia's death, he hid it well. "It sounds nice. I'd like to see all of it the next time I'm at your house."

"Which we can Tuesday . . . if you're free. My mom called last night. She's coming for a visit and she wants to meet you."

"Really?"

Milo laughed. "Trust me. From the moment I first mentioned you, she's been trying to orchestrate a meeting."

"Why did it take so long?" She stopped as they approached the booth, her curiosity in overdrive.

"Because I didn't want to scare you away."

"Meeting your mom wouldn't have scared me."

"A week after we started dating . . . yes, it would have. Trust me on this. She'd been trying to encourage me to get out in the world again within a year of Celia's death. When ten years slipped by, she was convinced I'd shut down on life."

"Had you?" she asked, the subject making her voice unnaturally quiet.

"No. You just hadn't found your way to Sweet Briar yet."

She looked up at him through lashes that were suddenly tear dappled. "Do you really mean that?"

"You have no idea," he whispered against her ear. Wrapping his arms around her, he gave her a tight squeeze. "She's going to love you just like I do."

For several long moments they simply stood there, the crowd sifting around them as they held each other close. Eventually his arms relaxed and she stepped back, turning toward the booth. "Looks like they've got a little bit of a line."

"Good. That means word's getting out. Especially now that we've got the room—both in the booth and the new chests—to store some outgoing items for those who really need it right now."

As they rounded the far corner of the booth, Tori stopped, a smile stretching across her face. "Rose!"

The elderly woman turned, dark circles framing her bottom eyelids. "Victoria." Leaning forward for a kiss, the woman thwarted her intention as a cough rattled her frail frame. "I'm sorry. I shouldn't be here. I told that to Dixie"—she poked a bony finger into the arm of the woman next to her—"but she wouldn't listen."

Tori turned her smile in Dixie's direction, her gratitude for her predecessor's accomplishments impossible to hide. "I'm glad she didn't. Sweet Briar has missed seeing you out and about."

"Well they better get their fill now. Dixie has but ten more minutes and then I'm heading home, with or without her. Even if that means I have to walk the whole way."

"Quit your complainin', Rose. I told you we'd head home after this. You'd do well to remember I did you a favor bringing you tonight. Ellie might have given that flag order to someone else had you not been here. They don't come in all that often, as you well know, so just quit, will you? I need to drop off this food." The woman hoisted two bags onto the booth's counter. "Been saving them for a while now, waiting for this festival to hurry up and happen."

Buoyed by the first real hope she'd felt in a while where Rose was concerned, she turned back to Milo, pointing at the large stand-up sheds on either side of the booth. "Are those the chests for the food?"

"They sure are. And they're perfect." He looked at Dixie. "I understand from Georgina that the idea came from you?"

The woman thrust her shoulders back. "It did."

"Well, then a thank-you is in order. It was exactly what we needed." He opened Dixie's bag and began sorting the cans for the volunteers behind the counter who were busy with other items. "Between that, and the anonymous donation . . . it was meant to be, I guess."

"You mean the donation that came via Martha Jane's money?" Dixie asked.

Rose's shoulders slumped.

Tori rushed to change the subject, her desire to make the outing a positive experience for Rose front and center. "So, are you enjoying the festival this year, Dixie?"

Obviously oblivious to her efforts, Dixie continued, her monotone voice drowning out the sounds of the crowd. "Well, if nothing else, at least Kenny was listening all those years ago in your class, Rose."

The retired teacher slowly turned. "What are you saying?"

"It's simple. You read Robin Hood with your class back then, didn't you?" Dixie asked, her arms crossed in front of her chest in authoritative fashion.

Rose slowly nodded as Milo's head slumped forward between his shoulders with a groan.

"Well, he certainly took the notion of robbing from the rich to a whole new level, didn't he?"

Chapter 19

She simply watched as Rose made her way into the sunroom, the elderly woman's slipper-clad feet shuffling across the floor at a snail's pace. Her posture, weighed down by age, seemed worse than normal, her shoulders stooped forward as if they were attached to a moving cable not more than a foot in front of her toes.

"You know how Dixie is, she's quick to speak and slow to think. And if I remember correctly, you're the one who told me that shortly after I moved here." Tori leaned forward, rested her elbows on her thighs and her chin on tented fingers. "I don't think she meant to be nasty, I really don't. I suspect she just thought she was being clever."

"Well, she's not," Rose snapped as she stopped in front of her fabric closet and flung the door wide. "Can you imagine the nerve of that woman suggesting that I somehow taught Kenny to do the things he's done? That I encouraged him to rob an old woman and then strangle her to death?"

"No." Because she couldn't. Especially when the woman making the suggestion was supposed to be Rose's friend. Could Dixie really be that blind to the fact that Rose was struggling right now? That she was questioning her impact on a man she poured her blood, sweat, and tears into for three decades?

But she knew the answer even before the questions stopped lining up in her thoughts. Dixie was clueless when it came to the feelings of anyone but herself. It wasn't that she was deliberately mean. She just hadn't been shown a better way. Or if she had, she hadn't taken very thorough notes.

"I knew I should have resisted when she showed up on my doorstep begging me to go to the festival with her. I didn't want to go. I just wanted to sit in here and sew, that's all. But she played on my sense of loyalty—claiming she needed to get out, to get a little fresh air in her lungs but was reluctant to do it without a friend. She said she was afraid someone would jostle her in the crowd."

"And they wouldn't jostle you? You're certainly more frail. . . ." The words trailed from her mouth as they registered in her ears. She jumped to her feet, closed the gap between them in two quick strides. "Rose, I didn't mean that to sound the way it did. It's just that I've been worried about you—"

The woman's bony hand lifted into the air and pointed at the top shelf. "Do you see that bolt of pale blue fabric up there?"

Tori followed the line from Rose's finger, her cheeks still warm from her blunder. "Uhhh . . . yes. Would you like me to get it down for you?"

"Yes. Please." Rose bent at the waist, a loud cough rattling her tiny body with such force she took hold of the door for support.

"Rose? Are you okay?"

"I'm fine!" she snapped after temporarily clearing her lungs. "Just get me down that fabric, will you?"

She did as she was told, grabbing hold of the silky weather resistant fabric with two hands. "Where would you like me to put it?"

"Over there, on my cutting table," Rose instructed before turning in the same direction herself, a pair of sharp fabric scissors clutched tightly in her hand. "I think Dixie just has green eyes. Always has, always will."

Tori set the fabric on the cutting table, then stepped to the side, her eyes trained on Rose. "Green eyes?"

"Like the green-eyed monster."

"Ahhh, I get it now." She marveled at the way the woman's tremor-filled hands stilled the moment she touched a pair of scissors or a tape measure or even a needle. It was as if her body needed a sewing task to remember its youthful qualities.

"I remember when I was first teaching at the school. When a class of children would visit the library, Dixie was the only one who could read the week's books. If she got a call or had to address a question from a patron, the children had to wait. The classroom teacher couldn't pick up where Dixie had left off."

Sensing her friend's need to talk, she simply nodded and kept listening.

"If I was recognized with an award of some kind, she always talked about the one she'd earned that was bigger and better. And if a student would come up to me when we were out and about, she'd cut in and remind the child of the last time he or she was at the library."

Rose rolled out her tape measure and stretched it across the fabric, her fingers instinctively reaching for a series of pins to mark the desired length. "Just tonight, when Ellie came over to ask me to make a new flag, you could see Dixie fuming, wondering why Ellie was asking me and not her. And do you know what she did?" Without waiting for an answer the woman continued on, her hand guiding the scissors through the fabric with ease. "She cut me off when I tried to answer by apologizing to Ellie for not having the time to make it . . . trying to make it seem as if she'd been asked first."

She suspected she knew the answer, yet she asked anyway. "Had she?"

Rose peered up, the scissors a mere snip away from completing their cut. "If the way Ellie's eyebrows scrunched up in confusion was any indication—and I'm quite sure it was—then the answer is no."

"I guess it's jealousy, like you said. Maybe even a self-esteem issue. Some people with low self-esteem climb into their shell and spend the bulk of their life looking outward from some safe place they've created. And then there's others who try to inflate it by tearing down everyone else."

"Like Dixie."

"Like Dixie," she repeated, stepping back from the table to give Rose as much room as she needed to rewind the remaining fabric onto the bolt. When it was ready, Tori returned it to its place on the top shelf of the closet. "But knowing that doesn't make the things she does any easier, does it?"

"It should, but it doesn't." Rose pulled her sewing box across the table and flipped its lid open. Reaching inside, she selected an array of colors and lined them up beside her favorite sewing chair. "But this time her green eyes hurt Kenny, too."

"How so?"

"By assuming the worst just like everyone else." Rose stared down at the pale blue fabric, her hands beginning to show signs of their tremor once again. "Everyone is convinced he murdered Martha Jane."

"I know."

Slowly, she grabbed hold of the cut fabric and carried it to her chair. "I even had my doubts for a little while. The more people commented on his temper, the more I saw it, too. But I know that young man. I know him as if he was my own flesh and blood."

Tori sat down beside Rose and patted the woman's hand. "I know you two are close."

"I'm not blind, Victoria. I know he has a temper—a bad one. And I know he has socialization issues and learning challenges, but he has always had a good heart. I don't believe that just disappeared in one horrible moment."

"One horrible moment," she repeated in a whisper as her thoughts traveled back to the very day Martha Jane was murdered, to a conversation Rose hadn't been privy to . . .

"She might not say sorry to someone dumb like me . . . but someone dumb like me can make her sorry. Real sorry."

She closed her eyes against the memory, Kenny's anger-filled words shooting a hole right through Rose's assertion that he may have committed the crime in a split-second spasm of anger.

But as damning as his words were in relation to Martha Jane's murder later that same evening, there were still things that didn't add up. Things that continued to nag at her subconscious every chance they got.

Like the perfect donation amount that was allowing her to get exactly what she wanted in order to finally complete the children's room . . .

The woman coughed again, the sound a heartbreaking reminder of the cruelty that was age. "Rose? Are you okay?"

"I'm fine, Victoria. Really. I'm just having a hard time kicking this cold. It's what happens when you get old." This time Rose's reply was more appreciative in nature, the resentment she'd exuded earlier at the same question a distant memory. "I love the symbols on our flag, they represent us so perfectly."

Tori cocked her head and waited for the woman to bring her up to speed, her thoughts still weighed down by thoughts of Kenny.

"I thought the flames would bother me after that little revelation Colby unearthed, but it doesn't. Now, instead of feeling anger toward the Yankees, I see that there's no trial that can't be overcome . . . even something as destructive as fire."

Flames. Flames . . .

"Oh! I know what you're talking about now." She grabbed hold of the brick-colored embroidery floss and turned it over in her hands. "And this is for the three bricks that—"

"Six. Six bricks."

"Uhhh, yeah, okay." She shrugged off her mistake, mentally replacing the bad information with the good for future use. "They represent the rebuilding phase, right?"

"Partly. But even more than that, I see it as a sign of our solid foundation no matter what." Rose took the floss from Tori's outstretched hand and replaced it with white and yellow. "Do you remember what these are for?"

She stared at the two separate bundles in her hand, her mind coming up blank. "No, I'm afraid I don't."

"The white will be used for a picket fence and the yellow will be—"

"The sunlight!" She looked from the bundles to Rose and back again. "To symbolize warmth and friendliness."

"Or gossip."

"Gossip?"

Rose nodded as she reclaimed the bundles and added them to the lineup beside her chair. "When I see a white picket fence, I think of old busybodies hanging over them, spreading the kind of gossip that destroys people's lives and reputations."

"It's not really that bad," she said, remembering her own starring role as the town's topic of gossip after Tiffany Ann Gilbert was found dead. "Eventually they get it right."

"But not before making people feel bad about themselves. They"—her pale and wrinkled face grew crimson—"I mean, *I*, did it with Colby and Debbie, and now everyone is at it again . . . this time about Kenny. Then again, he's been picked apart over fences since he was no bigger than my knee."

"Why?" she asked, her interest aroused still further.

"He didn't perform like the other children at academic fairs and school events. People couldn't grasp the fact that he was handicapped in a way that didn't require a cane or something outwardly obvious."

"That's sad."

"Yes it is. It's even sadder knowing that he's already been tried and convicted over every dinner table and picket fence in all of Sweet Briar before he's stepped one foot in front of a judge."

She leaned back in her chair, hooking her knee onto the seat cushion. "You said something once about Kenny . . . how he didn't grasp the concept of money. Can you tell me more about that?"

"I suppose." The woman paused her hand over the section of fabric she'd captured in a large embroidery hoop and sighed. "I noticed it when he was in my class as a kindergarten student. We were working on counting— which he did fairly well with. He tended to be okay when it came to reciting something by memory, almost as if the repetitiveness was able to seep into his head and hold on for dear life. Anyway, round about springtime, I introduced money . . . pennies, dimes, and nickels."

Tori nodded to indicate she was listening, her mind commanding everything her friend said to memory for further scrutiny at a later date.

"But somehow he couldn't transfer what he'd memorized about numbers to the coins. He simply couldn't understand that the penny was the same as one, the nickel the same as five, the dime the same as ten. And then, when I tried to show the increased value in relation to an object of greater worth . . . he completely shut down."

"Did he ever get it? Maybe as he got older and moved on through the grades?"

"No. Never. I tried taking him to the market with me one summer. Showed him a piece of candy next to a large roast beef. Asked him which was more important. He said the roast beef even though he was looking at the candy. But that was really no different than most kids that age. . . . Who wants a roast beef when they can have a swallow of sugar?"

Tori laughed. "I can relate."

Rose lifted her head slightly so she could see Tori best. "No wonder I can barely see you when you turn sideways."

"Is that why?" she joked. "Because Leona says I need a boob job."

The woman snorted in disgust. "Sounds like Leona. Why there are times I would love to—"

Tori waved her hand in the air in an effort to cut the conversation off in favor of the previous one. Besides, when Rose got on a Leona kick, it wasn't pretty. "Tell me more about Kenny and the money. Did you pay him for odd jobs around your house?"

"I tried to, but I knew it meant nothing to him. So instead of giving him the money directly, and risking the chance he'd toss it in the trash along with a candy wrapper, I started sending it to places where he might need money. I'd send thirty dollars over to Leeson's Market along with a list of items he needed. When he showed up, they'd simply hand him the things I'd requested. And he was happy with that."

For a moment Tori said nothing, her mind churning over everything Rose had said while her eyes followed every motion the woman made with her needle, the edge of the first brick taking shape inside the hoop. Finally a thought emerged. "So, if you'd told him to go down and buy himself some things to eat . . . and then handed him, say, a twenty dollar bill and told him to keep it under that . . . he couldn't do it?"

"No. He simply has no concept of money and/or the value of an item. If he pulled it off, it would be sheer luck."

Tori gripped the edge of her armrest, her subconscious feelings pushing their way to the foreground with undeniable force. "Then I don't believe the chatter over the picket fence. Because it doesn't add up."

Rose looked up, a brief flash of hope firing through her tired eyes. "You don't?"

She shook her head.

"Why?"

"Because Martha Jane's money was missing . . . for real, after she was murdered."

"Go on . . ." the woman said, her voice raspy with emotion.

"Well . . ." She stopped as ideas she hadn't realized she'd even been entertaining started pounding on the inside of her brain, waiting to be released. "For starters, why was he so angry this last time?"

"Because Martha Jane called him a criminal. She accused him of stealing."

"And he hadn't. We know that because I was standing there when she pulled open the drawer and saw her cash exactly where she'd left it."

Rose rolled her eyes. "Can you imagine being so

paranoid about your money you stuff it in a sock drawer and then forget when you switch the drawer out with another?"

"No, I can't." But that was beside the point. She continued, her mouth putting words to her thought process. "So then he was mad that she'd falsely accused him. Fine. We know that. We even know he was angry enough he wanted to make her pay."

"We do?"

Uh-oh.

She averted her eyes from her friend's for a moment as she tried to come up with something she could say that would lessen the impact of Kenny's words. In the end, though, she simply relayed the comment word for word. Rose's face drained of all color.

"Why didn't you tell me?"

"Why would I? You were already hurting enough."

Releasing the needle onto the fabric, Rose leaned back in her chair, her eyes staring straight ahead. Tori rushed to continue, to put Kenny's damning statement where it belonged.

"But what everyone is missing, is this . . . even if he killed Martha Jane—which I don't believe is the case—he wouldn't have stolen the money. And I say that for two reasons. First, money meant nothing to him, so why on earth would he take it?"

"And two?"

"And two, he was angry because she accused him of something he didn't do, right?"

Rose nodded. "He may have been deficient in a lot of things, but that boy—that man, now—knew when people made fun of him or spoke ill of him and it hurt him deeply. He wanted to show them they were wrong."

The words confirmed what was on the tip of her tongue. "Then stealing the money for real made no sense. All it would have done was prove her right and him wrong."

The flash of hope she'd seen for the briefest of moments ignited in Rose's eyes as the woman pushed the fabric off her lap and sat forward in her chair. "It would have proved her right and him wrong! That's it!"

Tori held up her hands, palms out. "But it's not enough. Not yet."

"He can't stay there, in that cell, it's killing him."

Reaching over, she patted her friend's hand. "I know that. And it's why I haven't been able to ignore this nagging feeling that he didn't do it."

"Then what do we do? How do we get enough proof to make everyone see he didn't do this?"

How indeed.

"Well, I think I—"

"*We*, Victoria, *we*. I want in on this, too."

She considered protesting, her protective side wanting to call out all the reasons Rose needed to stay out of it—her poor health, her high emotion, her age . . . In the end, though, she simply encouraged her in the one area she could excel more than anyone else. "You are . . . by keeping Kenny's spirits up. Visit him. Tell him that there are people who believe in his innocence."

"And what are you going to do?"

"Well, I think there's one fact we can't ignore. Proving Kenny's innocence is going to be mighty hard when he can't do much to help us. Add that to the fact that there are a lot of arrows pointing in his direction for this murder and, well, I think I need to go at this from a completely different angle."

Rose's brow arched.

"I need to do exactly what I did when every finger in the town was pointing at me for something I didn't do, either."

The woman's eyes dulled momentarily. "Not *every* finger, Victoria."

She squeezed Rose's hand. "You're right. Not every

finger. And that alone backs up what you need to do. He needs to know there are fingers that aren't pointing in his direction. It will carry him through the rough spots just like it did for me."

"That still doesn't tell me what *you're* planning on doing."

"Instead of trying to prove Kenny *didn't* kill Martha Jane, I'm going to focus on someone else entirely."

"Who's that?" Rose asked.

"The person who *did*."

Chapter 20

There were times she simply didn't know when to keep her mouth shut. It was the people pleaser in her that reared its head every time someone asked her to help—whether it was leading a tour, talking to a group of librarians for the state, adding an extra story-time session for a local scout troop, or making sixty-plus homemade scarves and hats over a two-week time period. Regardless of the request, she always said yes.

One might think she'd get a clue, as nearly every phone call that came into the library these days resulted in adding yet another red circle to her already overcrowded desk calendar . . . but no.

She just kept on adding circles.

Only this time, she wasn't sure if a red circle was truly appropriate. Trying to catch a killer seemed as if it should call for more. . . .

Dark purple, maybe?

"Miss Sinclair?"

Dropping her red pen onto her desk, she mustered a smile

at her assistant, a woman she treasured more and more with each passing day. "Hey, Nina, what's going on?"

"The man from the insurance company is here."

"He is?" She looked down at her calendar, saw the faint circle that had been overpowered by a larger one for yet another daily to-do. "I remembered this the other day . . . I even told Milo about it."

Nina cocked her head to the side, a sympathetic look lighting her dark eyes. "Should I send him in or do you need a minute first?"

"Where is he?"

"At the information desk."

She pushed her chair back and stood, then rounded the corner of her desk to join Nina in the doorway. "I'll see him there. If I can reduce the small talk and go straight to the reason he's here, maybe I can move on to the next thing before it's time to call it a night."

"Sounds like a good idea. Duwayne is big on not wasting time he doesn't have to waste." Nina trailed behind as they headed toward the main room, the hushed voices of their patrons bringing a smile to Tori's lips.

It didn't matter how chaotic her days were, or how overwhelmed her life was on any given day. The moment she stepped foot in her library, everything suddenly seemed not only doable but surmountable as well.

Entering the main room, she made a beeline for the dark-haired gentleman beside the information desk, his displeasure at the delay evident in everything from the tightening of his hand on the handle of his briefcase to the way he glanced at his watch again and again. "Mr. Fielding? I'm Victoria Sinclair, head librarian."

The man nodded and shook her hand, his grip limp at best.

"I know we're both busy people so I figured we'd get straight to the damage if that's okay."

His shoulders perked upward. "That sounds good. Real good. Lead the way."

Mindful to keep her voice as low as possible, she led the way around the room, pointing out the water line from the storm. "Essentially the bottom row, around the entire room, was affected by the water, though by the time I got in here, it was beginning to recede."

"You sure got everything cleaned up quickly."

"I didn't see any point in keeping any storm reminders around longer than absolutely necessary. Now, as you can see, that bottom shelf has been cleared of all damaged books."

"You didn't throw them away, did you?"

"No. They're in a series of boxes elsewhere in the building."

"What about the rug?"

"We got it up, turned a few power fans on it, and it bounced back fairly well."

"I see that." He scribbled something in a notepad. "If I determine the rug is salvageable— and I must say, it appears as if it is, thanks, no doubt, to your quick action—I will recommend a thorough and professional cleaning to remove any potential odor."

"That sounds good. I haven't noticed any yet, but the weather has been fairly good since the storm and it's enabled me to keep the windows open all day long."

Glancing up from his notepad, he studied her. "There's another room now, isn't there? A kids' room?"

"Yes." Beckoning him to follow, she led the way down the hall. "But, as you'll see, that room suffered no damage at all."

They stepped into the room, a small, gasplike sound emerging from the man's mouth. "Wow, this is spectacular."

"Thank you. We like it." She walked into the room

and spun around, her hands indicating the lowest level of shelving. "No water. No damage. Which made us happier than I can tell you."

He flashed his first smile. "Trust me, we're happy, too," he said as he began wandering around the room, peeking at titles and studying the various drawings on the wall. "Why didn't they have this kind of stuff in the libraries when I was a kid? Maybe I wouldn't have dreaded being dragged there by my mother quite so much."

"I don't know. But I do know that it's kids like you just described that prompted me to want to do this."

"Really?"

She nodded. "Of course. Sure, there's a part of me that wanted to reward the kids who already love the library. Take their enjoyment to the next level. But there was another part that wanted to find those kids who despise the library and despise books and capture their interest."

"You've certainly captured mine." He took a step forward then stopped, his hand digging into the costume trunk. "They get to play dress-up?"

Again, she nodded. "They get to act out their favorite stories . . . make them come alive beyond the pages of the book. Sometimes they act it out exactly the way it happened in the story. And sometimes they tweak a character to have a different trait . . . or change the ending to see what might have happened."

"Wow. I love this place. It's . . . I don't know . . . it's happy, I guess." He pulled out a gingerbread costume and held it up. "What story is this for?"

"Do you remember the line, 'you can't catch me, I'm the gingerbread man'?"

The man's face lit up. "I do! He has all these animals and people chasing him, trying to eat him, right?"

"Yes, that's the one."

He chuckled. "I bet the kids have a fun time acting that one out."

"They do."

He reached inside again, this time grabbing hold of a vest. "And what about this one?"

"That's for Robin Hood."

"Oh, yeah. He was a good guy. He did what most of us wished we could have done."

"Steal?" she teased.

"I suppose, if you get technical about it, it was stealing. But back then, as a kid, it just seemed like the right thing to do."

"How so?"

Turning the vest over in his hand, he opened it wide and slipped it on, the child size costume coming just halfway down his chest. "Well, the rich people already had everything they needed and they really didn't need anything else. Yet there were so many people who *did* need things—things like food and clothes and a place to live." He dug around in the chest again, pulling out the matching hat and placing it on his too-large head. "Kind of like what happens when a storm hits and people lose everything they own. When that happens . . . and those images are played on televisions across the country . . . I always wonder what the rich people are thinking while they're watching it. You know, do they feel bad? Do they wish they could help? Or do they just sit back in their leather chairs and change the channel with their remote control?"

She couldn't help but grin as he turned to check himself out in the wall-mounted mirror, his middle-aged body looking rather silly in the child's costume. "He was a hero for doing what he did," he finished.

"Funny how people don't see it that way when it's not happening on the pages of a book." The second the words were out, she wished she could recall them. Now was not the time to lament the injustice that was being done to Kenny Murdock. There would be time to work on that task after some of her red circles were tackled.

"I suppose. But I can tell you this much . . . if I'd lived in this town when I was a little boy, I'd have been wearing this costume every time I came here."

Peering over his shoulder into the mirror, she couldn't help but laugh. "I think you would have had some competition."

"From who?"

"A little boy named Curtis who loved his childhood trips to the library as much as I did." She took the hat from the man's outstretched hand and positioned it atop her own head. "He told me Robin Hood was his favorite book as a kid. That he, too, liked what the character stood for."

"How could you not?" He slipped the vest off and folded it neatly in half. "Anyway, is there anything that you want to *say* is damaged? We might be able to pull it off so you can get money to buy something you need . . . maybe more chairs? Or a table for the kids to sit at?"

"I appreciate that, but you and I both know that wouldn't be honest. Besides, we just got a donation that will cover a few things I've been wanting to do in here for . . ." Her voice trailed off, her mind transporting her back to a similar conversation not too long ago—a conversation where she'd listed each of her remaining dream items for the room. . . .

Feeling her mouth begin to gape, she covered it with her hand, a troubling notion taking shape in her thoughts as a face appeared before her eyes.

"Miss Sinclair? Are you okay?"

She shook her head against the thoughts that threatened to consume her where she stood. "I'm going to have my assistant show you the damaged books. I—I have to go, I have to . . . I have to look into something that just came up."

"Hey, I was only kidding about what I said. I wouldn't really falsify a claim."

Jogging toward the door, she paused her hand on the light switch, the sense of urgency her gut had created compelling her to keep moving. "Don't apologize. Please. That statement—joke or not—may have just saved someone's life."

Chapter 21

It made sense. Perfect sense, actually. But if she'd learned anything from her own experience as a murder suspect, the more convincing the evidence she could provide to the identity of the real killer, the better.

A conversation, where she happened to mention her wish-list items to a man who happened to respect Robin Hood for his actions, wasn't enough. Not yet, anyway. She needed to lay all the pieces side by side until the picture emerged with such startling clarity that his hand in Martha Jane's murder couldn't be denied.

But where did she start?

"The wish list," she whispered, her words echoing her thoughts. Breezing into the main room, she motioned Nina over. "Nina, something has come up that I need to address right now. Could you take a few moments to show Mr. Fielding the storm-damaged books?"

The woman nodded, her dark hair bobbing against her shoulders. "I'd be happy to, but is everything okay? You look upset."

"Not upset. Just surprised . . . and, I guess, a little hopeful that I can make a difference." She gave her assistant's hand a gentle squeeze and turned back toward the same hallway from which she'd just come, her office her destination of choice this time around. "Don't worry. I'll be fine. I promise."

The second she entered their shared office, though, her confidence began to slip. What if she was wrong? What if the thoughts swirling in her head were nothing more than a case of someone grasping at straws?

Was it worth getting Rose's hopes up for something that might be nothing at all?

No.

But she needed to bounce her suspicions off someone, see if what made sense to her made sense to anyone else. . . .

She dropped into her desk chair and stole a peek at the wall clock. Milo's school day was still in full swing, the final bell not set to ring for two more hours.

Her shoulders slumped. Could she really wait another two hours to share her thoughts with someone?

No. Not unless you want to explode . . .

Glancing around her desk she looked for something, anything, to keep her busy for the next two hours. There were books to order as per the second red circle on the calendar, calls to return, next month's event and activity calendar to schedule, and an order to be placed for the table and chairs in the catalogue. . . .

"The catalogue," she whispered. Bolting upright in her chair, she pushed the calculator off the booklet and started thumbing through the pages, her hand finding the dog-eared page with surprising speed. It stood to reason that if someone knew exactly what you were going to buy, he or she could give you the exact amount of money.

Curtis knew what she wanted. He'd stood there in the children's room with her, listening to her talk about the table and the chairs, the curtain and the brackets. But even with that kind of knowledge, he had no idea where she'd go to purchase those items.

She needed to talk to someone, someone who would hear her out and help her brainstorm all possible avenues. . . .

Eyeing the clock once more, she grabbed the phone from its base and punched in Margaret Louise's number, the digits as much a part of her memory bank as her favorite color and the sound of her late grandmother's voice.

The phone was answered on the first ring. "Why Victoria, I was just thinkin' 'bout you."

"We need to talk."

The woman's loud, boisterous laugh filled her ear. "That's what I reckon we're doin' right now."

"No, I mean in person."

"You found something out, didn't you?"

Had she? She wasn't sure. But it was worth following . . .

"I'm not sure, but I think so. Can you come over?"

"Are you at home?"

She shook her head, then realized the gesture was futile. "No. I'm at work. In my office."

"I'll be there lickety-split."

Replacing the phone in its base, Tori swiveled her chair around and stared out at the hundred-year-old moss trees that adorned the lawn of the Sweet Briar Public Library. From the moment she'd started working there, she'd loved this view—the trees, the occasional pedestrian meandering along the sidewalk, a few avid readers stretched out on benches with their latest stack of borrowed books. It was a view that gave her peace and afforded clarity at moments when she needed it most.

She had no idea how long she sat there, staring into space, but it was long enough for the ears she needed to show up at her door.

"I got here as fast as I could," Margaret Louise huffed

as she strode into the room and over to the pair of rattan chairs in the corner. "Of course I got stuck behind some old man drivin' at a turtle's pace . . . land sakes they seem to come out of the woodwork when there's places to go, don't they?"

"I'm just glad you're here." She stood and walked over to her friend, her body suddenly too antsy to be confined to a chair. "I don't think Kenny stole Martha Jane's money."

"You've said that before. So what's different now?"

"I think Curtis took it." *There.* It was out. In the open.

She stole a look at her friend, the woman's unusual silence making her suddenly less sure of her thought process. "Just hear me out, okay? It makes sense, it really does."

In a tone that sounded a lot like babbling to her own ears, she laid out her train of thought, including the who and why that had gotten her to the drifter's front door. "I think it was a day or two before the money showed up that he stopped by the library. I remember being surprised to see him because I hadn't necessarily pegged him as a reader—though, in hindsight, he fit the stereotype perfectly. He's quiet, a little brooding, and he drifts from town to town. What makes a better companion for someone like that than a book?"

"A needle and thread . . . a swig of moonshine . . . take your pick."

"Margaret Louise!" The woman's silly asides always made her laugh, and today was no exception. In fact, if she was honest with herself, they helped to lessen the tension that had her body in knots. "Could you follow along, just this once?"

As her friend shifted her weight a touch, the chair beneath her creaked and groaned. "Go on. But you might want to hurry it along. I'm not sure this pretty little chair can take my big ol' body much longer."

"Anyway, he came to drop off some books he'd finished reading. They were mostly popular titles and they were all in pristine condition. He said he bought them before he moved on from his last place of employment. He reads them once and then donates them to the library in whatever town he's in at that point in time."

"A carpetbagger with a bent toward philanthropy? Now isn't that a fine howdoyoudo?"

She cracked a smile. "We got to talking . . . about how libraries played a big part in each of our childhoods. He told me about the carpeted stairs he used to sit on as a kid while he looked through book after book and I told him about the little rocking chairs that I adored."

"I saw one of those rockin' chairs at Stu's week before last. I think Lulu would love one, don't you?"

"I do." She exhaled a strand of hair from her forehead and continued on, the words finally starting to lead to the part that mattered most. "I took him back to the children's room to show him what we've done and he loved it. I don't think I've seen a man react to that room the way he did . . . except for maybe Milo and Mr. Fielding."

"Mr. Fielding?"

"The insurance man who came by today to assess the damage from Tropical Storm Roger." She wandered across the room only to turn back and retrace her steps. "He started asking questions."

"Who did? The insurance guy?"

"Oh. I'm sorry. I know I'm rambling." She raised her arms into the air and then clasped them over her head for a moment. "Curtis started asking questions about everything in the room—the murals, the books, the costumes, the stage, you name it. He loved it all."

"Who wouldn't?"

She shrugged. "Anyway, we got to talking about the

few little things I still wanted in the room. I told him about the brackets and the curtain, the table and the chairs—" She stopped suddenly, her gaze fixed on her friend's. "I *told* him, Margaret Louise. I told him each of the items I wanted."

Understanding dawned on the woman's plump face and she nodded slowly.

"Now that doesn't explain how he could know the exact cost but—"

"I reckon it does." Margaret Louise struggled out of the chair and headed toward the one behind Tori's desk. "He saw the catalogue, probably knew tax wasn't an issue, and he added it up."

She stared at her friend. "What do you mean he saw the catalogue? When? How?"

"Don't you remember I told you about Dixie and how she still gets that catalogue? That she just got that same copy the other day at the post office?"

"I think so . . ."

"I even told you she'd dragged some poor soul into the corner just so she could show him everything inside."

It sounded vaguely familiar, so she nodded.

"Well, that was Curtis."

Tori swallowed over the lump that sprang in her throat. So maybe she wasn't such a nut after all . . .

"'Course I thought she was bendin' his ear. Never thought he was takin' notes."

Taking notes.

Tori held her hands up. "But wait a minute. Seeing that catalogue might explain how he knew the cost of the table and chairs . . . but"—she worried her lip inward—"that doesn't explain how he hit the nail on the head with the brackets and curtain. Especially when the curtain is from some specialty Web site Leona found on the—"

Leona.

It was the final card. It all made sense now.

"Margaret Louise, do you think you could find out whether Leona discussed the curtain with Curtis?"

The woman nodded. "Can I use your phone?"

"Absolutely. Just press line two."

Five minutes later they had their confirmation.

But was it enough? Could they take the wish list and the donation amount to the police chief and have it be enough to get Kenny released?

"I say we march over to Adelaide Walker's right now and ask him. See if his face turns red as a beet. 'Cause that's the way to spot a liar no matter how old someone is. I used it on Jake when he was a young-un and I use it on his *own* young-uns now. Works like a charm."

She had no doubt it would. But if they were right, and they confronted him, would he simply turn and run? Or, worse yet, would he strike out at one of them?

"I don't know, Margaret Louise, I don't know if that's such a good idea."

The woman pushed off the desk chair, patting her fanny pack as she met Tori at the door. "I've got a can of Mace and I know how to use it."

There were a million reasons why they should go straight to the police. And they all made perfect sense from a logical standpoint.

But there was some merit to Margaret Louise's suggestion. It would get them the kind of answers they were seeking in a more expedient route, which, in turn, would enable them to bring much-needed peace to Rose in the same fashion.

"Let's do it."

A look of surprise flashed across Margaret Louise's face, only to be chased away by a mischievous smile to rival all others. "Are you sure?"

"Sure as I'll ever be." Grabbing her purse and keys, she picked up the phone and punched in the code for the information desk. "Nina, I've got to take care of an important matter. I'll be back before closing. If for some reason I'm not, then"—she stole a glance in Margaret Louise's direction, the woman's excitement nearly contagious—"contact Chief Dallas. Tell him he's got the wrong man."

"The wrong man?" Nina repeated in her ear, worry evident in every nuance of her assistant's voice.

"The wrong man. Tell him it's Curtis . . . the man who was working for Martha Jane until her death."

Chapter 22

It was funny how an idea could seem to be smart one minute and, well, not so smart the next. The timing of that realization, though, needed to be a little better.

"Do you think this is such a good idea?" she asked as she followed Margaret Louise down the sidewalk and up Adelaide Walker's front steps. "I mean, do you think maybe Chief Dallas might be more effective at getting the truth? It *is* possible the red-face trick won't work on Curtis."

"It'll work. It always works." Pausing her knuckles just inches from the elderly woman's front door, Margaret Louise turned and met her eye. "Did you hear that?"

Tori looked side to side. "No. What was I supposed to hear?"

A soft tapping in the distance brought a grin to her friend's face. "That."

"Oh. Yeah, I heard that."

"I think that's our man."

She froze.

"Somethin' wrong, Victoria?"

"I—I . . ." She stopped, swallowed, and started again, this time with a voice that sounded a little less hesitant. "Let me do the talking, okay?"

The woman's shoulders slumped. "Really? I've been rehearsin' what I'd say the whole way over."

Tori laughed, the sound as much of a motivator as the feeling that evoked it. "You can rehearse and gab at the same time?"

"I can do many, many things at the same time, Victoria."

Slipping her arm around the woman's shoulders, she tugged her to her side. "I know. And you do them all well. It's just that—well, I want to confront him . . . if you'll be my backup."

Once roles were set and a basic plan formulated, they walked down the steps and around to the backyard, the sound of their feet barely discernable against the soft breeze that rustled the tree branches overhead. "Curtis?" she called. "Curtis, are you here?"

His head popped around the corner of the house. "Right here." As his gaze settled on Tori's, a tentative smile spread across his face, softening his features. "What can I do for you, ladies?"

"Well, we"—Tori motioned to the woman trailing her heels—"wanted to thank you. Your generosity was unexpected and wonderful all at the same time."

He slid his hammer into his tool belt and looked a question at them.

"In this day and age it's plumb hard to find someone so willin' to part with their assets simply to help someone else. In fact, it's mighty refreshin', young man." Margaret Louise slapped a hand over her mouth as her eyebrows raised upward with glee. "Just don't go tellin' that twin of mine I called you that. She'd have my head."

A smile did little to dispel the confusion on his face.

"I have all the item numbers written out on a pad of paper beside the phone. I'll call those in just as soon as I get back to work." She stole a glance in Margaret Louise's direction, the woman's unzipped fanny pack providing some relief as she contemplated her next words. "And I'll stop by Leona's this evening to get the ball rolling on the curtain."

His jaw tightened a smidge as she continued on, her words taking on a distinctly friendly tone. "The only thing I don't know much about are the brackets. Will those be tough to attach to the top of the stage?"

"I don't know what you're talking about," he said through teeth that were suddenly clenched. "What brackets? What curtain?"

Margaret Louise stepped forward, her pudgy hand slipping into her fanny pack. "Sure you do. And there's no sense in continuin' this modesty of yours. You did a good thing donatin' that money to the library and the collection booth. We needed it. Didn't we, Victoria?"

She nodded, her gaze fixed on Curtis. "We did."

"We needed it much more 'n she did, didn't we?"

Again, she nodded. "Robin Hood knew what he was doing, and so did you. It's a shame we don't have more like you around."

Curtis shifted from foot to foot, his gaze moving between the two women with rapid speed. "I didn't—I mean, I—"

"We know you stole it, Curtis. Kenny told us."

Tori's head snapped to the right as she stared at her friend and cohort. "He did?"

Margaret Louise stared back, her eyes narrowing on Tori's face as her own sported a telltale shade of red. "He did. He told me this morning . . . when I stopped by the station to see if he needed anything."

The man's face drained of all color as he wrapped his hand around the handle of his hammer. "Look . . . I didn't know what else to do. I figured if I called, they'd think it was me. One look in their computer system and they'd think it was me."

Tori looked from Curtis to Margaret Louise and back again, the man's words not at all what she'd expected. "What are you talking about?"

Raking a hand through his nearly nonexistent hair, he dropped onto the patio and leaned against the house, his voice shaking as he rushed to explain. "Who is going to believe the drifter in town?"

"Believe the drifter about what?"

"That he wasn't the one who strangled the old lady on the floor?"

She grabbed hold of Margaret Louise's arm for support. "What are you talking about?"

"That woman—Mizz Barker. She was dead when I found her."

The women stared at one another before turning, simultaneously, back to Curtis. "She was already dead?"

He nodded, his hand shaking as he finally pulled it from his hair. "I went looking for her because she hadn't paid me yet. I'd asked her that morning but all she did was holler at me for some tree I hadn't cut low enough. Then, after the tree, it was a piece of siding she saw dangling. And so it went . . . all day long."

"That sounds like Martha Jane," Margaret Louise mused. "Go on, we're listenin'."

"Once I had everything done that she'd badgered me about, I knocked on her door. When she didn't answer, I knocked again. And still she didn't answer. About that time I began to wonder if she ever had any intention of paying me . . . I mean, I'd heard the way she talked about me to you"—he motioned toward Tori—"that first day. She hated me."

She wanted to argue but she didn't. He was right. Martha Jane had thought very little of her employee.

"She hated most people." Margaret Louise. "It was just the way she was."

Curtis shrugged, his words continuing even as he fixed his focus somewhere in the distance, as if he was revisiting the day in question. "So I tried the door and it was open. I called to her as I went inside but she never answered. And as I walked through the house, calling her name, I found myself getting madder and madder with each step I took."

"And then what?" Tori prompted, her mind torn between the believability of the man's words and facial expression, and her desire to wipe the hurt and worry from Rose's eyes once and for all.

"I found her. Lying faceup on her bedroom floor, that heavy rope Kenny was using wrapped around her neck."

Tori closed her eyes as the man's words formed an image to match.

"Why didn't you call someone?" Margaret Louise asked as she placed her hands on her hips. "Why didn't you call the police?"

He propped his head in his hands for several moments, his silence giving them time to exchange looks. The problem was, neither of them knew what to believe.

Finally he spoke, his voice muffled. "Unlike Doug, I'm not a drifter because I like moving all the time. I'm a drifter because no one who requires an application will ever hire me."

"Why not?" Tori asked, her curiosity on overdrive.

"Because I embezzled money from my last employer."

Margaret Louise sucked in her breath while Tori simply processed the man's words. "Why aren't you in jail?"

"It was my brother-in-law. He didn't push for maximum penalty out of respect for my sister. But he's made sure I'll never get a job again."

"And you figured the cops wouldn't believe you about Martha Jane because of that charge?"

He looked up, his jaw tight once again. "I didn't *figure*. I *know*. Once a criminal, always a criminal."

She mulled his words. "Are you going to tell us you didn't take her money?"

His face turned red.

Margaret Louise beamed. "See? I told you. Works for 'em whether they're five or thirty-five."

Rolling her eyes, she turned back to Curtis. "Well? Are you?"

He shook his head. "I took it."

"Why?"

"Because she owed me."

"She didn't owe you that much," she stated frankly.

"You're right, she didn't. But when I opened that drawer and I saw all those bundles of hundreds, I couldn't leave them there. She was dead. She wasn't going to need them anymore anyway, so what difference did it make?"

"It wasn't yours, son," Margaret Louise stated matter-of-factly. "That's the difference."

His face flushed still redder. "But it's not like I hoarded it for myself. I spread it around . . . to people and places that needed it more than either of us did."

"Just like Robin Hood," Tori whispered.

Chapter 23

Try as she might, it was getting harder and harder to keep smiling. Even with the ever-growing pile of fleece scarves and hats on the coffee table.

Sure, she was appreciative of her friends' efforts, their contributions bringing her closer and closer to reaching her mental goal of sixty scarf and hat sets for the women's shelter.

But still, she just wasn't in the mood for idle chitchat and small-town gossip.

"I like that shade of pink, it's very soothing," Beatrice said from her spot across Dixie's empty living room. "It reminds me of a glass of pink lemonade on a quiet summer day."

Tori mustered a smile for the girl who, like her, had opted out of the dessert stampede in favor of completing their current task—Beatrice's shirt for Luke, and Tori's yet another hat and scarf. "Thanks. I like that shirt, too. Luke is going to love it."

"Do you really think so?" Beatrice asked, her cheeks

taking on a pinkish hue. "Green is his favorite color. And he likes race cars so much I wanted to make it look like the sort of shirt a race car driver might wear."

"And you're succeeding. He's going to love it." Setting the fleece on her lap, she leaned her head against the sofa and kneaded her temples. "I've had this headache all evening and nothing I do seems to shake it."

"Maybe eating something would help?"

"I wish it were that simple," she mumbled, only to pull her head upright as her words traveled around to her ears. "Beatrice, I'm sorry. I'm not trying to be a downer, I'm really not. Your suggestion about food is a good idea. I'll take a peek in the dining room once everyone is back and settled . . . maybe there will be something with a little less sugar."

"No need to apologize. I know you're worried about Rose."

"I didn't realize you—" She stopped, her own face growing warm.

"What? That I actually pay attention while I'm a wallflower?"

Her mouth gaped open.

Beatrice shrugged. "Well, I do. And I learn a lot that way—how things are done here, who is and isn't good friend material, where all the"—a giggle erupted over top of her words—"cute men are."

Tori laughed, too. "Take whatever Leona says with a grain of salt."

"I do."

"I didn't mean to belittle the way you are."

"I know. It didn't take a lot of cowering and sewing to realize you're the kind of person everyone wants for a friend." Carefully, Beatrice pushed her needle through the green fabric, attaching a NASCAR patch to the right breast pocket of Luke's shirt. "But it also hasn't taken a lot of listening and watching to know you're struggling with the whole Kenny thing—and yes, I know it's Kenny Murdock."

She had to smile. "I am. And thanks. It's been a long day."

"What happened?"

For a moment, she considered changing the subject, but in the end, she seized the opportunity to express her pent-up frustration aloud. "I thought I had it figured out, I really did. And it all fit so perfectly. But I was wrong."

Seeming to understand her need to talk, Beatrice simply nodded and waited for Tori to continue.

"I wasn't wrong entirely. I was right on who stole Martha Jane's money . . . he even admitted it when Margaret Louise and I confronted him. But what we weren't counting on was the fact that his actions were independent of the person who actually killed her."

"Independent?

Tori nodded. "He stole the money all right. He even stepped over Martha Jane's body to get it. He just wasn't the one who actually killed her."

Beatrice sucked in a breath, her eyes large and rounded. "How awful. How utterly awful."

"It is. But what's even more awful is the fact that it makes Kenny an even more likely suspect." She let her head drop forward as she looked down at the fleece once again, her drive to create a scarf dissipating rapidly. "After today, the one thing that didn't add up isn't an issue any longer. Which means money is no longer a viable motive."

"Leaving rage as the most likely choice?"

"I'm afraid so."

"I'm sorry, Victoria." Looking up from her charge's shirt, she eyed her closely. "How's Rose taking it?"

Like clockwork, her head began to pound still harder, the realization that she'd gotten her friend's hopes up for nothing heaping stress on top of stress. "She didn't know about Curtis. I didn't tell her. I didn't want to get her hopes up."

"Curtis?" Beatrice whispered.

Tori nodded.

"Does Leona know?"

"To the best of my knowledge, no. If she ever shows up tonight, I'm sure her sister will tell her."

"Wow." Beatrice looked back down at the shirt only to glance up once again. "But if you didn't tell Rose about your suspicions, how could she have gotten her hopes up?"

"Because I clued her in to my radar where the whole stolen money thing was concerned. And now she's out there, in Dixie's dining room, thinking I'm going to dig something up—something that will tell her everything is going to be okay . . . that Kenny is no longer a suspect in her neighbor's murder."

"Does everyone else know?"

"I think so. But Margaret Louise tried to pull most of them aside when she first got here for the sole purpose of keeping talk of Curtis to a minimum. At least until we have a chance to tell Rose."

"Why didn't you tell her when it first happened?"

Good question.

"I guess because I was so happy to hear she was coming tonight that I didn't have the heart to tell her something that might propel her back into her reclusive state."

A swell of voices in the hallway rose up, sending Beatrice back to her shell with nary more than an apologetic shrug.

"Would you believe he had the nerve to call me . . . from a jail cell of all places? To ask if I'd help him?" Leona swirled into the room, a sparkling gold clutch in one hand, the latest travel magazine in the other. "That's why I'm late. I had to dispose of the suit he bought me."

"You threw away that suit?" Margaret Louise asked, dumbfounded. "Why?"

Tori sat upright, her hands beginning to sweat. "Ladies . . . now is not the time to discuss this, remember?"

As if she hadn't spoken a word, Leona took center stage and addressed her twin's question. "I threw it away because I thought he'd spent his hard-earned money on me . . . not money he simply snatched from a drawer like a common criminal." Claiming a seat that had been previously occupied by Georgina, Leona sat down, crossing her shapely legs with a disgusted huff. "Can you imagine? Spending tainted money on *me*?"

"He was in love, what can we say?"

Leona shot a nasty look in her sister's direction. "Well of course, that goes without saying . . . but, really? Aren't I worth the blood, sweat, and tears?"

"What's going on in here?" Rose asked as she shuffled into the room carrying a piece of chess pie on a plate. "I came back from the bathroom and you were all gone." The elderly woman looked around the room, her gaze coming to rest on the newly arrived Leona. "Oh. You came."

Leona made a face. "I *am* a member of the sewing circle."

"How, I have no idea. You don't sew," Rose spat out as she made her way over to the vacant spot beside Tori. "But that's neither here nor there. So what was all that ruckus about just now? What did I miss?"

Debbie cast a worried look in Tori's direction, followed by one from each of the other members as well.

"Vic-toriaaa, what is going on?"

She swallowed.

"Victoria, I'm speaking to you."

She closed her eyes.

"What happened with Kenny?"

The direct hit made her eyes and her mouth fly open. The elderly woman's gaze grew cloudy. "You think I can't tell it's something important? Something I probably don't want to hear? Just tell me."

And so she did, her mouth filling in all the details her heart hated to share—the moment the suspicion about Curtis took hold, the way she and Margaret Louise had tag-teamed him with questions, and, finally, the absolute certainty they had that he was, indeed, telling the truth.

Rose listened quietly, the slight bob to her head the only real indication that she was following along. When Tori finished, she simply gathered her flag-making paraphernalia and stood. "So it's even more likely than ever that Kenny was behind Martha Jane's murder, is that right?"

Tori looked down at her lap.

"That's not Victoria's fault, Rose," Georgina interjected. "She was only trying to help."

"I know that," said Rose with a voice that was strained and tired. "I just hate to think that the little boy I taught to read . . . the teenager I cheered on from the sidelines . . . the young adult I supported emotionally after the death of his parents . . . could carry so much rage, so much disregard for another human being's life as Kenny did."

She glanced up through misty eyes, Rose's wooden acceptance of Kenny's culpability even worse than her denial had been.

"Rose, I'm sorry," she whispered.

"I know. And so am I." Rose took two steps toward the hallway and then stopped, turning back to the circle members with pain in her eyes. "If you don't hear from me for a few days, please don't send out the search party. I'm fine. I'm simply working on a flag for Ellie's shop."

"A flag? Why?" Debbie asked.

"Because she sold the last one." Dixie stood. "I'll show Rose out."

As the two women disappeared into the hallway, Tori

released a sigh that echoed around the room. "I feel awful."

Georgina stood and crossed the room to the spot Rose had vacated, a navy blue scarf in her hand. "I know it's hard to see a friend hurting in the way Rose is. But I want you to know that you did the right thing. It wouldn't have been right to let Kenny take on charges he wasn't responsible for. Murder is enough. He didn't need robbery, too."

She considered the mayor's words. "I just wish he'd been the one who'd committed the robbery instead of the murder."

"We all do, Victoria," Margaret Louise said around a mouthful of something powdery. "But the truth is the truth."

"Has anyone been in touch with Martha Jane's sister? What's going on with all of her things?" Debbie asked.

Georgina cast one final look at Tori before swiveling to address the rest of the circle. "We have. She's in a nursing home and can't make the trip out to get everything in order. She asked if we could find someone—someone trustworthy—to go through and inventory all of her sister's belongings before the moving crew comes in."

Heads turned as everyone looked at everyone else.

"Is anyone interested?" Georgina asked, her gaze moving around the room before coming to rest, once again, on Tori.

She shook her head.

"I can't. I have too much to do right now with the donation for the shelter."

Debbie pointed at the pile. "Looks to me like you're close to meeting your promise. Just tell us how many more you need and we'll get it done."

"I—"

"It might be good for you. I think this whole business

with Rose and Kenny has affected you." Georgina took hold of her hand and gave it a gentle pat. "Maybe seeing Martha Jane's home and her things will make you feel less guilty about Kenny. He murdered an elderly woman, Victoria. He needs to pay for his crime."

Georgina was right. Like it or not, Kenny Murdock had killed an elderly woman out of anger. No amount of digging her head in the sand and wishing it wasn't so could change that.

"Could I ask Rose to help?"

"Do you think that's wise?" Debbie asked, her brows furrowed. "I mean, wouldn't that be like adding salt to the wound?"

"Maybe," she admitted. "But maybe it would do for her what Georgina is hoping it does for me."

"It's worth a try," Dixie said as she entered the room again.

Georgina agreed. "When can you do it?"

"Would tomorrow work?"

"Tomorrow?"

She nodded. "I have the day off anyway, so I have the time. And besides, if it proves to be more difficult than either of us imagine, I'll have something to look forward to that night."

"Look forward to?" Margaret Louise asked as she cocked her eyebrow in blatant curiosity.

Again, she nodded. "Milo is making dinner."

Leona smiled wickedly as she uncrossed and then recrossed her legs. "You've been paying attention, dear."

She looked a question at her friend.

"Letting a man wait on you hand and foot—it's a lesson I tend to teach by action rather than words." The woman removed a speck of lint from her skirt as she peered at Tori atop her stylish glasses. "It pleases me to no end to know you've been paying attention so well."

"Leona, I'm not trying to get Milo to wait on me hand and foot."

The woman waved her off. "There's no need to thank me, dear."

Chapter 24

If she played her cards right, she'd have a good thirty minutes to try and coax Rose into accompanying her into Martha Jane's home. And what she couldn't do with words she planned to achieve by way of her elderly friend's mouth.

Rose Winters was pretty much a what-you-see-is-what-you-get kind of woman. She wore her emotions on her sleeve and put her expectations out in the open so there were no misunderstandings to be had. But if there was one weakness in her take-no-prisoners persona, it came by way of her sweet tooth.

A sweet tooth that was utterly helpless against the promise of pie . . .

Tori's late great-grandmother's pie recipe to be exact.

Grabbing hold of the foil-wrapped pie, Tori headed for her front door, her ankle boots making a soft clicking sound against the wood floor. There was a part of her that was dreading the task of walking through Martha Jane Barker's house—the same part that made her cry while reading the news and send checks to every charity that came knocking via her mailbox. But there was also a part of her that was almost looking forward to it as a way to say good-bye—once and for all—to a task she had failed to complete.

She flung open her front door and stepped onto the porch, the poignant smell of mums from her neighbor's yard filling the air. There were so many things she wanted to do around her place, little details and touches that would take it from the cozy place it almost was to the picture-perfect home she wanted it to be.

Maybe that afternoon, after inventorying Martha Jane's home, she could do a little planting of her own. Then again, she still had another hat and scarf set to make . . .

"I was hopin' I'd catch you before you ran off."

Tori turned the key in the lock and spun around, a smile stretching across her face. "Margaret Louise, what a nice surprise." She peeked around the woman's plump frame. "What? No little ducklings in tow today?"

"Not until after school." Pointing at the wicker chairs that graced her tiny porch, Margaret Louise flashed her most charming and irresistible smile. "Do you have a moment to sit?"

She glanced at her wristwatch. "Uhhh, a little, I guess."

"Good." The woman plopped down in the rocking chair and crossed her swollen ankles. "Last night, before you left, you mentioned having only one hat and scarf set left to make after everyone else committed to a particular number."

"That's right. Why? Can you not make the extra two?" Tori leaned forward in her chair and squeezed the older woman's knee. "That's not a problem. You've done so much already."

Margaret Louise shook her head firmly. "It's not that. I'm still fixin' to do the extra two."

"Then I'm sorry, but I'm not following."

"Please don't make that last set."

She looked a question at her friend.

"Please."

"I don't understand," she protested. "Has someone else agreed to make another hat and scarf?"

"Sorta. Though, *agreed* isn't really the right way to say it."

"I don't understand."

Margaret Louise met her confused gaze with one that was impossible to read. "Just hold off making that last set, okay?"

"It's okay to have an extra," she said. "They won't send it back."

The woman shook her head firmly. "I don't want this one to be an extra. It needs to be one you *need*. Please."

She studied her friend for a long moment, questions firing through her mind in rapid-fire succession. Why couldn't she make an extra set? Why all the secrecy? And could she coax her into coming to Martha Jane's house *with* her?

The last question made her sit upright, all thoughts of hats and scarves gone. "Wow. I guess I didn't realize how apprehensive I am about doing this," she mumbled.

"Doing what, Victoria?"

"Going through Martha Jane's house."

Suddenly, the woman's somewhat secretive aura was gone, in its place nothing but empathy. "Then don't go. Tell Georgina she needs to find someone else."

Oh how she'd love to be able to do that, to put the task off on someone else while she planted mums or read a book or readied the box for the women's shelter. But she couldn't.

"I can't back out now. I told her I'd do it."

"Tell her you made a mistake." Margaret Louise stilled the rocker with her foot. "Frankly, I found it to be rather nervy of her to ask. You're too busy as it is."

She waved her friend's worry off. "It's okay. It won't

take all that long. It's not like I'm actually packing anything up . . . just making a list. Besides, I'll have some time to relax tonight when I have dinner with Milo and his mom."

The woman's eyebrows tilted north. "His mamma?"

She nodded.

"You're meetin' his mamma tonight?"

"I am."

Slowly, Margaret Louise's mouth stretched wide, an inner sparkle making her eyes shimmer with excitement. "You can't be trekkin' 'round that house, Victoria. You need to be here . . . gettin' spit-shined."

"Spit-shined? What am I? A shoe?"

The woman rolled her eyes, a gesture that did little to mar her excitement. "Meetin' a man's mamma is important. Why, I remember the first time I met Melissa. She was just pretty as could be even with the way her knees were clackin'."

"Excuse me?"

Pushing herself out of the rocking chair, Margaret Louise took hold of Tori's hand and pulled. "I reckoned she was scared. But, even so, it broke my heart to learn a few years later that she was afraid she'd worn the wrong outfit."

The woman stopped at Tori's door and held out her hand. "Keys?"

"Margaret Louise, I really have to get going."

"Not yet, you don't. What you've got to do is pick out your dress. It's not every day you meet your beau's mamma for the first time."

"Margaret Louise, it's really not a big deal."

"Hush, Victoria." Inserting the key into the lock, she turned and pushed. "Now let's get somethin' real purty picked out."

Police Chief Dallas was waiting when she pulled up, his feet resting on the front railing, his backside in a narrow brown rocking chair. "Was beginnin' to think you forgot all about this," the man said as one foot and then the other dropped to the ground with a thud.

She stepped onto the sidewalk with the covered plate in her hand, the man's presence all but eliminating any hope she had for roping Rose into the task at hand. "I'm sorry. Something came up as I was leaving the house."

He narrowed his eyes. "Everythin' okay, Miss Sinclair?"

"Everything's fine," she replied, a smile lifting her cheeks upward as she recalled the reason for her delay. There was no doubt Margaret Louise's timing had been less than stellar. Yet there was also no denying the fact that she'd loved every minute of their unexpected shopping trip through her bedroom closet. It was the part of having girlfriends that she adored most. "But I don't suppose there would be time for me to head next door to Rose's house to see if she'd like to help?"

Rising to his feet, the police chief shrugged. "There's time but it won't do you no good."

Her shoulders rose and fell beneath her maroon-colored sweater set. "Why not?"

"Last I saw her, she was sittin' on a park bench in the middle of town square sewin' on a Sweet Briar flag just as if she were Betsy Ross," he said, chuckling at his own words. "If I knew how to paint, I'd have had to capture her in that very spot. She looked so peaceful."

"Peaceful?" She dared to hope the man's words were accurate.

"Looked that way to me." He pointed at the covered dish. "Mind if I take a peek?"

"No. Not at all." She held the plate steady as he worked at a corner of the foil. When he'd folded enough of the foil up to afford a look, a long low whistle escaped his lips. "Is that chocolate mousse pie?"

She nodded.

"I mean, is it *real* chocolate mousse pie?"

"If you mean real as in homemade . . . yes, it's real. It's my late great-grandmother's recipe."

He whistled again. "My mamma makes one just like that, bless her heart."

"Do you see her often?" she asked as she caught sight of Doug and waved.

"She's in a nursin' home now. Don't remember her own name, let alone mine. Why"—he stopped, scratched his head—"I think she was makin' her pie when we finally realized she was losin' her mind."

He nodded before she could respond, his mouth continuing to move a mile a minute. "Yup, I remember now. It was Thanksgivin' and we were all waitin' for dessert . . . waitin' for her pie. And when it was finally time, and we took a bite, we realized she'd made a mistake."

"Forgot the eggs?" she asked.

"If only it were that simple," he said, his laugh one of pain as much as humor. "She used the gravy packet from the chicken instead."

She felt her mouth gape open.

He nodded affirmation of his story, his gaze leaving her face in favor of the pie in her hands. "Haven't had a real one since."

She, too, looked at the pie.

So much for bribery . . .

Inhaling deeply, she handed the pie to the police chief. "I decided to skip the gravy this time, so there's no guarantee."

A smile that rivaled the sun broke out across the man's face as he took the pie from her hands. "You sure?"

"I'm sure."

"That's mighty sweet of you, Miss Sinclair." Motioning toward the door with his chin, he stepped onto the sidewalk and headed toward his car. "I'll just wait in my car until you're done."

"You don't want to come with me?" she asked.

"Nah, I've got some eatin' to do." He bobbed his head in her direction. "I owe you one."

"Let's hope I don't have to collect."

She watched as he set the pie on the roof of his car and peeled back the foil, her mind playing through the million reasons she shouldn't be there. Unfortunately, it was the one reason she should that propelled her through the door.

"This is the last time I agree to a favor," she muttered under her breath as she stepped into the entryway and looked around, the sterility of the plain white walls coming as little surprise.

For as rigid and full of herself as Martha Jane was, her attitude was an indication of unhappiness—the kind of unhappiness that often came with living a colorless life. Pulling a notepad and pen from her purse, she began walking from room to room, jotting down everything she saw.

First came the front parlor, a room she'd missed during her one and only trip into the house thanks to the back-door entrance she'd taken. A floral sofa protected by a plastic covering sat at an angle to the window, an old record player gracing a nearby table. Pictures and books, spread across four separate wall-mounted shelves, completed the room.

She moved on to the kitchen. A china service for eight, silver for ten, crystal stemware for twelve, and an oak table for one were the highlights of the room, rounded out by a cabinet with barely enough to keep a fish alive.

Room by room she made her way through Martha Jane's house, evidence of the woman's solitary life alive and well around every corner—a single glass next to her reading chair, a stack of dog-eared crossword books beside the couch, a single dirty plate in the dishwasher.

It didn't take a rocket scientist to see that Martha

Jane Barker had died in the same manner she'd lived her life—by herself. But knowing that didn't make it better. The woman may have been rude and, at times, downright nasty, but no one, not even Martha Jane, deserved to have their life snuffed out because of someone else's rage.

She blinked back a tear that threatened to make its debut down her face, Georgina's words filtering through her mind with startling clarity.

"Maybe seeing Martha Jane's home and her things will make you feel less guilty about Kenny. He murdered an elderly woman, Victoria. He needs to pay for his crime."

Georgina was right. Kenny had done something wrong, something that simply couldn't go unchecked. Sure, she hated that his crime and his impending punishment were such a source of grief and sadness for Rose. But, in the end, it was a reality that needed to be played out. For Martha Jane, first and foremost.

Peeking into the three-season room off the back of the house, she stopped, her eyes imagining the way the homeowner had looked just one day before she was murdered. The woman had been so uptight, so judgmental, her scorn for the storm workers as tangible as the tattered screens in the window.

What made some people so disdainful of others? What made them think they were better than other people simply because of the house they owned or the clothes they wore?

They were questions for which there were no answers. None that made sense, anyway.

She jotted down a few notes—flower cart, three ceramic pots, a single dark brown wicker chair with matching ottoman, one yellow throw pillow, and a radio that had seen better days—before moving back into the hall.

As she approached the last room, she felt her feet slow, memories of her final conversation with the victim juxtaposing themselves with the conjured image of a lifeless body, a thick outdoor rope wound around its neck.

"Oh, Kenny, don't you see? You proved her crazy ranting to be right." She shook her head against the spoken words, their presence almost deafening in a house that was much too quiet.

She drew her hand up in a fist when she reached the closed door only to pull it back down when she realized there was no one to answer a knock. Inhaling sharply, she turned the knob and pushed the door open, the smell of stale air assaulting her nose as she stepped into the room.

Bypassing the assorted contents, she strode over to the window and slid it open, the addition of fresh air in the room a welcome reprieve. For a moment she simply stood there and looked out, the thin line of trees that separated the home from its closest neighbor offering a sense of peace and tranquility hampered only by the near-constant hammering somewhere in the distance.

Hammering done by men Martha Jane had called lazy. Like Doug and Curtis.

Curtis.

"That man should be up on the roof patching holes instead of writing notes in that notebook of his. Writing doesn't fix things. A hammer and nails does."

She spun around, determined not to let her thoughts travel to the man she'd been so certain was the answer to all Rose's problems. What good did it do? Curtis stole the money. He didn't murder Martha Jane.

Kenny did.

Pulling her notebook from under her arm, she readied her pencil above the empty page, her hand meeting the paper as she scrawled the name of the room at the top.

1. Full-size bed. Mahogany.
2. Two matching nightstands.

3. A Victorian lamp.
4. A mahogany-trimmed mirror. Oval.
5. A mahogany six-drawer dresser.
6. A dark cherry jewelry box.

She slid each drawer of the jewelry box open, taking time to document each and every piece of jewelry it contained—pearl necklaces, a silver charm bracelet, diamond stud earrings, a tennis bracelet, and so it went, each item nicer and more elaborate than the one before.

When she was finished recording a description of each piece, she slid the drawers shut, her gaze lingering on the details of the box before moving on to the next item. The pine and glass flag case hung just off to the side, its pale blue contents drawing her eye, as they had that first day.

She marveled at the embroidered detail on the flag—the way the sun's golden rays bathed the picket fence in warm light, the ferociousness of the flames, the sturdiness of the six bricks . . .

"Beautiful," she marveled aloud. It was the kind of work she hoped to start doing thanks to Rose. Watching her friend begin the process of duplicating the town's flag the other night had inspired her to take her own sewing to the next level.

Now if only she could find an extra hour or two a day . . .

"And while I'm at it, maybe I can find a few flying pigs."

"Miss Sinclair?"

She whirled around, the sound of footsteps in the hallway catching her by surprise. "I'm back here, Chief. In her bedroom."

He poked his head around the door. "Almost finished in here?"

"I am. I just have to write down the contents of each drawer."

"*Clothes* is sufficient. Especially now that the money is gone."

Sliding the capped pen into her mouth, she nodded, the man's words filtering their way into the recesses of her mind. "Do you know how much, exactly?"

"We know that from the false report she filed just before her death."

"Did he donate it all?"

The man nodded. "What he didn't donate, he used on Leona Elkin."

She stifled the urge to laugh. "Will she have to testify?"

"Probably. Though, between you and me and these four walls, she brought every last thing he bought her to the station last night. Tried to heave it in through the bars of his cell."

"He didn't give her any knives, did he?" she quipped.

"Nah. Seems he tried to do good with the money he stole . . . a modern day Robin Hood of sorts."

She closed her eyes against the image of Curtis in the children's room, pure joy on his face as he spied the Robin Hood costume. It was nothing short of a shame that a man who seemed so gentle in spirit could travel down such a wrong road.

"How's he doing?" she asked, the question surprising her as much as it seemed to the chief.

"Okay, I guess. He's a real quiet fella'. Just sits on the bench and writes in a notepad he asked for. We let him have it because it seemed harmless enough."

"And Leona? How did she seem beyond the heaving incident?"

Shrugging, he shook his head. "I reckon she'll land on her feet."

She made a mental note to call Leona all the same. A shock was a shock no matter how tough you pretended to be. The fact that the shock came in such a public way only increased the disappointment factor.

"You ready to go?"

Looking around the room one last time, she nodded. "Yeah. I think I got everything."

The chief pulled his hands from their resting place above his belt and led the way to the door, his heavy footsteps echoing through the room, nearly drowning out the hammering in the background.

"Wait. I need to shut the window." She hurried over to the back wall and slid the window into place, locking it at the top for good measure before heading back across the room. "I opened it to get a little fresh air." Pausing midway, she met the chief's eyes. "Where did you find her?"

He pointed just in front of her feet. "Right there."

She stared at the spot he indicated, the dead woman's face suddenly clear in her mind. "It's a shame," she whispered. "A real shame."

Chapter 25

Somehow she'd managed to fool herself into thinking dinner at Milo's would be nothing out of the ordinary. That the presence of his mother—albeit for the first time—would merely provide an extra person for conversational purposes. . . .

However, the moment she peered into the full-length mirror on the back of her bathroom door, she knew otherwise.

Who had she been trying to kid? She was meeting Milo's mother.

Mothers could make or break a relationship with a mere look—a raised eyebrow, a twitching nostril, pursed lips, you name it. And how she'd been able to convince herself otherwise was a complete mystery.

Then again, trying to get sixty hats and scarves made while juggling a full-time job with her pathetic attempt at helping Rose and, well, overlooking the importance of this particular dinner made sense.

In a roundabout, I-didn't-see-it-coming kind of way.

But now that it was here, she was freaking out. Big-time.

Willing herself to remain calm, she buttoned her blouse all the way up to the neck only to unbutton the top three and then button them again.

The peal of the phone from the other room made her jump and she rushed to answer it before it went to voice mail. Snapping it open, she held it to her face.

"Hello?"

"Victoria? How ya holdin' up?"

She exhaled a far louder sigh than she intended. "Do you think this outfit is really okay?"

"I most certainly do," Margaret Louise said, her voice morphing into a laugh that helped ease some of Tori's tension. "That color sets off your eyes real nice like."

"But what about the shirt? Do I button every last button?"

"Do you want to look uptight?"

"No." Looking down at her chest, she undid the top three buttons. "Okay, I undid some."

"How many?"

"Three."

"Three? Are you tryin' to offend Milo's mamma?"

She buttoned another.

"What happens if she doesn't like me?" she asked, the question bothering her more than she'd admitted up until that point.

"Then she needs her head examined."

She felt the corners of her mouth tug upward. Just a little.

"What do I say?"

"Just be yourself. The same exact girl her son fell in love with in the first place."

A thought struck her from left field, making her clutch the phone tighter to her face. "Margaret Louise? What happens if she adored Celia so much I simply fall short?"

The ensuing silence in her ear made her pull the phone back to check their connection. When she was satisfied they hadn't been disconnected, she held it to her ear once again. "Margaret Louise? Are you still there?"

"I'm here. I was just tryin' to imagine how I'd feel if Jake lost Melissa and then started datin' again ten years later."

She swallowed. "And?"

"I'd be happy for him. I'd reckon that whoever she was, she must be mighty special to reach his heart."

Nodding, she stepped back into the bathroom and peered into the mirror. She'd pulled her shoulder-length brown hair into a clip at the base of her neck, tiny tendrils of hair escaping to frame her heart-shaped face. The green of her blouse pulled out its matching shade in her eyes, just as Margaret Louise had said, the effect bringing a smile to her lips.

"Okay," she said into the phone. "I think I'm ready."

Balancing the plate of raspberry tortes in her left hand, she knocked on the door, the butterflies she'd managed to corral back at the house taking flight once again. The sound of footsteps inside did little to help the situation.

"Tori, you're here," Milo said as he flung open the door. Reaching for the plate with one hand, he leaned forward for a kiss, his lips brushing her forehead before meeting hers. "Mom is so excited to meet you."

Nerves made her glance at the floor only to be thwarted by her feelings for the man standing just inches away. "I'm excited . . . and a little nervous . . . to meet her, too."

He slid his free arm around her shoulders and tugged her close to his side. "There's nothing to be nervous about. She's going to love you just like everyone else does."

"From your mouth to—"

A woman of similar size and stature to Tori rounded the corner, her eyes glistening. "You must be Victoria." She reached around her son and clasped Tori's hand inside her own. "I've heard so many wonderful things about you I feel as if I already know you."

Her eyes grew misty as she met Milo's eyes. "Thank you. Your son is a very special man."

"That he is. Now, come sit with me so we can get better acquainted." The woman stopped midstep and turned. "Oh, forgive me for being so dense. My name is Rita. Rita Wentworth."

It didn't take long to realize Margaret Louise had been right. Rita had watched her son suffer the grief of losing his wife and then pick his way through the years that followed, his steps aimless with the exception of his job.

"I always knew Milo would make a fine teacher. His cousins looked up to him as if he was some sort of superhero. They loved to play with him, creating adventures they'd continue each time they saw each other. But, even more than playing, they loved to spend quiet time with him. Reading. Talking. Learning."

Tori stole a glance in Milo's direction, the man's cheeks slightly pink. "What?" she teased. "This is fun for me. Your mom is filling in all the gaps I can't know."

"I just hope she doesn't fill in a gap you don't *want* to know." He made a face, then reached across the sofa and entwined his fingers with hers. "Enough about me, Mom. I think it's time you get to know Tori a little better."

"Oh, I'm sorry, dear. I called you Victoria earlier. I hope I didn't upset you." The woman worried her brows.

Tori held up her hand. "Not at all. In fact, all of my friends here in Sweet Briar call me Victoria."

Rita looked surprised. "I didn't realize there were many women your age in this town."

"There aren't. Not many, anyway." She met the woman's eyes across the coffee table. "My friends range in age from twenty-three to eightysomething and I wouldn't trade them for anything in the world."

Milo nodded. "You remember Rose Winters, don't you, Mom?"

"Rose Winters . . . Rose Winters . . ." The woman tapped her index finger on her chin for a moment. "Oh yes, of course. She's the woman who retired the year you started at the school, isn't she?"

Again, Milo nodded. "She's one of Tori's closest friends."

"Really?" Rita asked as she returned her undivided attention to Tori. "How do you know her?"

"Through my sewing. I was invited to join the Sweet Briar Ladies Society Sewing Circle when I first moved here. The women in that group have become my dear friends."

The woman beamed. "How lovely that you don't see age as a stumbling block."

Tori shrugged. "Friends—true friends—are hard to find. I'd be foolish to close myself off from one simply because we were born at different times."

"I can see that you were right all those years, son." Rita swiped at a tear as it made its way down her gently lined face. "You always said you'd know when you found the right one. And you most certainly did."

Milo rose from his spot beside Tori and made his way around the coffee table, his tall lanky form sinking onto the cushion beside his mother. "Thanks, Mom."

For a moment she didn't know what to say, the raw intensity in the room almost too much to take in all at once. Eventually, though, the pair looked up, their matching smiles trained on her face.

"You two are going to make me cry," Tori whispered.

"Too late." Rita pulled her hand from her son's grasp and gestured for Tori to join them, the woman's welcoming arms doing little to stop the flow of emotion that threatened to make her face blotchy and her nose run. "So tell me more about you. Milo says you're a librarian?"

And so they talked about everything. Her job. Her hobbies and interests. The children's room at the library. Ideas she had for future expansion. And her nearly complete project for the women's shelter in Chicago. When she was done, she inhaled deeply, the experience of meeting Milo's mother nothing less than wonderful.

"See? She's Wonder Woman," Milo touted.

Tori waved him off. "Hardly. I just like to keep busy even when I probably should slow things down every once in a while."

"I know. Which is why I'm afraid to ask you a favor."

She stared at him. "You're different. What do you need?"

He looked from Tori to his mom and back again, his shoulders drooping a smidge. "I wouldn't ask if I had another option. Not because I don't want you there—I do. But because you have too much on your plate already."

"Get to it, son," Rita said.

"Yes, please," she agreed.

Raking a hand through his hair, he finally cut to the chase. "I need another career for Thursday. I have two lined up every other day, just not then. You'd only need to talk for about ten minutes and then take a few questions from the kids."

"I'd love to," she said. And she meant it. Nothing pleased her more than working with kids. To be able to pair it with Milo for a little while only made it better.

"Lovely," Rita said under her breath. "It does a mother's heart good to see her child surrounded by such wonderful people." Pushing off the sofa, the woman reached her hand toward Tori's. "Come see what Milo's friend did for him."

Looking a question at Milo, she stood and followed Rita to the bookshelf that ran the entire length of the living room wall. "My husband was a decorated veteran. When he died he had a full military funeral."

She stopped beside Milo's mother as the woman pointed to an upper shelf. "I wanted Milo to have the flag that had been on his father's casket before it was lowered into the ground. Franklin would have wanted him to have it."

Milo joined them by the shelf and picked up where his mother left off. "I kept it in that chest in my room with the intention of making a case for it eventually. Unfortunately, I never got around to it with work and all."

She followed his gaze to the dark cherry and glass flag case propped on the top shelf. Inside it was the perfectly folded flag that served as a final link between father and son. "Oh, Milo, it's perfect . . . But when on earth did you find the time to make that? You've been so busy with the collections booth."

"I didn't make it, that's how. Sure, I could make something like it if I tried, but to track down the various parts he found in order to give it a true heirloom feel . . . I wouldn't have a clue."

"He?"

"His friend, Victoria." Rita clapped her hands together. "Can you believe that?"

She dropped her eyes from the flag to Milo. "Who?" she repeated. "Who made it? It's gorgeous."

"Doug."

"Wow. I had no idea he was so talented."

Milo pulled her close, his mother grinning ear to ear from the sidelines. "I didn't realize just how far his talent went, either. But we'll both get to see his ability in greater detail on Thursday when you come for career day. He's my other presenter that day."

"If it's okay, I'd like to come, too," Rita said. "It'll give me something to do. Sons aren't supposed to be so"—the woman gestured around the room—"neat and organized. It leaves visiting mothers with nothing to do."

Chapter 26

Tori walked up her porch steps, her arms heavy with papers and charts detailing the ins and outs of the library's coming year—budget proposals, structure improvements, catalogue additions, and a request that would make Dixie Dunn a happy woman.

"I was beginning to wonder if you were having a rendezvous with Milo after work. And then I remembered his mamma is in town."

Her foot froze on the top step. "Leona? Is that you?"

The woman, dressed in a hunter green pantsuit, stepped out from behind the shadow of the rocking chair, a furry mound cuddled in her arms. "It most certainly is."

"What are you doing here?" The second the words were out, she braced herself for the lecture on southern etiquette she knew was sure to come.

Leona, of course, did not disappoint. "That kind of question might be normal in Chicago, dear. After all, you must be on guard at all times for fear someone will rob you blind."

She rolled her eyes, a gesture that didn't go unnoticed.

"Goodness gracious, Victoria. Don't you know how perfectly backwoods an eye roll like that is?"

"And you're going to stand there and tell me you don't roll your eyes on occasion?"

"I don't. I look skyward, for guidance . . . at times when my patience is tested."

"Are belles known for impatience? Because you've led me to believe they smile twenty-four/seven in the hopes of landing a man."

The woman's eyes rolled upward.

She dropped her stack of papers to the ground and clapped her hands. "See? You just rolled your eyes."

Leona shook her head. "No. I was looking for guidance."

"For what?"

"To get through to you."

She stared at her friend. "What are you talking about?"

"Belles don't *land* men, dear. They're simply the flower that attracts the bees."

"The flower that attracts the bees," she repeated. "Hmmm. And when that flower gets stung? What then, Leona?"

"You bloom brighter and prettier and attract an even bigger bee."

"To make the first bee jealous?"

Leona made a face. "To show him what he's missing."

"What happens when the first bee is . . . I don't know . . . maybe . . . *behind bars*?"

Even in the gathering dusk she was able to see the color drain from her friend's face. She rushed to make amends. "I'm sorry. I shouldn't have said it that way. It's just, well, I've been wondering how you are."

"We're fine, aren't we darling?" Leona looked down at Paris, sleeping soundly in her arms, then offered a barely discernable shrug. "I went to his hearing yesterday. His judge is very handsome."

Her mouth hung open. She willed it to move long enough to voice the question screaming in her head. "You're not . . ."

"His robes are really quite dashing."

Shaking her head, she picked her papers off the ground and gestured toward the door with her chin. "Would you like to come in?"

"How refreshing. Of course, dear."

She led the way into her cottage, their heels making soft clicking sounds on the hardwood floor. "What can I get you? Water? Soda? Tea?"

"Nothing right now." Leona strode into the living room and lowered herself onto the plaid armchair. "So tell me about Milo's mother. Margaret Louise told me you met last night."

"We did. She's wonderful." She breezed across the living room and into the kitchen, depositing the stack of papers onto the table. "We seemed to hit it off well."

"Just make sure you hold your position, dear. That's extremely critical at this juncture."

She poked her head around the corner. "Hold my position?"

"As Milo's woman." Leona lifted Paris up and gave him an air-kiss. "Trust me on this, dear. You give that woman an inch and she'll take a mile."

"You don't even know her," she protested.

"I don't have to. Milo is an only child, isn't he?"

"Yes."

"And her husband passed away, didn't he?"

"Yes."

"I wouldn't give her half an inch if I were you." Pulling Paris back onto her lap, Leona ran a flawlessly manicured hand along his back. "When is she leaving?"

"I don't know," she said, shrugging.

"Oh dear."

"What?"

"That's not a good sign."

"She's coming to his classroom on Thursday to hear me speak with his class about being a librarian."

"It's starting already, dear. Be firm. Be very, very firm." Leona looked around the room, her gaze skirting the sewing alcove and the dining area. "I suggest you find a crisis around here . . . something that needs Milo's help. Just to get him from her clutches for a while. Show her who really makes him run."

Tori held up her hand. "Enough. Rita is a sweet woman. She doesn't have her clutches on Milo. She wants him to be happy."

Leona's eyes rolled skyward. After a long moment, she simply shook her head. "That's what they all say, dear."

Any thought she had toward protesting never made it to her lips thanks to a gentle knock at the door.

"Are you expecting someone?" Leona asked as she looked toward the door.

"No."

"It never ceases to amaze me how rude people can be . . . simply dropping by unannounced."

She bit her tongue over the desire to make an observation about pots and kettles, deciding, instead, to simply answer the door. When she reached the front entry, she peeked out through the sidelight that ran the full length of the door.

Rose.

Feeling a sense of relief bubbling up, she pulled the door open. "Rose . . . what a wonderful surprise," she said as a snort rose up from the living room. "Is everything okay?"

The elderly woman pulled her arm up, a bag swaying from her hands. "I have a few hats and scarves for you."

She reached out, took the bag from the woman's hand, and motioned her inside. "I can't wait to see them."

"I made them in a mint green and pale yellow combination." Rose stepped into the living room and stopped, her feet rooted to the ground. "Oh. It's you," she sniffed as she made eye contact with Leona.

"Yes it is." Leona's eyes traveled down and then back up Rose's frail frame. "How are you, Old Woman?"

Rose shuffled across the room and over to the sofa. "You really must quit talking to yourself. People might think you're a little"—she held her index finger to her temple and moved it in a circular motion—"crazy. They might even think you need to be locked up like that young man you were mooning over."

"I don't moon over anyone," Leona proclaimed as she tightened her grip on Paris. "I don't need to."

Tori sighed at the first sign of a smile on Rose's face in entirely too long, the woman's words bringing a similar expression to her own face as well.

"So you've finally accepted the unavoidable?"

Leona stared at her. "What are you talking about?"

"You ignored the part about you being old."

"And crazy," Tori chimed in.

Leona turned her fiery look in Tori's direction. "I'm sorry, dear, I don't believe I heard you correctly."

Rose chuckled. "Hearing is the first to go, Leona."

Tori laughed out loud, much to Leona's chagrin.

"Victoria, I was hoping we could sew together for a little while . . . if you don't have any"—Rose stole a glance in Leona's direction, the woman's fuming breaths further deepening the smile on her wrinkled face—"other plans, of course."

"I can sew and talk at the same time. In fact, now that you mentioned it, I could really use the chance to slow the day down a little." She turned back toward the kitchen. "Can I get you anything, Rose?"

"I'm fine. But perhaps Leona would like a good stiff drink."

"You took the words right out of my mouth, Old Woman."

An hour turned into two and then three, dusk morphing into night as their needles continued to move in and out of their respective projects while Leona filled the room with idle chitchat and compliments for Paris's every twitch.

When Rose had completed her final hat and scarf set, she pulled a familiar piece of pale blue material from her bag and carefully unfolded it on her lap.

"So Ellie sold a flag?" Leona asked.

Rose nodded. "Gives me something to do to take my mind off things."

"I'm sorry about Kenny, Old Woman. I know he meant a lot to you."

Tori met Rose's eye before they both turned and looked at Leona. "Why, Leona, that sounded almost . . . almost genuine."

Leona made a face at Tori. "I know she believed in him. And I know it hurts when someone disappoints you."

"Then I'm sorry about your young man—even if he was too young for you," Rose said with a garbled voice. Bending slightly at the waist she coughed, the sound rattling her chest. When she was done, she simply sat up tall as if all was well. "For what it's worth, I liked that young man. At first I thought he was quiet because he was unfriendly. But as the days went by and I saw him working around Martha Jane's and then Adelaide's, I came to realize he was just the kind of man who liked to process before he spoke."

"He had aspirations of being a writer," Leona explained.

"Ohhh, okay, that makes sense now." Tori looked up

from her final hat and scarf, her shoulders weary from being hunched over her lap for hours on end. "That explains the notebook he kept so close while he was working."

Leona nodded. "He wrote down snatches of conversations he heard, sounds that caught his attention, mannerisms people had. He said they'd help him one day."

"Such a shame the way this generation seems to think things should just be handed to them instead of earning it." Rose slipped her embroidery hoop into place and sealed it tight. "Forty years ago, people didn't steal money. They earned it. And they didn't kill people because they got their feelings hurt."

Tori rolled her shoulders forward and then backward, Rose's words solidifying the fact that the woman was on the road to recovery as far as Kenny Murdock was concerned. "I went through Martha Jane's house today and jotted down every item inside. And while I was doing that, I realized this whole thing shouldn't be about Kenny. It should be about Martha Jane. We owe her that much."

Rose nodded. "Working on this flag helped me accept that as well."

"How?" Leona asked.

"Because it calms me in a way that allows my head to be heard over my heart." Rose pulled the brick-colored embroidery floss from her bag and threaded her needle. "I've got just one more brick to go. . . ."

Tori sat up tall, peering at her friend's latest project from across the coffee table. "I see . . . you're adding the top one now." She mentally counted the rectangles. "Wait. There's six. Aren't there supposed to be more?"

Leona shook her head. "No. Just six."

She thought back to Martha Jane's final day, to the conversation they'd had in the woman's bedroom.

"There can't be. Martha Jane said they added more. To emphasize the notion of strength in the town's foundation."

"They *did* add more," Rose explained, as she pulled the needle and thread up through the underside of the flag. "And this *is* more."

She closed her eyes, willed herself to return to the room she'd inventoried just the day before. "No, it's not. You've got six bricks there and Martha Jane's flag had six bricks, too. There's no difference."

"In order to make a difference from six, there would have to be ten and the section is not big enough to hold ten bricks," Leona mused. "Or they'd have to make them so tiny no one would *know* they were bricks."

Rose nodded. "Six is right."

"There were three on the original flag and they increased it to six." Leona scooted forward in her seat and then stood, her hand firmly wrapped around Paris. "I need to get him home. He needs his beauty rest."

Rose snorted.

"Well he does," Leona protested as she headed toward the door. "He gets bags under his eyes if I keep him out too late."

Rolling her eyes, Rose snorted once again. "Do you hear this, Victoria?"

The sound of her name snapped her back to the here and now, all thoughts of bricks and flags leaving her dazed and confused. "Wha-huh?"

"Dear?" Leona asked, stopping at the door. "Are you okay?"

"What? Oh, yeah, I'm fine. This flag thing just has me a little perplexed is all. I really thought Martha Jane's flag had six yesterday but"—she pushed her final hat and scarf off her lap and rushed to meet up with Leona—"I must just be confusing it with the one Rose is working on."

"It happens to the best of us," Rose said.

"Speak for yourself, Old Woman. My memory is crystal clear."

"That's more than we can say for your judgment."

Leona turned, a knowing smile stretching her mouth wide. "No need to worry. I'll be getting plenty of help in that department very soon."

"What are you talking about?" Rose asked.

Tori dropped her head forward. "You don't want to know."

"Yes, I do."

Tori inhaled deeply, shaking her head at Leona even as she laid out clues for Rose. "He sits at a table, waves a gavel, and . . . wears a uniform of sorts."

Rose cocked her head to the right. "A judge?"

"That's right, a judge." Leona pulled the door open, then turned to help Paris wave good-bye. "Perhaps I can get him to go a little easy on Kenny."

Chapter 27

She loved everything about her job—the books, the research, the ability to excite a reluctant reader, and the opportunity to get paid while doing it. Yet of all the things she loved about being a librarian, working with kids was her favorite. Their minds were like sponges, ready and willing to soak up a new fact or a different way of looking at something.

It was why the children's room had been so important to her when she took the job at Sweet Briar Public Library. And it was why she made sure to include special children's activities each and every month regardless of the time of year.

Having a chance to speak with them about becoming librarians was simply icing on the cake.

She looked around at the faces assembled around her, some hanging on every word she said, others picking at their friends, the carpet, their shoes, and whatever else they could find.

But that was okay. The world needed people in all sorts of careers.

"Have you read every single book in the library?" a little boy in the back row asked.

Eyes widened around him. "Have you?" echoed a few more voices.

"While it might be neat to say I have, I'm happy to say I haven't."

The students looked at one another in surprise.

"Why?" asked the same little boy.

She looked from Milo to his mom and then back to the children on the carpet. "Because I'd be sad if I didn't have any books left to read."

The little boy tilted his head a hairbreadth. "I hadn't thought of that. I'd be sad, too."

A redhead turned around. "You like books, Pete?"

Pete nodded. "It's my favorite thing to do."

The redhead's mouth hung open.

"I like them even more than playing kickball or collecting bugs."

"Me, too." Tori smiled at Pete. "That's why I became a librarian."

"But boys can't be librarians," the redhead countered.

Milo pushed off the wall and stood in front of his class. "Of course they can. And if Pete decides to be a librarian one day, I think he'll do a great job." Turning to Tori, he smiled, his eyes saying more than his third graders were capable of understanding. "Well, class, shall we give a round of applause to Miss Sinclair for telling us a little bit about what it takes to be a librarian?"

His question was met with loud clapping and even a few whistles. "Thank you, class. I look forward to seeing your faces at the library."

She left the rug in favor of the empty chair beside

Milo's mother, the woman's pleased smile warming her from the inside out.

"You did wonderfully, Victoria. The children really enjoyed your talk," Rita whispered as her son worked to quiet his students.

When they were silent once again, he pointed to the man who'd just entered the room. "I have another career for you to hear about that I think you're going to enjoy as well. Mr. Doug here is going to tell you about what it takes to be a woodworker."

"What's a woodworker?" a little girl with blonde pigtails asked.

The redhead rolled his eyes. "Someone who works with wood, dummy."

Milo opened his mouth to correct the student only to shut it again as Doug took charge of the room. "What's your name, sweetheart?" he asked the little girl.

The child looked down, embarrassment coloring her face bright red. "Cindy," she whispered.

"Cindy," he repeated. "That's a beautiful name for a beautiful little girl." Turning to address the redhead, his voice took on a slightly tougher tone. "Everyone has different gifts. Some have an ability to play sports, some an ability to write, some can fix just about anything that's broken, and others can teach children like Mil—I mean, Mr. Wentworth, does."

Heads nodded. "I'm no good when it comes to books. No one ever really taught me to love them like Miss Sinclair does, so being a librarian was out for me."

"You could learn to like them," Pete said.

Doug nodded. "You're right. And I think I'll start workin' on that once I get back home to my kids. In fact"—he leaned against the edge of Milo's desk—"I'm considerin' a book on Sweet Briar's history as a souvenir for my son."

"Don't bother," the redhead said. "The history is all

wrong anyway. Moonshiners destroyed the town, not Yankees."

Doug looked a question at Tori across the room. She shrugged and gestured toward Milo with her head.

"Derrick, now is not the time."

The redhead crossed his legs and sulked as Milo nodded at Doug to continue.

"I work with wood. I fix things that are broken." He looked around the room, his knack for keeping kids interested more than a little impressive. "That's why I'm here in Sweet Briar, you know. To help people fix their homes after the storm you just had."

Cindy frowned. "My house had a broken window. But Daddy fixed it right up."

"See? That's the kind of stuff I do . . . 'cept I tend to do more with wood than glass."

Doug held up his finger and then walked into the hallway only to return with a small table in one hand, a window shutter in the other. "Anyone know what these things are?"

Pete raised his hand. "That one"—he pointed to Doug's left hand—"is a table . . . like the kind that goes between chairs or next to a bed."

Doug grinned, dimples carving holes in his cheeks. "Very nice." He looked around, then nodded at Cindy as he lifted his right hand in the air. "Do you know what this is?"

"One of those things that covers the window before a storm."

"A shutter. Very good." He set them both on an empty desk. "Does anyone know where I got them?"

The redhead popped up, his demeanor a bit more humble. "The hardware store?"

Doug shook his head.

"Leeson's Market?" another child asked.

Again, he shook his head.

"Ebay?"

The adults in the room laughed, including Doug.

"Anyone else?" he finally asked.

"You made them," Cindy stated.

"Very good. I made them." He wandered back out into the hall, this time reappearing with his tool belt.

The little boys in the room leaned forward.

"Wow."

"Those are so cool."

"My dad would go crazy over that."

One by one, Doug pulled each tool from his belt as he told its proper name and gave a brief explanation of its function. When he was done, he took a few questions and then looked toward Milo to bring his portion to a close.

"Class . . . you've seen a table and a shutter that Mr. Doug has made. And they're all special and all important things that people need. But sometimes, people who work with wood can make something extra special. And it's called a keepsake." Milo skimmed the faces of his class. "Does anyone know what a keepsake is?"

A brunette in the front nodded. "It's something that means a lot to a person. Something they keep forever and ever."

Milo smiled. "Very good, Stacy. It's something a person keeps forever and ever." Stepping into the middle of the circle, he motioned to the children to turn and face him in the center. When they'd done as they were told, he continued. "My father was in the military my whole life. And when he died, he had a special funeral service. When it was over we were given a flag to honor his service to our country."

The children nodded, their eyes wide on their teacher.

"For a long time I didn't have a place to keep the flag . . . somewhere I could display it for people to see." Milo waved a hand in Doug's direction. "Then Mr. Doug made me a very special case so I could display that flag."

The students turned to look at Doug.

"Would you like to see it?" Milo asked.

Sixteen little heads bobbed up and down.

He stepped back out of the circle and around to the back of his desk. "I have it right here." He reached behind his chair and pulled the dark cherry wood and glass case into the air. A smattering of *oohs* and *ahhs* erupted around the room, followed by sixteen sets of hands clapping.

Doug's face grew red. "Thank you. Now I better hit the road and let you guys get back to work." He waved to Tori, then headed toward the door, Milo on his heels.

"Can you keep an eye on the case while I walk Doug out?" Milo asked.

She nodded, then turned toward the flag case in time to see the little redhead barreling toward it at top speed. "Would you like to see it up close, everyone?" she asked, jumping to her feet.

"Can we?" Cindy asked.

"Absolutely." Lifting the case from the desk, she walked over to the circle of seated students and squatted down to their eye level, holding the case out for them to see.

"What's that?" Pete asked.

She looked at the little boy standing beside her. "What's what?"

"That." He pointed at three letters crudely carved into the back of the case.

Pulling the box closer, she examined the carving more closely. "It looks like an *M* . . . and a *T* . . . and a—"

"*B*!" Pete added. "*M.T.B.*"

"I think you're right," she said as she studied the letters. "*M.T.B.* it is. . . ."

"What do you think it stands for?" the little boy asked as more heads peeked around the back of the case to catch a glimpse at the letters.

"Mark . . . Thomas . . . Bughead," Derrick said. "Yeah, that's it. Mark Thomas Bughead."

She couldn't help but smile. Third-grade boys were an entity all their own.

Pete rolled his eyes, then lowered his voice so only Tori could hear. "What do you think, Miss Sinclair?"

She read the letters again . . .

M.T.B.

"*M.T.B.*," she repeated. "*M.T.B.* Hmmm, you've got me, Pete. I have absolutely no—"

In a flash she was standing in the middle of Martha Jane's bedroom, the elderly woman practically smacking Tori's hand for getting too close to her prized possessions . . .

"My great-grandfather, Matthew Tucker Barker, made that box, his initials are even carved into the bottom."

"His initials are carved into the bottom," she whispered as sixteen sets of eyes trained on hers.

Chapter 28

It took everything she had not to pull Milo out the door the second he returned, the picture that had begun to form in her head begging to be discussed and dissected. But, once again, the opportunity to do so rested on the ringing of the final bell.

Something that was still a good thirty minutes away.

"You okay, Tori?" he asked as he waited for his students to return to their desks. "You look as if you've seen a ghost."

She swallowed back the urge to scream. "The *truth* is more like it."

"The truth? What's that supposed to mean?"

"Mr. Wentworth? Todd just kicked the back of my chair."

He looked up at the ceiling and sighed.

"We'll talk later." She turned toward the door only to stop midway and retrace her steps. "Can I take this with me? I promise I'll be careful . . . with the flag."

"Yeah, sure, I guess." Handing the case to her, he held

it a second longer than necessary. "Can you at least tell me if you're okay?"

"I'm okay," she repeated. "But call me as soon as you're done for the day. We need to talk."

He studied her for a moment, his eyes a dead giveaway to the pull he felt in her direction. "Can you hang tight until then? Because if you can't, I can get another teacher to cover me."

"No. I'll wait. It's only thirty minutes."

A glance at the clock confirmed her words, chasing the worry from his eyes. "Okay. Thirty minutes."

She looked down at the case in her hands, her eyes riveted on the crude carving on the back.

M.T.B.

Could it really be?

She knew the answer. Felt it with every fiber of her being.

But why? Why would Doug take a flag case from a dead woman's home? Unless . . .

Her feet froze in the hallway as a reality she hadn't even considered reared its head with such clarity it couldn't be ignored any longer.

"Maybe she wasn't dead. Maybe he killed her," she whispered, her words echoing against the tiled walls of Sweet Briar Elementary.

But why? Was a case really worth murdering someone?

She had to know.

Flipping her phone open, she dialed Rose's number.

"Hello?"

"Rose, it's Tori . . . I mean, Victoria."

"You sound awful."

"I have to ask you a question. But I don't want to say why I'm asking just yet. In case I'm wrong."

"What is it?"

She inhaled, mustering up every ounce of courage she could find. "Do you, by any chance, have an extra key to Martha Jane's house?"

Silence was followed by a faint sound in the background. "I have one right here in my drawer."

"Can I borrow it for a few minutes?"

More silence followed.

"Rose? Are you still there?"

"You said no questions, right?"

She smiled in spite of the knowledge she held. "Yes."

"Then you may borrow it."

"You're a lifesaver, Rose."

Rose sighed in her ear. "If that were the case, Martha Jane would be alive."

She let herself in the back door, her feet sounding suspiciously guilty as she made her way down the same hall she'd traveled just the day before. Only this time there was no notebook in her hand. Simply a key . . .

A key that would hopefully lead her to the truth once and for all. A truth she was more apt to see with a focused eye.

Once again, the bedroom door was shut, the room closed tight by Chief Dallas. And, once again, she turned the knob and pushed the door open, the same stale air that had greeted her the day before welcoming her back for a second visit.

Only this time she didn't head straight for the window. Instead, she made her way over to the dresser, her gaze focused on the jewelry box on the top of the mahogany dresser.

"*M.T.B.*," she whispered as she took hold of the box and turned it upside down.

Sure enough, the same crude initials she'd seen just an

hour earlier were duplicated on the bottom of the box. Initials Martha Jane had said her great-grandfather carved into the bottom of the piece.

She set the box down and lifted the frame off the nightstand. Once again, the same dark cherry wood was used, the same three letters carved into the back.

She turned toward the case on the wall, the same case she'd inventoried just the day before, the use of pine suddenly standing out from the rest in a way she couldn't believe she'd missed.

Pulling it from its nail, she turned it over and studied the back.

Not a single solitary initial anywhere.

Aware of her heart beating double time inside her chest, she turned the case over once again, her gaze drawn to the town's chosen symbols—the flame, the white picket fence bathed in sunlight, and the bricks.

Six bricks.

"Six," she repeated aloud.

She closed her eyes and willed herself to return to the moment she'd stood beside the elderly woman and learned about the town's historic flag. But there was nothing.

Opening her eyes, she stared at the details of the flag.

The picket fence bathed in sunlight represented warmth and friendliness—that she could remember. It had struck a chord with her, one she'd shared with Martha Jane.

"Hogwash is what it is. Except for the pile of bricks. That one at least is accurate. Or was for about three weeks . . . before the founders ordered a new one on account of their feeling that six bricks represented strength better than three."

"Then why are there six?" she mumbled as she counted the bricks for the umpteenth time, the final total one she could see as easily as she could count.

Turning the case over once again, she swiveled each

of the three metal flaps to the side and pulled the back cover out and onto the dresser. Once that was complete, she grabbed hold of the flag and lifted it from the case, slowly unfolding it across the bed. The fabric, the stitching, and the thread were exact duplicates of Rose's current efforts.

Which meant one thing . . .

The flag stretched before her now was a new flag.

But why would someone replace the old flag with a new—

"*. . . the souvenirs I bring back from each trip helps. Teaches them things, too . . .*"

She covered her mouth as a series of chilling conversations swept through every corner of her mind.

He'd been to Chicago . . .

"*Brought my kids back a jar of water from the lake. Didn't work so well. My son and my daughter each want something different . . .*"

And then, less than an hour ago, he'd mentioned an idea he had for his son, something that would document Doug's time in Sweet Briar . . .

"*. . . I'm considerin' a book on Sweet Briar's history as a souvenir for my son . . .*"

She swallowed against the bile that rose in her throat.

Doug had said his children didn't like to share. Which meant one thing. His daughter still needed something from Sweet Briar . . .

"The town's very first flag would certainly fit that bill," she whispered, the sound of her cell phone cutting through her words.

Looking at the display screen, she heaved a sigh of relief and headed toward the window. "Milo, hi. I'm so glad you called."

She tucked the phone under her cheek and slid the window up, the late afternoon breeze lifting her hair from her face.

"So what's going on? Why did you look so upset when you left? And why did you want my flag case?"

"Because it was the clue I've been looking for." Spinning around, she leaned against the wall beside the window, her gaze riveted on the outstretched flag that adorned Martha Jane's empty bed.

"Clue?"

"To Kenny's innocence."

"I thought you'd given up on that."

She inhaled deeply, the truth she'd assembled over the past hour bringing a sense of peace she hadn't felt in days. "I had."

"So what changed?"

"Reality."

"Huh?"

"I know who killed Martha Jane. And it wasn't Kenny. I'm positive of that now."

A sound outside the window startled her and she pushed off the wall for a closer look.

Nothing.

Nothing except for one of Paris's many kinfolk.

"It wasn't until I saw the initials on the back of your flag case that I started to put two and two together," she continued.

"Initials? What initials?"

"On the back of the case. Martha Jane told me about them that day I was here . . ." Her words trailed off as she heard another sound, this time coming from the hallway outside Martha Jane's room. "Milo, can you hang on a second? I think Rose might be looking for me . . ."

A large calloused hand reached around the corner and through the open doorway, Doug's face emerging just as he smacked the phone from her hand. "Did you tell him?" he hissed through a mouth that no longer sported the endearing smile she'd come to associate with the drifter who'd shown up on Rose's doorstep looking for work.

"Tell who, what?" she asked as she looked down at the still-open phone. "Milo! I'm at M—"

His hand swept down and grabbed the phone, shutting it inside his strong hands. "You couldn't leave well enough alone, could you?"

She backed up, her legs bumping into Martha Jane's bed. "Was a flag really that important?"

"It shouldn't have been. But that old hag came in just as I was takin' it off the wall. She started squawkin' about lazy bums and good-for-nothin' drifters and I snapped." He leaned his face toward hers. "I just snapped. It happens."

"Murdering an innocent woman doesn't just *happen*."

"It does when she threatens to have you arrested."

"You were trying to *steal* from her, Doug," she shouted. "What was she supposed to do?"

"She was supposed to stay away until I'd gotten the damn thing off the wall and out of the room."

"How did you even know about it?" she asked as she tried everything she could think of to buy herself some time.

"Anyone within a quarter-mile radius heard her talkin' to you that afternoon. About her precious money . . . her precious flag . . . the two lazy bums working just outside that window"—he pointed toward the back wall—"and that idiot who hung around Rose's house all the time. The one she was so certain stole her money."

"Idiot?" she hissed through clenched teeth.

"Did you ever hear him talk? That guy could barely string a sentence together without tripping over his words. But he worked out well for me."

She stared at him, anger raging through every muscle. "You mean he was the perfect scapegoat."

He nodded. "Couldn't ask for better."

"And now?"

His face clouded. "You mean with you?"

Fear begin to surface through the anger as she realized no one knew where she was except Rose. And she'd all but begged her not to ask questions . . .

"I suppose you'll have an unfortunate fall . . . unless you have a better idea. Something I can duplicate from a book, perhaps?"

A book . . .

She felt her mouth turn upward a smidge. "They're going to figure it out."

"Who?"

"The cops. Milo. Rose. Everyone. They'll figure it out when they go through the notebook I gave Chief Dallas yesterday. Martha Jane's sister will realize the flag case doesn't match . . . that the flag is wrong."

He shrugged. "And what if she does? I'll be long gone by then." He jumped forward, his face mere centimeters from hers. "I am a drifter after all, right?"

"You mean a carpetbagger, don't you?"

Doug whirled around as Tori's anger ballooned into full-fledged fear—for the woman standing in the doorway with a telephone in her hand.

"Get out of here, Rose!" she shouted. "Go! Now!"

"I heard what you said"—Rose stammered—"about Kenny. And I heard what you did to Martha Jane."

He looked back over his shoulder, Tori's gaze following his to the open window.

"Two of us can't fall, Doug," she pleaded, her worry for her elderly friend far more tangible than the fear she had for herself. She could put up a fight. Rose couldn't.

"I don't see why not." He reached out, wrapped his elbow around Tori's neck and dragged her toward the door. "It's not like Rose has anything left in her."

"Freeze. You're under arrest," Chief Dallas yelled as he moved into place behind Rose.

The elderly woman nodded toward the policeman, a slow but deliberate smile making its way across her face. "I've got more left than you know, young man."

Chapter 29

She woke to the sun streaming through her window, her mind relatively quiet for the first time in days.

There'd been nothing to keep her staring at the clock, nothing to make her reach for the phone in the middle of the night, nothing to make her stomach feel as if she were perched on the top of a ninety degree hill with no seat belt to hold her in place.

In fact, there'd been nothing but peace . . .

A peace that came from knowing the truth had finally been revealed, freeing a wrongly accused man and putting the right one behind bars in the process.

It was as it should be.

Although the part about Curtis still bothered her.

How could a man who donated books to a library and acted like a kid on Christmas at the sight of a favorite childhood costume steal money from a little old lady? A dead one at that?

It was the one piece of the puzzle that still made no

sense. And it was the piece that would gnaw at her until it finally did.

The phone beside her bed began to ring, the melodic sound bringing a smile to her lips.

Milo had been so sweet when he'd arrived at Martha Jane's house, the worry in his eyes further proof that she meant as much to him as he did to her. He'd panicked when they'd been disconnected, his mind picking through everything she'd said and coming up empty.

Rose, however, had called to fill him in. . . .

Right after she called Police Chief Dallas and explained the entire situation to him as she'd heard it through Martha Jane's open window.

She reached for the phone, her mind conjuring up the sound of Milo's voice before he uttered a single word.

"Good morning," she said, her voice still heavy with sleep.

"Is it true?"

She sat up in bed, her hand nearly dropping the phone in surprise.

"Leona? Is that you?"

"Who else would it be?"

"Milo."

"He hasn't called yet?"

She shrugged as her eyes strayed back to the clock. "No."

"It's his mother. I warned you."

"His mother has nothing to do with this, Leona. He's probably just asleep. It is a school holiday, you know."

"You could have been killed yesterday."

She paused, the real meaning behind her friend's words sifting through the phone. "You sound as if that bothers you."

A moment of silence was followed by a slight sniff. "And that surprises you, dear? You are my protégé, after all."

"Your protégé?" she repeated.

"If I don't teach you the ways of the south, how will you ever learn?"

Grinning, she scooted back down in her bed. "Margaret Louise? Rose? Debbie? Melissa? Should I go on?"

"But that's not *my* southern."

"Ahhh. So there *is* a difference after all. I knew it."

"There are some similarities, of course, but my version is . . . well, better. Unique. Like me."

"Oh, you are unique, Leona."

"Thank you."

She glanced over at the framed photograph of her and Milo at the Re-Founders Day Festival and a thought occurred to her. "How's the judge?"

Leona's smile was audible through the phone. "Heavenly."

"And his robes?" she teased.

"The perfect cover."

"The perfect cover?"

"For what's underneath . . ."

She cleared her throat. "Okay, that qualifies as too much information, Leona."

The woman laughed. "Then I'll let you guess. It's more fun that way."

"So is that why you called this morning?" she finally asked. "To make sure I was okay?"

"Of course, dear. I feel as if you're my responsibility. It's why I really wish you'd heed my advice on Milo's mother. If you don't, you'll always be in her shadow—the woman who doesn't cook quite as well as his mother, the woman who doesn't keep house quite as well as his mother, the woman who doesn't care for him quite as well as his mother."

"We'll be fine, Leona." She rolled onto her side, her gaze glued to the tiny dust particles that danced in the sunlight. "I guess I'll see you Monday night? At our circle meeting?"

"Where is it this week?"

"Rose's house," she answered as she noticed the rainbow of light that played on her bedroom floor, the window beside her bed serving as a prism.

Leona started to speak, then stopped and cleared her throat before trying once again. "Is it true?"

She strained to make out her friend's question. "Is what true?"

"That Rose saved the day?"

"It is."

Silence fell across their conversation, each woman lost in thoughts the other could only imagine. But it was Leona who finally broke the silence.

"Not bad for an Old Woman."

She nibbled her lower lip inward, the image of Rose standing in the doorway of Martha Jane's bedroom with a look on her face that left no doubt she was still a force to be reckoned with. "No, not bad at all."

"I suppose I should say something supportive when I see her next."

"That might be nice."

"Perhaps you could offer me a suggestion in that regard . . ."

"How about something like, I'm glad you're okay, Rose. I admire you for what you did for Victoria."

A slight hesitation in her ear was soon followed by the faintest of snorts. "Gushing is only necessary for *a man*, dear."

She shook her head. "Then whatever you come up with will be fine, I'm sure."

When they hung up, she rolled onto her back once again, her gaze finding the ceiling out of boredom. Why hadn't Milo called?

A knock at the door caught her up short, a smile stretching across her face once again.

He didn't call because he opted to come over, instead. . . .

Swinging her legs over the edge of the bed, she stepped into the fuzzy pink slippers that awaited her feet each morning. A quick peek in the mirror beside her nightstand confirmed what she knew to be true . . .

She needed a shower.

But it could wait. Especially when Milo was at her front door . . .

Grabbing her robe from the bottom of her bed, she slipped into it on the way to the door, the satiny fabric cool against her skin.

She stole a peek through the sidelight, her smile fading a smidge as she realized it wasn't Milo knocking at her door.

It was Georgina. With a letter in her hand.

Unlocking the door, she swung it wide open. "Georgina, what a nice surprise."

The town's top elected official breezed into Tori's home, her trademark straw hat perched atop her dark hair. "Doug did all of it."

"I know."

"He stole the town's first flag, murdered Martha Jane, *and* stole her money."

Stole her money?

Tori shook her head. "He stole the flag and murdered Martha Jane. But *Curtis* stole her money, remember?"

"That's what he said . . . originally. But once Doug was safely behind bars he changed his story."

She trailed Georgina down the hall and into her living room, her fellow sewing member and friend claiming the same plaid armchair that Leona sought each time she came for a visit. "What do you mean he changed his story? He told Margaret Louise and me that he stole it. What reason could he possibly have to lie about that? Especially when the lie landed him in so much hot water?"

"He saw Kenny lurking behind the house on the night Martha Jane was murdered. He assumed, like everyone else, that Kenny was behind it. When he stumbled across the cash stuffed in a hole behind Rose's house, he assumed Kenny had stashed it there. He figured if he got rid of it, that would be one less crime Kenny would be tied to."

"And you believe him?"

"Chief Dallas suspected something was off when Curtis said the body had been faceup."

"It wasn't?"

Georgina shook her head. "No."

She considered the mayor's words. "So he took the money he found and donated it to the library and the collection booth?"

"Among other things." Georgina pulled her hat from her head and rested it on the armrest of the chair. "He put some in an envelope for the youth center in town, and still more in an envelope for a drifter who had a sick baby at home."

"He took the quality he liked most about Robin Hood and gave it a twist," Tori whispered as her mind worked to process everything she was hearing.

"What are you talking about, Victoria?"

What *was* she talking about?

Shrugging, she wandered around the room, her mind suddenly too jumbled to think clearly. "He still gave to the poor . . . he just did it from start to finish every step of the way."

Georgina looked a question at her.

"He took it from Kenny as a way to *help* him. And he gave it to people who needed help, too."

"Only it wasn't Kenny who'd stashed the money in the hole."

"Doug?" she asked, although she knew the answer without asking the question.

"He's in a lot of trouble," Georgina confirmed.

"I figured as much."

"So what happens with Curtis now?"

"He's a free man. The judge believed him when he said he was trying to help. . . ."

"Sounds like a lenient judge—" She stopped, a possible explanation sneaking a smile across her lips. "Would this judge happen to know Leona, by any chance?"

Georgina grinned.

Tori exhaled a loud sigh. "I should have known."

"I think Leona truly cared for Curtis."

"I think so, too." She raked her hands through her already rumpled hair, then pointed at Georgina's left hand. "What's that?"

The woman glanced down. "Oh. I forgot. It's for you."

"For me?"

"Yes."

"From who?"

"Why don't you open it and find out."

Taking the envelope from Georgina's outstretched hand, she turned it over, slipping her finger beneath the seal.

She peered inside, her mouth going dry.

"It's money."

"I know."

"He had some left?" She sank onto the couch. "I don't feel right taking this again. Not when it should really go to Martha Jane's sister."

"It wasn't part of her money."

"It wasn't?" She pulled the contents from the envelope, her finger flicking through the hundred dollar bills. "There's two thousand dollars here."

"It was apparently money Curtis had been saving ever since he started drifting around, chasing storms for work."

"I can't take this."

"There's a note." Georgina plucked her hat from the armrest and stood. "I'll leave you to it. I've got to head over to town hall and check on a few things."

When she was gone, Tori pulled the thin white sheet of paper from the envelope, her gaze falling on the perfect penmanship of a man who valued words as much as she did. . . .

Dear Tori,

I'm sorry for any heartache and confusion I may have caused. For what it's worth, Sweet Briar is the first place that felt like home in years. Your library brought me back to a time that made me very happy and is the reason I'm finding my way back to that place after too many years away.

Please use this money for something new and different in the library. A workshop? A speaker? A new section geared toward teenagers, perhaps? I leave the specifics up to you, knowing that the booklovers of Sweet Briar are in good hands with you as their librarian.

Best wishes,
Curtis

"Thank you, Curtis," she whispered as she took one last look at the donation, the man's generosity and kind words blurring her vision.

A second, softer knock at the door took her by surprise. She peeked outside.

Margaret Louise and Lulu stood on the porch, Lulu's eyes glowing with excitement.

Yanking the door open, she bent down and spread her arms wide, Lulu stepping into them without a moment's hesitation. "Hi, Miss Sinclair!"

"Hi, yourself." She released her grip on the child just enough to get a good look at the little girl's face. "You look like you've got something special to tell me."

Lulu shook her head. "Nuh-uh."

"You don't?"

"Nuh-uh."

"Land sakes child, where'd you learn to talk like that?"

"Jake Junior."

Margaret Louise grit her teeth. "I swear, when I get hold of that child . . ."

"I don't have something to *tell* you, Miss Sinclair. I have something to *show* you."

She flashed a quick glance at Margaret Louise over the top of Lulu's head. "You do, do you?"

"Uh-huh." Reaching out for the bag her Mee-Maw carried on her shoulder, Lulu set it on the ground at her feet. "Mee-Maw said you needed sixty hats and scarves for a special place that helps big girls."

"That's right, I do," she said even as she furrowed her brows at her friend. "I have fifty-nine right now . . . which means I need how many more?"

"None!"

She made a face at the little girl. "I need sixty and I have fifty-nine. How many do I need, Silly?"

"None!" Lulu repeated.

"Lu-luuu . . ."

The little girl reached into the bag and pulled out a wrapped package. "Open it," she instructed.

"Now?"

"Yes." Hopping from foot to foot, Lulu watched every move Tori made, her gaze never straying far from her face.

She gasped as the last piece of paper fell to the ground. In her hand was a hat and scarf set in a brilliant royal blue fleece.

"I made it . . . all by myself!" Lulu shouted with pride.

A lump sprang in her throat as she looked from the fleece to the little girl hopping happily beside her. "You did?"

"Mee-Maw helped me."

Tori swiped at a tear as it streaked down her left cheek only to be followed by one on her right. "Lulu, it's beautiful. Absolutely beautiful."

"I wanted to help, too."

Gathering the child in her arms, she closed her eyes and inhaled the potpourri of cookies, Play-Doh, and innocence that was Lulu Davis. "I couldn't have done it without you, sweetheart. Thank you."

She lifted her face toward the late afternoon sun, the warmth letting her know she was traveling in a westerly direction.

"Is there a reason I have to be blindfolded?"

"There is."

"Can I get a hint?"

"You mean like a clue?" Milo asked, his voice deeper than usual.

"Yes, exactly."

"No."

She pouted her lip outward. "Why not?"

"Because you figure out clues better than anyone else I know. Giving you a clue would be like telling you exactly where we're going."

"And that's so wrong?"

"It is if I want it to be a surprise."

"I'm not sure I like surprises," she countered.

His hand stopped her forward progress. "Then I suppose we should turn back."

"Well, I mean if you don't want to . . . I understand."

He laughed. "If you listen really hard, maybe you'll get your clue after all."

She did as she was told, an assortment of voices springing to life around her.

There was Margaret Louise.

And Leona.

Debbie, Colby, and the rest of the Calhoun bunch.

Georgina.

Dixie.

Jake and Melissa.

Rose.

Nina and Duwayne.

Beatrice . . .

"You can take your bandana off now."

Reaching behind her head, she undid the knot Milo had secured like the former Boy Scout he was. As the fabric slid from her eyes, her mouth gaped open.

"Surprise! Happy Birthday!"

She looked from face to face, the reality that was her life in Sweet Briar staring back at her with more love than she could have ever imagined.

"How did you know it was my birthday?"

Nina glanced at the floor. "I saw it on your calendar . . . underneath one of those red circles you keep adding all the time."

"You should have told me," Milo insisted. "Don't you think that's a piece of information I might have liked to have?"

"It's just a day. It's no big deal."

He cupped her face in his hands. "It's the day you were born and that makes it a very big deal."

She blinked against the tears that threatened to turn her into a pile of mush. "I couldn't imagine spending it with people I love more. You've truly helped make Sweet Briar feel like home."

Beatrice stepped from the crowd, a covered cake plate in her hands. "I made you a cake. I hope you like it." Slowly, the twenty-three-year-old lifted the cover from the pan, her face falling as she looked inside. "Oh no, oh no . . ."

Tori looked into the pan, her shoulders beginning

to shake as the picture registered in her mind. "Kenny Rogers?"

The girl's face flushed bright red. "I must have grabbed the wrong one by accident."

Rose muscled her way to the front. "Is his party at five?"

Beatrice looked at the ground.

"Because if it is, I could drop you off on my way home."

Tori made a face at Rose. "Beatrice, it's okay. I like Kenny Rogers, too."

The woman's face brightened. "Really?"

"Well, sure. But I have to ask . . . how did you land an invite to his party?"

"I didn't."

"Then how do you explain the cake?" Debbie asked not unkindly.

"Well, he sends me a card on my birthday every year. The least *I* can do for him is make a nice cake."

Margaret Louise nodded from her spot beside Rose. "Is that buttercream frosting?"

Beatrice nodded.

"Homemade?"

"Yes."

"Well, then, ladies—"

Milo, Colby, and Jake cleared their throats.

"Ladies *and* gentlemen . . . the least *we* can do is eat his cake." Margaret Louise grabbed a knife from the picnic table and slid it into the sweet treat. "Here's to Kenny . . . and Victoria. May your year ahead be filled with all good things."

Sewing Tips

- When you need to remember to leave part of a seam unsewn as in the hat pattern, or for inserting a zipper, placket, or such, mark the spot where you need to stop sewing by placing two pins next to each other.

- Since stitches can be difficult to remove from Polarfleece, it can save time in the long run to stitch slowly and carefully.

- To take advantage of the wicking properties of Polarfleece, you have to have the right side of the fabric facing away from your body. Sometimes, the right side of Polarfleece can be difficult to determine. One way is to check the selvage edge. Stretch the selvage and watch which way it curls. The side toward which it curls is the right side. Remember to mark the wrong side of your cut pieces with chalk so that it will be easy to tell later.

- A hot iron can melt Polarfleece.

- Use long pins with bead heads when pinning Polarfleece. Smaller pins can get "lost" in this type of fabric.

- Create a pin disposal receptacle by taking a little jam jar, gluing on the lid, and punching a pin-head-sized hole in the middle. Any time you find a blunt or bent pin or needle, pop it through the hole into the jar. Doing this can eliminate concerns about putting loose pins in the wastebasket.

- If you need to sew a seam allowance that isn't marked on your sewing machine, apply a strip of painter's tape as a guide.

- Chopsticks make great tools when turning projects, finishing corners, and stuffing batting.

- Write down all the alterations and note anything else that is relevant right on your pattern. Then if you decide to use the pattern again at a later date, you won't have to rely on your memory.

- For thick seams that are difficult for your sewing machine, like hems on jeans, use a hammer and a board. Lay the thick seam on the board on the floor and give it a few good hits with the hammer. (This can also help relieve any frustrations you have with your sewing project.)

**Have a sewing tip you'd like to share?
Stop by my Web site,
www.elizabethlynncasey.com,
and let me know.**

Polarfleece Hat
and Boa-Style Scarf Set

Experience:

Beginner

Materials for both projects:

*2 yards Polarfleece fabric (Solid colors work well because
the wrong side of the fabric will show on parts of this
project.)*
Matching thread
Straight pins
Chalk or marking pencil
Sharp scissors
Decorative button or appliqué (optional)

Quick and Easy Polarfleece Hat

Cut a rectangle of Polarfleece measuring 16" high x 22"
wide.

With right sides together, pin the 16" sides together. Sew a ½" seam, stopping 4" from the end. Trim seam allowances closely.

Along the top of the hat where you left 4" of the seam unsewn, cut 4" slits at ½" intervals to create fringe. Turn hat right side out.

Cut a strip of Polarfleece ¾" by 8". Gather the fringe together and secure by tying the strip tightly around the base of the fringe.

Create a cuff by rolling the bottom edge up twice. If desired, the cuff can be secured in place by sewing on a decorative button or appliqué through all layers.

Boa-Style Polarfleece Scarf

Cut three strips of Polarfleece (four if you would like a fuller scarf) measuring 10" wide by however long you'd like your scarf to be (54" is a good length).

Use a marking pen to make a line down the center of one of the strips.

Stack all of the strips on top of one another, with the marked strip on the top of the stack. Secure in place with straight pins.

Sew down the center line through all layers.

At 1" intervals, cut through all layers from the outer edges of each side toward the center, stopping about ½" from stitching.

Penguin Group (USA) Online

What will you be reading tomorrow?

Patricia Cornwell, Nora Roberts, Catherine Coulter,
Ken Follett, John Sandford, Clive Cussler,
Tom Clancy, Laurell K. Hamilton, Charlaine Harris,
J. R. Ward, W.E.B. Griffin, William Gibson,
Robin Cook, Brian Jacques, Stephen King,
Dean Koontz, Eric Jerome Dickey, Terry McMillan,
Sue Monk Kidd, Amy Tan, Jayne Ann Krentz,
Daniel Silva, Kate Jacobs...

You'll find them all at
penguin.com

Read excerpts and newsletters,
find tour schedules and reading group guides,
and enter contests.

Subscribe to Penguin Group (USA) newsletters
and get an exclusive inside look
at exciting new titles and the authors you love
long before everyone else does.

PENGUIN GROUP (USA)
penguin.com